Also by Douglas Lockhart

FICTION

Skirmish
Song of the Man Who Came Through
Sabazius
The Paradise Complex
The Mar Saba Codex

NON-FICTION

Jesus the Heretic
The Dark Side of God
Going Beyond the Jesus Story

PLAYS

Julia Flips Her Lid

douglaslockhart.com

This is a work of fiction. Names, characters, businesses, places, events and incidents are either the products of the author's imagination or used in a fictitious manner. Any resemblance to actual persons, living or dead, or actual events is purely coincidental.

AN IMPERFECT SPY

Douglas Lockhart

AN IMPERFECT SPY

Vanguard Press

VANGUARD PAPERBACK

© Copyright 2023
Douglas Lockhart

The right of Douglas Lockhart to be identified as author of
this work has been asserted by him in accordance with the
Copyright, Designs and Patents Act 1988.

All Rights Reserved

No reproduction, copy or transmission of this publication
may be made without written permission.
No paragraph of this publication may be reproduced,
copied or transmitted save with the written permission of the
publisher, or in accordance with the provisions
of the Copyright Act 1956 (as amended).

Any person who commits any unauthorised act in relation to
this publication may be liable to criminal
prosecution and civil claims for damages.

A CIP catalogue record for this title is
available from the British Library.

ISBN 978-1-80016-576-2

*Vanguard Press is an imprint of
Pegasus Elliot Mackenzie Publishers Ltd.*
www.pegasuspublishers.com

First Published in 2023

**Vanguard Press
Sheraton House Castle Park
Cambridge England**

Printed & Bound in Great Britain

Acknowledgements

Yet again do I owe a special debt of thanks to my partner, Robin Mosley, for her patience, support, editorial skills and many helpful conversations as this book took shape; Jean Curthoys, Jeff Malpas and Lynn Martin for taking the time to read the manuscript and make pertinent suggestions; David Challis for advice on medical matters and Pegasus for putting up with an old curmudgeon like myself.

What is the difference, in morality, between the totally anarchic criminality of the artist, which is endemic in all creative minds, and the artistry of the criminal?
—John le Carré
A Perfect Spy

1
A Little Turbulence Ahead

The sound of rain beating steadily on the windowpanes of the study fitted perfectly with John Hennessey's mood. In a tone that suggested he ought to have known better, Laura Greene said she was temperamentally unsuited to marriage, that marriage was a bubble, a membrane of imposed permissions. Not exactly a serious proposal on Hennessey's part, more a clutching at straws, but so sententiously received that he regretted having made it. Ten days later he was in London working with a new young editor on the manuscript of his latest novel, Tasmania's plummeting midsummer temperature all but forgotten. But not Laura's look; he could not get that out of his mind.

London had been Hennessey's stamping ground since the age of fifteen, when, for their boy's sake, his parents had decided it was time to leave Belfast and start a new life. 1951. His parents' version of love strained to breaking point, their marriage across the divide a bone of contention among friends as well as enemies. A new life and confirmation over the next eight years that their boy had a promising future, that if he curbed his tongue there was no knowing where he might end up. An honours degree in classics under his belt at twenty-one and on into the army to do his two-year stint. His mother chagrined by the sight of her son in a British uniform, his father equally put out when, later, the glories of academia were swapped for the uncertainties of the artistic life. Write? Fiction? His father had been incredulous. He might as well have chosen the priesthood, he said wryly, a few weeks before his death.

The on-street window of the café Hennessey was in visibly buckled when the bomb went off. The IRA's brief ceasefire with the Provos was over; the men with lava in their veins had spurned the British Government's attempt at negotiation. Another false dawn. British soldiers back on the Falls Road with Wessex gunships clattering overhead. Eyes-in-the-back-of-your-head stuff. No insignia. Visual parity between officers and men to fool the snipers. The classic one up, one down formation as they moved through the streets. But the centre of the cyclone elsewhere. An IRA hit list with the queen and other members of the royal family marked for assassination. A security scramble. Soldiers in bulletproof vests toting SA80 machine guns patrolling Buckingham Palace. Armed police forming what the papers described as a 'Ring of Steel' around royal buildings. Fifty or more terrorists armed with Semtex operating in cells on the British mainland — a nightmare for Britain's intelligence chiefs.

Hennessey's own negotiations had faltered more than once. The place of an editor he knew and respected had been taken by someone who wielded a Biro like a knife — another kind of surgery going on elsewhere. Time enough left over in which to catch a show, walk the Embankment or drink far too much red wine in the company of friends. Still on edge, however, as he headed for Heathrow and that leap around the Earth's curvature. A glance back, and a wave, as he disappeared into the international terminal and left a jittery Britain.

On his return to Tasmania, he found that Laura had taken off for Sydney only hours before — to speak at a conference. A great opportunity to strut her stuff, the note said, in her scrawly handwriting. The gods laughing as they moved the first piece in a game of chess bereft of rules. She returned to Hobart the following day, on a morning flight, the sun struggling to penetrate a canopy of thick cloud. Waiting behind glass he watched her plane touch down, then walked round to the passenger entry as she descended and crossed the tarmac.

"It's twenty-five degrees in Sydney!"

They hugged and separated, and she remarked immediately on the breakdown of the ceasefire and what was happening in London. It had turned into a lottery, she said, as they headed for the carousel. One minute you were minding your own business, the next you were dead and in bits. Just like that. She snapped her fingers. What an irony if it had been him passing in that moment.

"That's why I rang."

A passionate lady, Laura Greene, in the sense of opinions strongly held. A forty-eight-year-old lecturer in literature with a fiery temperament. Five-eight in her heels with short, dark hair. Slightly overweight, but attractive. A beautiful summer's evening in London when they first met, in a Knightsbridge pub. Laura the talker introduced by friends; a visitor from the antipodes to whom he had been instantly attracted.

"So how did it go with the book?"

He made a wry face, said that a fair compromise had been reached on its length. The conference? Nothing terribly new, she said. She had given a paper on the horror fiction of H P Lovecraft, answered a few questions, listened to two other lectures and skedaddled to have dinner with Emma and Michael.

"You didn't have to rush back because of me."

She smiled at the slight undertow of his words.

As they drove towards Hobart, he spoke again of his fear that Ireland was headed for a civil war. That was why the Brits would not pull out. They were afraid the IRA and the Anglo-Irish militants would go for each other's throats. A pause. He could remember his mother's family arguing the toss over who was properly Irish and who was not. His parents had almost separated after one of those bouts.

"I really can't imagine what it must have been like."

"You don't know the half."

A silence as they crossed the Tasman Bridge and headed into the city of Hobart. Then Laura saying that Alix was a lovely little girl, and that Michael doted on her.

"She's a bright kid."

"Emma sends her love."

He did not reply; a nod sufficed.

"You, okay?"

"I'm still jetlagged."

"How was everyone?"

"The same."

He had thought of staying on in London for another week, but in the end had decided not to because of Laura.

They were back in their flat before she broke the bad news: Dean had published *A Daughter for Cain* under his own name, she said. He had used the D H Lawrence quote and changed the title to *The Second Strength*. She produced a slim paperback from her handbag and handed it to him. An effusive review in *The Australian* had alerted her to Dean's effrontery.

On the cover, a yellow rose suspended on a black background. On the back, a photograph of a bearded Gavin Dean in a striped shirt, sunglasses and flat cap, his hands held out towards a manual typewriter.

"What a cheek!"

"Wait till you read the blurb."

Beneath the photograph lay an outrageous collection of words likening Dean to a character out of a John Le Carré novel — nothing at all like the quiet writer he had now become. The biographical sketch told how he had left his beloved Sydney at the age of twenty and roamed Australia pursuing a variety of unusual professions, how he had often been at odds with society and the establishment, and how he had later extended his roaming to various parts of the world as a foreign correspondent and documentary film maker. He now worked in Los Angeles, in the film industry, and was busy writing a new novel that laid bare the shenanigans of the Catholic Church.

"Marks Books?" said Laura.

After eight rejections, Hennessey had placed *A Daughter for Cain* in a drawer and closed it.

"The reviewer really liked it."

Hennessey leafed through the little paperback. "How can he hope to get away with this?"

"Dean's probably not his real name."

Hennessey laid the book face up on the dining room table to avoid looking at Dean's expression of triumph.

"You'll have to get yourself a lawyer."

"Lawyers are expensive."

"I'll help with that."

They had bumped into Dean and his companion — an attractive brunette — while staying in some holiday units when they first arrived from London. In publishing, according to his card. Dean the publisher talking to Hennessey the writer. "I only publish sexy westerns." Laughter all round. Interested in what

Hennessey was presently working on; he had some excellent contacts in the industry. The god of chance smiling on Hennessey in a twisted kind of way. A copy of the manuscript posted to Dean in Sydney with the hope that he might be able to drum up some interest in said book — the last communication with Dean in three years. No trace of the man at his business address in Bondi when Laura's friend Emma tried to check him out. The office that had once been a shop empty and deserted.

Tall, with wispy, sand-coloured hair, Mr Dean. In his late fifties, quietly spoken and well dressed. Amusing. His companion — Heather Barton — fluent when speaking of the London theatre scene. A nice couple. A business trip. An immediate con, of sorts. And so neatly done; not the slightest suspicion that the pair were anything other than what they appeared to be.

Hennessey flew to Sydney the following morning and consulted the Copyright Council and the Arts Law Society. Everyone was suitably shocked. According to Andrew Balchin of Balchin & Partners, a court injunction would be served on the distributor when Hennessey's UK agent confirmed copyright. Checks would also be run on Dean and the English publisher. And all to be done at minimal cost through the Arts Law Society because Balchin & Partners had a social conscience and Hennessey's finances were not robust.

A bit of a shock when, not long after, he found three scruffy plainclothes detectives on the doorstep. Two men and a woman, the smaller of the men unshaven and mean looking, the other clean shaven and smiling, but with ever such a slight cast to his right eye. Her arms folded across a stained tee-shirt; the female had come across as the more sinister. Identification produced. A chat requested. All of them trekking down the hallway to the lounge with Hennessey up front. Amazed when told that he was dealing with the local drug squad in connection with his book. A detailed explanation given of his relationship to Gavin Dean that eventually made sense to them — but only after a deal of questioning and a couple of telephone calls. An accidental meeting the reason for his initial interaction with Dean. A fluke. One of those things. Two meetings with Dean and Heather Barton over a glass of wine before the scene was set for skulduggery. A tense few minutes before the calls were put through and they realised he was not the potential villain they had hoped he might be.

Full of apologies for the communiqué they had received from Bondi that morning — about as daft a reading of a situation as their colleagues in Sydney could have come up with. The small detective tried to make amends by giving Hennessey a rundown on Gavin Dean's exploits: a police record that ran back to '56. Juicy items such as drug trafficking, assault, robbery with violence, prostitution and massage parlour racketeering all part of his portfolio. Armed. Four aliases that they knew of. Had escaped from police custody twice. Fraud his specialty. Warrants out for his arrest in Victoria and New South Wales in connection with the importation of hard drugs.

"Gavin Dean is his real name?"

A nod from the man with the squint, who seemed to be in charge.

Stretched to the limit, it was admitted. A disease eating away at the big brown continent. Every major city in the world with the same problem. Massive amounts of money being made by people totally devoid of conscience. Kids at school running the gauntlet of dealers in addiction and death. An erupting boil on the hide of Australian society; a running sore for which, it seemed, there was no final, curative treatment.

"And your being Irish..."

The woman speaking, her glance conspiratorial.

The suspicion had been that something was going down when they heard about the book and Hennessey's connection with Dean. The name 'Hennessey' had set alarm bells ringing. Ireland was now one of the drug capitals of the world, with Dublin leading the rest of the country in spent syringes and Mafia-type assassinations. An award-winning crime journalist had been shot in the face and chest for trying to expose Dublin's leading criminals. Irish godfathers were vying with Europe's best.

Hennessey nodded, smiled his most understanding smile. "There's no mention of my book having been stolen in the report?"

An apologetic look from the pack leader. They were only interested in what the book may have been used for.

"Such as?"

"To bring hard drugs into the country."

"So why put his own name on it?"

The book picked up again, looked at back and front. The photograph was for real?

"He didn't have a beard when we met him, but it's him okay." Hennessey paused; then, because he could not think of anything else to say, he said, "He's added four lines to the end of the last chapter."

The lines in question dutifully glanced at, the book replaced on the little coffee table.

"Well, that just about wraps it up. For now. Hope we didn't give you too much of a fright, mate."

They were on their feet; it was as if someone had given a telepathic signal.

"If you want to contact us, use this number. Ask for Detective Sergeant Brownley. That's me."

A nod from Hennessey; then a question. "Do you really think he used the book as a cover to import drugs?"

Brownley shrugged and said that it was Dean's style to do something of the kind.

"But you're only guessing?"

"It's his style."

"You've met him?"

"Never had the honour."

"Do you want a copy of the book?"

"Not necessary."

"What do I do now?"

A blank stare from Brownley.

"About the book."

"Civil, I'd say." He glanced at the smaller man. "You'll have to get him into court."

"The book's a separate issue?"

"We're drug squad."

The house was empty of them minutes later. Hennessey stood near to the window and watched as they climbed into a big white Ford parked under a no-standing sign. A sad trio. Actors out of an episode of *Hill Street Blues* looking for a decent script. He turned back into the lounge, stood for a moment, then wandered through to the kitchen to make coffee.

In the morning paper Pat Buchanan's push for the White House and a suicide bombing in Israel merged with fifteen thousand men and women in Belfast asking for their ceasefire to be returned to them. A collage of horror. Men and women worldwide trying to fathom their existence. Frustration and hate and uncertainty and sheer bloody-mindedness scrunched together in neat columns of newsprint. He stared at the paper's heading: ULSTER'S FALSE DAWN. Below, a photograph of a child playing next to a wall on which had been inscribed: EITHER BALLOT OR GUN — OUR DAY WILL COME.

He closed his eyes, opened them again as the telephone rang. BBC *Panorama*? He listened amazed as someone rattled off a list of questions about Gavin Dean and drugs and cross-examined him on his answers. No, he had no idea where Dean was or how much of anything had been imported into Australia. Yes, a British publisher had been involved, and there were reviews from British newspapers. On and on his caller went at breakneck speed, as the pounds sterling mounted. Minutes later he was talking to someone at *The Sunday Times*. How had they found out, he wondered. A tip-off from someone in the local squad? More likely a mainland stringer, a listener and watcher with the Federal Police. There was money to be made if you understood the system.

2
Interrogation

A friend of Hennessey's in London subsequently pried some interesting information out of Marks Books. Question: How had a book designated for the Australian market ended up carrying reviews from British newspapers? Reply: they would have to address that question to Mr Dean; Marks Books were not publishers; they were printers only. One thousand copies of the book had been printed and sent straight to Australia; the company's responsibility had ended there. Hennessey's lawyer requested documentation, and a police enquiry into Aranda Publications, the Sydney distributor, brought skulduggery to light.

The managing director of Aranda was Gunther Harrenstein, a German immigrant of almost fifty years' standing. Harrenstein had a clean record, had known Dean from a past interaction, but claimed to be afraid of him because of a violent episode. He had agreed to handle the books because he couldn't see how the arrangement could go wrong. Dean's name and photograph were on the book, and he had been shown reviews that proved that everything was, for once, legitimate and above board.

"Reviews?" said Hennessey.

Two, according to Andrew Balchin.

But there was a postscript, and it did not make sense. On handing over the books, Dean had said that any profits made could be kept by Aranda. He was not interested in the money, just in the books being properly distributed. When the police suggested that this was a rather odd way to do business, they were told that just about everything Dean did was odd. Hennessey immediately saw another reason: no record of the transaction. So, was Harrenstein lying? Was the story of the transaction merely a tactic, Dean's cute way of keeping the law off his tail and Harrenstein in his debt? Hennessey knew he would have to meet Gunther Harrenstein before that question could be answered. And so, he decided, because he was piqued by Dean's behaviour, and because the police only seemed interested in what the books may have been used for, to do some snooping on his own. It would do no harm to quiz Harrenstein and see where it led. As it turned out, however, his gentle 'quizzing' of Aranda's managing director not only confirmed his suspicions, it also resulted in an invitation from the Hobart drug squad to visit their inner sanctum. The request came within hours of his return from Sydney, and that fact was not lost on Hennessey.

Driving round to where Garibaldi's Italian restaurant had once been, Hennessey parked his Renault 12 and looked for the doorway with the pull-down metal shutter Brownley had described. It was on the left of a fenced-off area, two of the squad's white Fords being in evidence. The unattended reception desk suggested the foyer of a cheap hotel. He dinged a counter bell and waited. A woman appeared. It was the same woman in the same dirty tee-shirt who had visited the flat. She said nothing, merely smiled and showed him into a large, gaunt room containing an assortment of desks and chairs, a row of filing cabinets, a cumbersome photocopier and a large safe of ancient vintage. A glass-fronted office graced one corner. Detective Sergeant Brownley's greeting was similarly low key, the reception of a third individual altogether different. Emerging from the office, a casually dressed, lightly tanned man in his mid-thirties made an immediate impression on Hennessey as he approached.

"Detective Inspector Palfreyman," said Brownley.

Hennessey grasped the extended hand.

"Please!"

Hennessey seated himself as directed.

"So, what have you got for us, Mr Hennessey?"

Hennessey handed over the newspaper cuttings he had extracted from *The Australian* and the *Sun-Herald*. One had a photograph of Dean sunning himself somewhere.

"I see the beard's come off."

"You've got a copy of my book?"

A nod and a smile; Palfreyman had thought it pertinent to acquire a copy. "I'm told you spent some time together."

"We met for drinks on two occasions."

"Talk to you at all about what he thought was important?"

"We talked mostly about my work, then about the book he eventually made off with. He told me he liked it because it dealt with real issues."

"What did you make of Gunther Harrenstein? Let anything of interest slip?"

Hennessey found Palfreyman's manner of speaking and sudden change in direction of interest. "He's under surveillance?"

"You know he is."

"He said he'd warn Dean, if he made contact — didn't want to suffer the repercussions of him being arrested while on the premises. Absolutely frank about that."

Having selected a chair with arm rests, Palfreyman sat back grandly. "What did you make of Herr Harrenstein?"

"He lied to me."

"What makes you think that?"

"He contradicted himself."

"You think they're in this together?"

"Could well be."

Something about Palfreyman bothered Hennessey. There was a laziness in his blue eyes, a tone in his voice that suggested education. Acting on instinct, he said: "What exactly is your interest?"

Turning to Brownley, Palfreyman handed him the cuttings and asked for copies to be run off. When the man was out of earshot he came straight to the point. He had taken the liberty of checking up on Hennessey when Dean's name cropped up, first through Interpol, then through Scotland Yard. Nothing. Then out of the blue a Ministry of Defence blip had appeared. The smile returned. National Service Signals captain in Germany '59 to '62. Stationed in Bielefeld, then Hanover, then Berlin.

"You accessed my military file?"

"You vetted German civilians wanting to work for the British. That must have been interesting."

Hennessey stared at Palfreyman.

"Would you care to elaborate?"

"Haven't we strayed from the point somewhat?"

"It's relevant, believe me."

"Who exactly am I dealing with?"

"Tell me about the vetting you were engaged in."

Hennessey kept his eyes on Palfreyman's face. "Some applicants required more scrutiny than others — it depended on the department they were qualified to work in. There was a huge floating population after the war, some of it still afloat in the late fifties and sixties. Papers lost. Burned. New papers acquired. That kind of thing."

"How long were you involved with Intelligence?"

"Who says I was?"

"We know you were."

"If you know that—"

"Decent rank."

"They bumped me up to captain so that I could function with a little more authority. We were all terribly young."

Brownley approached, but Palfreyman waved him away.

"They didn't bump you up to captain and ask you to sign the Secret's Act so you could listen in to a few Germans being interrogated. You're being modest, Mr Hennessey. You also spent some time in ciphers." A smile. "You're naturally conservative according to your file, yet surprisingly flexible when you need to be. You are, in other words, a contradiction in terms." Before Hennessey could respond, he added: "How good is your German?"

"Passable."

Doubling back, Palfreyman said he was part of a police unit looking into how crime was organised in Australia. It was a new unit. Experimental.

"I was beginning to think you were Intelligence."

"Nothing so grand; but we do sometimes act as an intermediary with ASIO."

"I smell politics."

"Unavoidable."

"Organised crime?"

"A grand slam clean-up of the cesspool, Mr Hennessey. The cesspool you were about to dive into."

"What makes you think I was about to do that?"

"Your visit to Aranda." Another smile. "We were still checking you out when you decided to do that."

"And my being Irish."

"That, too. We had to find out if you had a record."

"My military file is so readily available?"

"One big happy family."

Hennessey hesitated. Then he said, "I couldn't sit back and do nothing. This lot were only interested in what my book may have been used for."

"It's your intention to continue ferreting?"

"You'd rather I didn't?"

"We don't want you getting under our feet." Said quickly, but not by way of a reprimand. "You might even be of help. Friendly chat and analysis? An innocent stumbling about in the thicket?"

"To what end?"

"Our mutual benefit?"

Hennessey's mind was racing. "What exactly are you suggesting?"

"That you keep on doing what you're doing." Palfreyman's expression was a mixture of amusement and curiosity. "You could perhaps start by chatting to a man called Norman Giffard in Sydney. He got out of Pentridge about three days ago."

"You've already talked to him?"

"No point in our talking to him."

"Why should he open up for me?"

"Because you've got a lovely story to tell, haven't you. How you were conned to hand over the manuscript of your novel to a perfect stranger."

"Giffard is known to Dean?"

"We think it was Dean who put him inside."

"Why?"

"Punishment."

And again, Hennessey hesitated. "What you're suggesting isn't normal practice."

"Unusual situations demand unusual solutions, Mr. Hennessey." The smile returned. "It's entirely up to you, of course."

"And if I decide not to?"

"Then you would have to bow out." Palfreyman produced a card and handed it to Hennessey. "Think it over. Call me if you're interested. I'll be here for the next few days." Hennessey glanced at the card and Palfreyman added, "OSI: Office of Special Investigation."

***

A large manila envelope arrived for Hennessey the following morning; it was from his lawyer. The cover letter was short and to the point: Marks Books were continuing to deny all responsibility. A bill of lading and a delivery note had been provided; it showed that one thousand copies of *The Second Strength* had been sent to Australia. Also supplied was the name and address of the consignee in Sydney.

Hennessey's manuscript had apparently been given to Marks Books by a Miss Dyson and returned to her in person on completion of the job. But they had retained the plates for the purpose of printing a further edition if that were required.

Hennessey scanned the bill of lading and the delivery note copies with interest. Shipping company: OCL Australia/New Zealand. Vessel: *Australian Venture*. Port of loading: Tilbury. Number of packages: 18. Gross weight: 175 kg. Measurement: 0.301. Address of consignee: 87 Portobello Avenue, Vaucluse, Sydney. And on the delivery note: 999 books, value of consignment four thousand pounds sterling. The police had been to the Vaucluse address, but Miss Dyson had flown the coop.

He put the letter back into its envelope and laid it on the mantelpiece. Then, looking up the number for the *Sun-Herald*, he punched it in and asked to speak to Rose Munroe, the writer of a half-page feature lauding Dean's praises. Could he hold the line, a voice asked.

"Rose Munroe speaking."

"My name's John Hennessey," said Hennessey, wondering how exactly to phrase what he had to say. "I'm trying to get some information on Gavin Dean, the author of the novel you reviewed some time back — *The Second Strength?*

"What do you want to know?"

Hennessey smiled into the receiver as if by way of apology. "I know you're going to find this difficult to accept, but Dean didn't write that book, I did. I sent the manuscript to him thinking he was going to help get it published, but—"

"You sent the manuscript to him?"

"It's a complicated story. Suffice it to say—"

"I dealt with Mr Dean's public relations people in person, Mr. Hennessey. Everything was above board. Their representative was a Miss Tyson. She—"

Hennessey laughed outright. "You're sure it wasn't Dyson?"

Rose Munroe cut Hennessey short. If he had proof for what he was asserting, then he should go to the police. With that said she delivered a curt goodbye and terminated the call. Annoyed by her dismissal and realising his mistake in not mentioning straight off that the police were already involved, he rang back hoping to make her see sense, but was told she had already left the building. Defeated, and not a little angry with himself for having handled the situation so inadequately, he replaced the receiver and stood contemplating his next move.

3
Crooks with a Philosophy

Thirty-five years since he had put his signature on that sheet of paper, the space in between a mass of contradictions, desires and half-fulfilled ambitions. A different man now; yet in many ways still the same man. Captain John Hennessey of the Royal Army Signals Corps reporting for duty. Duty? Now there was a word to conjure with. No question of his employing his talents because it was his 'duty' on this occasion; merely assisting and reaping the benefits of official backing and support. He laughed to himself as the sheer lunacy of the situation hit home: it was Palfreyman's intention to use him, feed him names and locations and let him loose like a dove among hawks. If he got his craw wrung it would be just his bad luck. But he would, of course, agree to help, he already knew that. Not because he was enamoured of authority figures, but because the idea of Dean playing the sensitive writer made him see red.

Anger, then lethargy as he realised how difficult it would be to track Gavin Dean down on home territory. Then anger again as he read those reviews and relived defeat at the hands of Rose Munroe. A shake of the head. There were no criminals of any kind in his books, just ordinary people involved in their own particular brand of dishonesty.

He waited two days before contacting the enigmatic David Palfreyman; he had no desire to appear eager. On being told that he would cooperate, Palfreyman's suggestion was that they meet in a Greek café in Salamanca Place, but Hennessey insisted that they meet on the same spot as before. When he arrived, Palfreyman was in the little glassed-in office, and there was the hustle and bustle of a busy squad going about its duties.

"You'll have to sign a waiver," said Palfreyman, indicating vaguely that Hennessey should be seated. Then, "I strongly suggest you stick within the guidelines we set for you."

"What do you have me down as?"

"Talented?"

Hennessey huffed a laugh.

"Our suspicion is that Dean is part of a group of serious malcontents, perhaps even some kind of leader. He's also a sociopath. He hates society and everything it stands for.

"Someone like Dean hating society is news?"

"It's more than that. Our sources suggest he's being nurtured."

"I didn't smell politics when talking to him."

"Psychopaths don't retire. Mr Hennessey."

"A moment ago, he was a sociopath."

"He was diagnosed as having strong psychopathic tendencies while in Pentridge. Nasty, nasty temper."

"Totally in control when I met him."

"The woman with him," said Palfreyman, distracted by some horseplay in the big room, "the one said to have been in a car crash."

"I didn't know she had been."

"Well, she wasn't. Someone beat her to a pulp, and we think it was Dean." His tanned face took on a kind of boyish innocence. "Do you know where they met? How they met? In Pentridge. He was doing a three-year stint for armed robbery; she was part of a theatrical group that put on shows, for the prisoners. They got together the moment he was released."

"Harrenstein said she was in Melbourne."

"She's presently with her mother. I wouldn't advise contacting her."

"I have the feeling you're holding out on me."

"One step at a time, Mr Hennessey."

"How am I supposed to have come by this chap Giffard's name and address? He'll want to know."

"Tell him the truth. Tell him the police mentioned him while discussing Dean with you, that being a journalist you knew how to follow through." Palfreyman's smile was suddenly wicked. "Spice it up for him with a description of the local squad dropping in on you. He'll love that. And a bit of the brogue, if you can."

"I've never worked as a journalist."

"You're being pedantic."

"And if Giffard won't talk?"

"*Make* him talk; I'm sure you'll think of something."

Hennessey could smell disinfectant; it reminded him of school. Palfreyman also reminded him of school, of a head prefect he had come to distrust.

"Hold on to things like air tickets and receipts; I won't be able to reimburse you without them." Palfreyman sat blinking. "There will, of course, be a small remuneration for your efforts."

"You're putting me on the payroll?"

"Not quite. You've been classed as a freelance source of information, in loose terms, an informer. Informers are paid for what they come up with."

"Doesn't signing a waiver change that somewhat?"

"Yes, it does. It says you're an honest Joe helping us out, not just a betrayer of confidences."

"So, what is Dean really up to?"

Palfreyman stared straight ahead for some seconds, then he looked at Hennessey and said, "A game to ease his conscience? It would be funny if it weren't so serious. Dean published a pamphlet criticising the Australian penal system while in prison. It's a ripper. They all have some way in which to hide the truth from themselves."

"That truth being?"

"That they don't give a damn about anyone or anything but themselves."

"Some of them have had pretty rough treatment since the day they were born. Can you blame them for looking after number one?"

"It's more than that." Palfreyman embarked on a weary truth. "There's a hell of a difference between looking after number one and ripping off every other person you meet as if it were a divine right. That, as you well know, is Dean's basic philosophy. If it stands still, con it. If it talks back, bash it."

"He was quite attentive with Heather. Looked after her the way you would expect a husband to look after his wife. They looked and sounded like an ordinary married couple."

"The silly bitch bit off more than she could chew." A shake of the head. "Why do they do it? One minute they're teaching Sunday School, next minute they're running drugs." Palfreyman laughed to himself; it was a cruel laugh. "I'm afraid I don't have much sympathy for her, Mr Hennessey. She was an educated woman; she must have known what she was getting herself into."

"Call me John," said Hennessey.

"She gave him legitimacy, John, an appearance of decency. She knew what he was capable of."

"Maybe she thought she was making a statement."

"That may have been going on, but I doubt it. She would have to have been blind as a bat not to detect the contradictions he embodied."

"Crooks with a philosophy?"

"A *loose* system of reasoning."

"And you think Harrenstein's involved?"

"We can't say for sure; that's where you come in. Harrenstein came to Australia from Germany with his parents in '47 at the tender age of five and has turned into a model citizen. The father, a Doctor of Medicine, arrived in '46 by himself, then returned to Germany for his family. Both parents are dead."

"Why the one-year delay?"

"There was a vetting period of nine months."

"Was the IRO functioning then?"

"IRO closed down halfway through '51. Its legal and political functions were spliced into the United Nations; its resettlement function was taken over by another governmental body."

Palfreyman's familiarity with the International Refugee Organisation's role and subsequent demise confirmed Hennessey's conclusion about him. He asked how the German mass migration scheme had worked and was told that a migration agreement had been signed between the Australian Government and the Federal Republic of Germany in 1952. Migrants coming in under the scheme had from then on travelled almost free of charge, both governments contributing to the fare. Or, conversely, they had come in under the landing permit scheme. This scheme had been based on the sponsorship of individuals by relatives or friends in Australia, accommodation and maintenance being guaranteed by the sponsor.

"Your interest in Harrenstein was triggered because of his association with Dean?"

"Dean has the habit of keeping interesting company."

Hennessey chewed on that. "I didn't get to Germany until '59. When I came out of ciphers, they gave me a little office with an interpreter and a typist back-end of nowhere."

"You used an interpreter?"

"I didn't want the interviewees to know that I spoke German." An apologetic smile. "We caught a few small fish that way."

"What did you do with them?"

"Told them politely that they were not required."

The Australian immigration interrogators had had the same problem, Palfreyman said. They had accepted low-ranking Nazi sympathisers into the country for reasons of quota: screening officers had been allowed considerable latitude if the individual was highly qualified. Nothing had been said in the press about this change in policy until 1960, and that in spite of the furore set up by the Australian Jewish lobby.

"Human beings caught up in a bloody nightmare," said Hennessey, eyeing Palfreyman with interest. "Even the innocent felt guilty." Then in a tone that made Palfreyman glance at him, he said, "So who exactly am I dealing with?"

A pause before Palfreyman answered, then everything out in the open, because it was time. "We're a war crimes unit with extended powers attached to the DPP in Canberra."

"Dean's role?"

"A work in progress."

"Knowing Dean alone was enough to make Harrenstein of interest?"

"It made you of interest."

Hennessey's laugh was muted.

"I've been as straight with you as I could be," said Palfreyman.

"And the larger picture is what?"

A pained look from Palfreyman. "That's something I can't discuss, at least not at the moment." The smile returned. "Let's see how things turn out with Giffard."

"I see you've reverted to the American acronym."

In accordance with the cliché, Palfreyman's eyes widened.

"I cut my teeth on the OSI's interrogation manual. It was standard text in '59." Hennessey's smile was again apologetic. "Sorry about that; old habits die hard."

4
Limbo

Hennessey felt light of foot as he left the train at Marrickville, walked up the ramp to the main road and doubled back across the bridge. He loved the strangeness of new locations, and Marrickville's Vietnamese stores crammed with exotic vegetables, fruits and strange packets delighted him. As a child he had spent a lot of his time staring at things, inspecting things, touching things. Intrigued by shape, texture and colour, he had contemplated becoming an artist, but in the end had succumbed to the rhythm of words.

Norman Giffard had not succumbed to the rhythm of words; he chewed on them as if they were pieces of stale bread. Standing on the sagging timbers of a decrepit veranda with grass growing up through its boards, Hennessey thought it all over before it had even begun.

"I can't help you." Giffard's voice was atonal. "I don't know where the bastard is, and I care less." Then, with a distinct edge, he added, "What brought you to my bloody door?"

Palfreyman had not exaggerated the man's size; he was truly enormous. Blurting out that he knew Giffard had been in Pentridge because of Dean, Hennessey waited for the blast.

"Where the hell did you pick up on that?"

"The police," said Hennessey.

Giffard's reaction was immediate; he made to close the door.

"Give a fella a chance!" said Hennessey.

"Fuck off!" said Giffard.

"Fuck off yourself!" said Hennessey.

The door flew open, and Giffard came out fast, very fast for a big man. Hennessey backed off, saying that all he wanted to know was where Dean was holed up.

"And if you knew?"

"I'd have him arrested. There are warrants out for his arrest in two states."

"What's it to you?".

"He swindled me. He published a book I wrote under his own name. It's all over the bloody place."

Giffard digested that. "The police told you about me?"

"One of them let it slip that you'd probably been done because of Dean, that you'd just got out. Is it true he dobbed you in?"

It was written on the big man's face that his mind was working; he ignored Hennessey's question. "They gave you this address?"

"I pried it out of a prison official — fifty bucks did it." The words Palfreyman had framed formed on his tongue. "I'm a freelance journo."

"I can't help you."

"Can't or won't?" asked Hennessey.

"Take your pick," said Giffard.

"Don't you want to see him behind bars?"

"What I want has got fuck all to do with you."

"We're in the same boat."

Giffard's laugh was sour. "Dean's one of the luckiest bastards alive — as I'm sure you already know. Where did you meet him?"

"Hobart."

"He's got a brother in Hobart. Maybe you should ask him where wonder-boy is."

"I will."

The big man laughed again. "You're out of your depth, mate. I'd jack it in if I was you."

"The police aren't doing anything."

"The police are fuckwits."

"I'll find him," said Hennessey. "I will."

"Then what'll you do, kick the gun out of his hand?" Giffard's tone was derisory. "Go home, mate, he'll wring your silly bloody neck."

"You're obviously afraid of him," said Hennessey.

"Of course, I'm afraid of him! You don't fuck around with someone like Dean. He's nuts!"

"Did you know he almost killed Heather?"

"That's no surprise. She was asking for it; silly bitch thought she understood him."

"You probably want him as badly as I do."

"You don't know what the fuck I want."

"How long were you inside? Three years? Must have seemed like forever."

"You've done time?"

"I was in the army."

Giffard tone was suddenly conspiratorial. "A bomb would do the trick, mate. Know anything about bombs?"

"We could nail him if we worked together."

The big man stared at Hennessey. "What help could you be to me?"

"You know the streets, I know—"

"You know bugger all, mate, that's why you're here."

"I can go places you can't go, ask questions you can't. I could be useful." Hennessey went on implacably, holding Giffard's attention with the flow of his words. "Think about it." Producing his pocket diary, he scribbled a contact number on a blank back page and tore it out. I'll be there for a few days."

Giffard accepted the piece of paper from Hennessey without comment and stepped back into his dismal hallway.

"I'm your best chance of nailing him," said Hennessey.

"I'm your best chance of staying alive," said Giffard.

***

Hennessey stayed on in Sydney for three days with Laura's friend Emma and her husband, but Giffard did not make contact. Disappointed, he booked a flight back to Hobart, his intention being to track down the brother. Why hadn't Palfreyman mentioned Dean's connection with Tasmania? And why was a man like Giffard so afraid of Dean?

Emma was intrigued by Hennessey's description of Giffard. She hoped he knew what he was doing. A pause before she spoke again. How had he managed to get a fix on Giffard? Hennessey explained without going into detail.

"You could get into real strife with this business. I suggest you be very careful, John."

They talked on, and he was eventually forthcoming about the rough patch he and Laura were going through. She was probably glad to see the back of him, he said.

Emma let Hennessey talk without interruption; she was a good listener. He fell silent on having said that it wasn't all Laura's fault.

"I know she can be difficult."

Hennessey did not reply.

"You enjoyed your time in London?"

"IRA messed it up for me. I was afraid to open my mouth in case someone thought I was trying to hide my accent.

"You've only got the trace of an Irish accent."

"Exactly."

"Where did you stay?"

"Knightsbridge." A pause. "Laura and I met in Knightsbridge."

Emma heard the cry in that pause.

"You miss London?"

"I don't miss the struggle to survive."

She remembered the day she had first met Hennessey; he had looked so out of place in his tweed jacket and cavalry-twill trousers. He had loosened up a bit since then, but still refused to wear short-sleeved shirts. In some ways more English than the English, but Irish in his heart of hearts. And quite at home in Australia, as far as she could tell. He seemed to understand the surface laziness of the Australian temperament, the continual attempt to disarm seriousness. In fact, he had settled in with remarkable ease, according to Laura.

"She's maybe jealous of your success."

"It's my not earning enough that's the problem. Money is Laura's gauge of success."

Emma was taller than Laura, and slight of build; Hennessey suspected a passionate nature. Laura was passionate, in a mechanical kind of way; her love making sometimes reminded Hennessey of marching by numbers. Not that he was much better; his nature did not allow for flamboyant acts. Yet he longed for them, somewhere in his mind. And Laura, too, he imagined; it was often in her look that he had not managed to cancel the distance between them.

For want of something to say, Emma doubled back to the reason he was in Sydney. She wondered who Dean was planning to morally screw right that minute.

"I suspect he's got a good mind."

"Then why doesn't he use it?"

"He thinks the world is there to supply his needs, that it owes him."

"You sound like the psychologist I used to be."

"He got passed my defences, Emma — I have to respect him for that."

"Takes a sharp one to get past Laura."

"He's a professional."

"You intend to keep going with this?"

"If I can," he said, realising that that was true.

On the return flight to Hobart, he read about the anti-Semite Vladimir Zhirinovsky's claim that Pat Buchanan was a brother-in arms, then about Newt Gingrich trying to stop Buchanan's ascendancy from annulling Bob Dole's attempt to sideline Bill Clinton. A faction on the right was threatening American democracy. Republican respectability was on the line, Buchanan's mania for conspiracy theories and his outspoken belief that Christianity was superior to all other religions was proving difficult for the Republicans to handle. Hennessey turned a page and was informed that skinheads wearing swastikas had attacked an alternative bookshop in Nottingham, and that eight kilometres away another far-right mob had been in action. Thirty-two people had been arrested. As his plane began its descent, he folded his newspaper and placed it on top of the few overnight things in his briefcase, the paper's block capital prophecy of a landslide victory to the Liberal Party at the coming general election staring up at him. Closing the lid, he snapped the catches back into place and prepared himself for the routine of landing, a routine, which for him, was anything but routine.

5
Assignation

David Palfreyman looked relaxed, but he was in fact on edge; he was being quizzed by Jack Murchinson in a gentle voice, and that always spelt trouble.

"What exactly are you getting at?" asked Palfreyman.

Murchinson blinked out a reply. "When the OSI was set up our brief was to build expertise and accumulate information. We've done that. Our capacity to obtain and evaluate information is second to none, yet we're behind the eight ball."

"They're getting clever."

"Overnight they've got clever?"

"They're being advised."

"That's the diagnosis, but by whom?"

Palfreyman admitted that they were not getting the results they had hoped for, that the groups under surveillance were keeping a remarkably low profile. Then a little more brightly he said, "Hennessey's up and running; he's seen Giffard."

"And?"

"Nothing so far."

"He's happy to play along?"

"He signed the waiver."

Hennessey had been fascinated to learn of Australia's early impatience with the trial process for war criminals. Palfreyman had been forced to open up when he realised Hennessey was familiar with OSI priorities. Yes, they were after war criminals, but things were now a little more complicated than in the past. The feeling in Australia in the post war period had been that the community wasn't interested in endlessly pursuing low-level suspects at home. Australia had done her bit through the International Military Tribunal in Tokyo, and through trials in the British zone in Germany. That, it had been felt, was sufficient. The OSI had been vigilant against serious war criminals penetrating the intelligence screen, but as with those Hennessey had interrogated in the sixties, the rest had either been innocent of any crime or guilty of no more than a moral lapse under stress. This view had later been expanded to include belatedly identified members of wartime organisations aligned with the Third Reich, and therein lay part of the problem now being faced. High-ranking German intelligence officers had been awarded entry into America, Britain and Australia on the proviso that they assist in the refining of Allied intelligence procedures, and although this was denied by successive governments, evidence to this effect kept surfacing. Old these individuals may now be harmless in terms of views long held; they were not.

Returning to his previous grievance, Jack Murchinson said, "They've developed a sixth sense, David, and I don't like that. Our ability to handle this is being questioned. Not directly, you understand. Not to my face. But it's in the air."

"It's not ASIO's territory."

"No, but what's going on encroaches."

Palfreyman's instincts made him hesitate; it was bad policy to be too clever too often in Murchinson's company, but it was equally dangerous to appear inattentive or complacent. With that in mind he said he would move things up a gear.

"Yes, you do that," said Murchinson.

***

It was raining heavily, and a huge fire was blazing in the dining room of Tasmania's Cradle Mountain lodge in spite of it being summer. The temperature had again dropped way below the seasonal average. Gavin Dean scanned the dinner menu leisurely, chose east coast scallops curried and pan fried for entree, venison medallions with wild mushroom ragout, red currant sauce and pumpkin dumplings for mains, plus a dessert of Grand Marnier parfait ice cream in a nougat basket with fruit coulis. Then he headed for the wine bay, it being the habit of this particular establishment to let their patrons choose their own bottle and return it to the table. As he entered the trellised enclosure, a Sydney voice drawlingly remarked on the oddity of there being Australian and Tasmanian wines in different compartments. Wasn't Tasmania part of Australia? the voice asked. There was a guffaw in response. When Dean returned to his table he was grinning.

"What's so funny?"

Patricia Dyson, the new woman in Dean's life, had returned from the toilet to find an empty table.

He reiterated what he had overheard.

"Hah!" she said.

"Fucking Tasmanians," he replied.

"You're a fucking Tasmanian!"

"Not in here," he replied, touching his forehead.

According to the guidebook, Lake St Clair Lodge was set in a wilderness of high peaks and deep valleys situated on the boundary of the lake and Walls of Jerusalem National Park in Tasmania's far west. Covering a vast area and containing a jumble of rugged mountains, these parks nestled in deep forested valleys and alpine moorlands. The text eulogised limpid tarns, rock-walled lakes fed by crystal clear streams and falls of snow in midsummer. On this occasion the snow had been swapped for torrential rain.

Patricia Dyson reached for the bottle he had chosen and stared at its impressive label. "Any good?" she asked.

"Tops," he said back.

They sat in silence after that, thinking their own thoughts, their gaze straying this way and that as the dining room filled with an assortment of people.

"What time's he flying in?" she asked.

"Around ten; but it's a hell of a night."

"What's he coming in for again?"

"To see your tits."

It was just his way of talking, she knew that, but it still infuriated her; he was so bloody-minded about everything. Ask him a question and you got the minimum response, or a belittling remark. Or a reply that didn't make sense. Ask him for even the smallest favour and you got no response at all. It was as if he were switched off inside, as if he had hung up the receiver on his emotion.

They had flown into Launceston from Sydney that afternoon, hired a car and headed for the hills. A holiday, he had said at first, smiling at her sweetly. She had realised later that his sweet smile had been silent laughter at her little girl's gullibility, at her willingness to once again take what he said at face value. Like with that bloody book. But there were compensations; he was loaded. She had a good idea where the money came from but didn't care. She enjoyed the surprises as they came and did what she had to do. What she had to do was look after his needs and run his errands. Emotions he might lack but urges he had aplenty. She wondered sometimes where his stamina came from at his age. And there were moments when he did seem to loosen up, when his eyes softened, and she could almost imagine him kissing her for her own sake. But it never lasted; he destroyed any such moment immediately and fled. It was as if he sensed the approach of something in himself, he would not, or could not, accept. So, she very quickly gave up on him, and that in spite of her feelings for him.

Gavin and Trish; Trish and Gavin.

It was she who had travelled to England and arranged with Marks Books to print *The Second Strength* and have it shipped into Australia. She had read the book on the flight back to Australia and had been struck by its sensitivity; a sensitivity she knew Dean did not possess. Yet his name was on the cover, and there was a photograph of him on the back.

Not quite the double act he and Heather had been.

Dean thought about Heather quite a lot, but not in terms of endearment; she was 'stupid-bitch' Heather in his mind in spite of her education and refinement. She had been willing to turn a trick or three but chickened out when faced with the real stuff. Different story entirely when he had got down to the business of how to dismantle the whole fucking system. Not so keen, then. A flushed face and a little frown when she realised, he was deadly serious, that there were no limits to how far he would go. Trish would never be a Heather, not ever, but she looked good on his arm, could put it on a bit, and knew when to shut up. Heather had not known when to shut up.

"So, what are you going to have?" asked Trish.

He blurted out his choice.

"I think I'll have the rack of lamb."

The man flying in was Tom Coates; he had his own plane and there was a bit of a strip only a few kilometres away. Not so easy landing at night with limited ground lights, and in such a Godforsaken spot, but Tom was used to bumping his machine down in the middle of nowhere, and everything had been carefully arranged. Except the rain. The rain had swept in unexpectedly from the mainland. Dean checked his watch, caught the attention of a waiter and handed him the bottle. With a glass of wine in him he would feel better, more able to respond to Trish's need for conversation.

"Not a bad dump, eh?" he said.

"You've been here before?"

"Three times," he said, remembering Heather's delight at the quality of the food.

"On your ownsome?"

"Yup."

"I'll bet," she said back.

He laughed at her expression, drank down a couple of glasses of wine in quick succession and began to feel amorous. It was a spicy Tasmanian pinot and it reminded him of Trish's more intimate parts. So, what did it matter if Tom didn't make it; he and Trish could have a nice time and stay on another day waiting for the weather to change. A day or two perhaps. She'd like that; he'd like that. He was here on business, but play could always be fitted in.

Dean's business interests were varied. He had been involved in club rackets, illegal gambling, race-fixing, prostitution, drug trafficking, armed robbery and even forgery. Even publishing, after a stint with Aranda. But his most astonishing skill — if the rest could be considered skills — was his capacity to lie. He could lie standing up or lying down. He could lie while telling the truth. He could lie looking you straight in the eye. He could lie after admitting that he had just been telling you lies. And he could lie believing that his lies were the truth. That, perhaps, was the greatest test of his lying skill, indeed of anyone's skill in lying; he had the capacity even to deceive himself. It was an astonishing fact, but he could sometimes believe his own lies to such an extent that the truth seemed to be the lie. And so it was with the stolen book, the book that mad Irish bastard was claiming to have written; Dean now felt as if he had written the bloody thing himself, and that, as far as he was concerned, was as good as having actually done so. Taking out his new-fangled mobile phone, he punched in a number.

"What's so funny?" asked Trish.

"I'm ringing a friend," he said back, keeping his eyes on her. "Someone I haven't spoken to in years."

"You remember his number?"

"I never forget a number."

Dean's memory for numbers was phenomenal; he was also very good at mental arithmetic.

"Ah," he said suddenly, putting on quite a different voice. "I'd like to speak to John Hennessey."

"Speaking."

"Ah," he said again, as if deliberating over something. "You've come up in a spot taxation check, Mr Hennessey. Purely routine. A letter to this effect is on its way to you. Yes, it's always a bit of a shock. Sorry about that. Yes, it is rather late, but it's midnight oil here at the moment. Irregular? Not at all. A courtesy, if you like. New policy."

Not for one second had he taken his eyes off Trish's face.

"Goodbye."

"A friend?" said Trish.

Dean's smile blazed out at her; it was as if someone had switched on a light inside his head. "So don't ever become my enemy, Trish," he replied.

***

Hennessey glanced at his watch: nine-fifteen and the rain bucketing down outside. Laura due back late because of some damned meeting. Odd time for the tax office to call but done affably enough. He thought about that as he made his way through to the kitchen. A warning from the tax office? How likely was that? When Laura came in around eleven Hennessey was in bed asleep, a book lying where it had fallen, a half-finished cup of coffee on the bedside table. Waking him with her thumping about, she told him of her annoyance at a colleague's intellectual impertinence and her fed-up-ness with just about everything.

"You're very late," he said.

"Some of us went on for a drink afterwards." She opened the wardrobe and hung up the dress she had been wearing. "Tuffnell had another go at me; it really was the last straw." Her state of mind showed in the way she moved her arms, and her head. "I think I'll resign."

"That's a bit drastic."

"What am I supposed to do?"

"Confront him."

"I've already confronted him."

"I rather got the impression he was gently mocking you the last time we were in his company."

"This was not gentle mocking, John; he went out of his way to insult me tonight."

"How? In what way?"

"By saying that my liking for textual analysis proved I was a rabid postmodernist. Literature wasn't there solely to be analysed and understood; it was there primarily to be read and appreciated."

"He has a point."

"Of course, he has a point; but there's more to reading than that. A student's appreciation of literature is heightened by analysis; analysis reveals a text's subtext, its underbelly. You yourself do not write solely to amuse."

"Understanding isn't always understanding in that sense. It can also be insight."

"Insight is *knowing* something."

"Yes, but not always consciously."

"There's no such thing as unconscious knowing, John."

"What about meaning?"

"What about it?"

"The word 'meaning' can be written down, and in being written become consciously known, but meaning itself doesn't belong to the category *meanings*: meaning isn't meaningful in that sense."

"It's still a word."

"Only when it's written down; prior to that it's an experience, Laura. Experience transcends meanings. Experience is timeless; it exists as the context within which meanings arise."

"Which is language, John."

"Not language, Laura; *psyche*."

"Psyche *is* language."

"Psyche is *soul*, Laura."

"You believe in souls?"

"No, I believe in *soul*."

"You've lost me."

"Sorry," he said back.

***

Tom Coates's little plane did not turn up that evening, or the next, or the next; the edge of a tropical storm kept Tasmania shrouded in rain clouds for over a week.

***

Hennessey had his accountant check with the tax office, but no such call had been made, or authorised. Ringing David Palfreyman, he discussed the call's significance. Palfreyman was intrigued. If the caller was Dean, then his feathers had been ruffled.

The sun reappeared on the Saturday to the delight of Hobart's marketeers. Wandering through Salamanca's market, Hennessey inspected stall after stall of books and records. Laura disliked markets: she preferred regular shops and arcades. On this particular Saturday, however, she did not head to the CBD; she headed instead for a little café in North Hobart, found herself a table and ordered coffee. A man joined her soon after, a man of such good look's heads turned in his direction. Bending, he kissed her on the cheek.

"I couldn't do it," she said immediately. A hopeless little squeak came out of her. "He's so vulnerable at the moment."

Mark Bishop signalled to the waitress, who came immediately. He wanted a short, black coffee and a piece of their delicious almond cake.

The girl nodded and sped off.

"I told him I was thinking of giving up teaching. Because of Tuffnell. He thought I was being overly sensitive, but that just isn't true. Tuffnell's insufferable."

Mark Bishop had heard a great deal about Laura's colleague. She would be better off out of it, he said.

What he had to understand, she said again, but with a new twist, was that Hennessey was not a bad man, or a mean man, just an impossibly self-centred man. And sometimes an incomprehensible man. Her face registered deep hurt and disappointment. He did not seem to need her; she felt superfluous. And he was now so preoccupied with his stolen book she wished she'd never happened on that review.

"It's a bizarre story."

"He's now helping the police in some way."

"You're still unsure?"

"I can't quite fathom why it's me you're interested in." She waved a hand vaguely in the air. "You could have your pick…"

"You're special," he said back.

"In what way?"

"In the way that I like."

She hiccupped a laugh and looked away. Then, apropos of nothing, she said that she wanted to write, and that Hennessey thought that a bit of a joke.

"He's said so?"

A shake of the head.

"How can you know then?"

"I know *how* he thinks; he doesn't think I'm up to it."

"Might just be he doesn't like the idea of there being two writers under one roof."

"That, too, probably," she admitted.

"What will you write about?"

"Stuff. Life."

"Novels?"

"What else?"

A silence.

"Are you having second thoughts?"

"No. Not at all!"

"So, what's wrong, Laura?" A searching look. "Tell me the truth."

She allowed his question to sink right into her before replying, then she said, "I didn't expect it to hurt this much. It really hurts, Mark."

"It ought to," he replied.

6
When Things Are A-cookin'

Norman Giffard's long strides carried him down Pitt Street at a terrific pace. Able to see well ahead because of his superior height, he observed his quarry enter a shop doorway and disappear. Seconds later he was in that shop, but there was no sign of the man he had been following. As there was no other exit, he enquired about his quarry's disappearing act, and was told by the young male assistant that no one of that description had entered. "You're sure about that?" The youth repeated his blunt denial. Staring into what were a youth's pockmarked features, Giffard reached out, grabbed the prissy little tie and pulled the pimpled face towards his own. The young man said nothing, did nothing. "I'll ask you again," said Giffard, not bothering to repeat his question. The young man relented.

"Upstairs?"

A nod from the boy.

"I'll wait." Giffard looked around. "I'll be over there in the corner next to that curtain, and you keep your mouth shut." Said in one breath and followed by, "Don't do anything silly." Going across to where he had indicated, he eased the curtain back and saw the treads of a staircase. Glancing back at the boy, who had not moved a muscle, he sat down on a nearby chair.

Ten minutes passed; customers came and went. When the curtain eventually moved, Giffard said, "Hello, Dave, long time no see."

Dave Hollows spun round, his face a study in confusion. Gathering his wits, he said, "I didn't know you were out."

"Out of sight, out of mind?" Giffard laughed. "I'll tell you, Dave, time just flies when you're having a good time." His huge hands were cupped around one knee, and he was rocking backwards and forwards. "I thought about you often. Just about every day in fact."

"We'd never have got away with it."

"What are you trying to say?"

"Look, you can't blame me for what happened. He was onto us."

"How?"

"I don't know how; he just was. I knew by the way he was acting."

Giffard stared up at Hollows for what seemed an age; then he said, "So where is he?"

"I dunno. He could be any bloody place."

"What's upstairs?" Giffard nodded at the ceiling "A little earner?"

"A mate. I dropped in for a chat."

"The kid knew he had to keep his mouth shut. Why was that do you think?"

"The kid's got brains."

"More than I can say for you, Dave."

"Look, I'd tell you if I knew where he was, but I don't."

"Maybe I just want my old job back."

"Yeah, that'll be right."

"Pass it on."

"You can't be serious."

"I've paid my dues, learned my lesson."

"Don't cause trouble for me, Norman."

"Me!" Giffard's expression was one of surprise. "Not me, Dave. I know where my bread's buttered. Tell him that."

***

Greed had got the better of them; betrayal had put Giffard in prison. Dave had saved his own neck by informing on Giffard early on, as if doing Dean, a favour, but he'd never been sure of Dean's smiling gratitude. Was it for real; or was it game playing? Was he in the clear; or was he being played with as a cat play with a mouse? What neither man knew was that Giffard had looked into his own darkness and come out of prison a changed man.

Laura Greene, on the other hand, had not looked into her own darkness; she was convinced the source of her problems lay elsewhere, that Tuffnell and Hennessey were the fulcrum of her despair. In Myer's department store she caught sight of herself in a mirror and hurried on perturbed. She would resign. No, she would stay on and teach literature the way she knew it ought to be taught. No, she would resign. She would get together with Mark and start a new life and write a novel and show Tuffnell *and* Hennessey what she was made of.

***

"Gifford's on the move." Palfreyman had the phone cradled neatly between ear and shoulder; it was lunch time, and he was sipping coffee between sentences. "Yup. We've had someone on it since you chatted with him. He still hasn't contacted you?"

"Not so far," said Hennessey.

After learning of the OSI's activities in Australia, Hennessey had questioned Palfreyman further and been treated to a mini history lesson. In 1931 the Melbourne-based League of National Security — an offshoot of the White Guard organised in 1923 by the Australian Army chief of staff, Sir Brudenell White — had hatched precise plans for taking over the state in case of a Bolshevik emergency. In possession of arms, this organisation's distrust of democracy's ability to ward off communist infiltration had been so great that Australia's Military Board had had to intervene to stop regular officers from joining its ranks. Called, among other things, the White Guard, this movement had recruited five hundred men and broken a police strike in

1925. By 1935 it had had an estimated eighty thousand recruits at its beck and call. There was of course no similarity between what had been going on then and what was happening now, but by a twist of logic some far right groups had evolved the bizarre notion that they were now the guardians of Australian's soul. Palfreyman's laugh had been derisory. If you added the ravings of white supremacists to the mix, you had the makings of a problem. And this was not to exaggerate the situation; it was a legitimate fear given the concentration of disparate ideas in Australian society that seemed to be coming together. The fact that such notions were being translated into a kind of mad ultra-right philosophy suggested a phobic core with an agenda that went beyond mere rhetoric.

"How about another chat with Harrenstein? Telephone him. Let it drop that you've been speaking to Giffard and that you've got a lead on Dean's whereabouts. If there's anything to the relationship that should make him react."

"Giffard might not like that."

"Who's going to tell him?"

"He won't take kindly to being used as bait."

"You're both after the same thing. Dean might even think you've teamed up with Giffard if he's in with Harrenstein. That would be nice."

"With your resources I'm amazed you haven't been able to locate Dean. Is he so clever?"

"He's got loads of nerve. Always does the unexpected."

"Giffard must have some idea as to his whereabouts."

"I doubt it. He's blundering about in the open in exactly the way one would expect."

"He told me I was out of my depth. Why tell me to pull my head in then proceed to put his own neck on the chopping block? That doesn't make sense."

"The bit about the bomb was interesting."

"He was teasing me."

"He's got a history of violence."

"He probably attracts it."

Palfreyman changed the phone to his other ear. "You'll talk to Harrenstein?"

"Of course."

***

Harrenstein's reaction to Hennessey's telephone call was to say the same things as before, but in an altogether different tone; it was as if the impersonal nature of the telephone robbed him of his acting skills. Yes, he would do whatever was required. No, Dean had not been in contact. No, he had not heard of Norman Giffard. Yes, a court order had been issued and all of the books had been retrieved. Well, almost all. Nineteen copies had sold, which left him with a lot of books cluttering up his stock room. Could Hennessey have them collected as soon as possible? Harrenstein's curtness reminded Hennessey of how the man had sounded as he dealt with staff. But what he was hearing now was more than Harrenstein's business voice, it was a barely disguised rudeness. As far as the little German was concerned, the pressure was off, and Hennessey was no longer of any importance.

"I'll have a friend collect them sometime this week."

"Sooner the better," said Harrenstein.

Hennessey took the plunge. "I think I may have a fix on Dean; Giffard let something slip."

"That's good news."

"Yes, it is, could be the break we've been hoping for."

"We?"

"The police? Myself?"

"Of course," said Harrenstein.

"If it works out, he's in for one hell of a surprise." Hennessey moved on: "Anyway, I've got to go. Thanks for your help. I'll arrange to have the books collected."

"Let me know if you get lucky," said Harrenstein.

"I'll do that," said Hennessey.

***

Laura didn't give a damn about Dean or the stolen book; she was at that moment occupied with more important matters: her thoughts. She had flirted with Mark Bishop at a party and given in to what she believed to be her need about a month later. Chance and a cup of coffee. Chance and a lot of talk about nothing. Chance and back to his place knowing what was about to happen. She moved down the hallway towards the lounge amazed still at her own brazenness. A look and it had been on. Something in the eyes, in the shape of the mouth. Availability. A sudden flush and they had been driving across town to his flat. A key in the door and a hallway not unlike the one she had just traversed and straight into bed. As quick as that, the act of betrayal. But betrayal was perhaps too strong a word; she had not felt at all like a betrayer as they tumbled about. At least not immediately. The act of betrayal had come later when what had been no more than a mad escapade had turned into what they now called love.

"You're back," said Hennessey.

Laura sighed theatrically. Hobart was no longer the sleepy little backwater it had once been. She took off her jacket and examined the patches of perspiration under each arm. It was beginning to feel like Sydney. People everywhere. Packed cafés. Traffic. Fumes. She had been glad to get out of it. And then, as if by way of an afterthought, she informed him that she had bumped into Mark Bishop and that they had gone for coffee. Did he remember Mark? Yes, the architect. She bantered on about some proposed development across from Salamanca and said that Mark was against the whole idea. Because of its height. It would cast a shadow right across to the buildings on the opposite side. Sheer madness. A travesty of everything sensible and the bloody council was all for it. On and on she went, moving around all the time, agitated, her face sharpened by her supposed annoyance.

During a lull, he said that he might have to go back to Sydney.

"More snooping?"

"I want to get to the bottom of this book nonsense. Why don't you come with me?"

His invitation seemed to trouble her; she stood blinking.

"You need a break. A couple of days in Sydney would do you a world of good. Us."

She screwed up her face. She couldn't. Tuffnell would find out and she'd never hear the end of it.

"Tell Mike you've got to have a couple of days off."

"He can't spare me right now."

"Confide in him. People like to be confided in."

She shook her head. No, that was not possible. Tuffnell would not take kindly to having to share her lectures; it would be playing right into his hands. He would have to go by himself. He said that he did not want to go by himself. That seemed to annoy her. Her agitation became even more pronounced. What was the point? He would be snooping, and she'd be left on her own. She might as well stay in Hobart. She had things to do. She would be in the way. She was tired. Sydney was not what she needed right that minute.

"What do you need right this minute?

"Lots of space and time to think." Said quickly, emphatically. The dam was about to burst, and she knew it. "I've had all I can take of just about everything and everyone."

"What does that mean?"

She hesitated, knowing that there would be no way back once she got started. Then, falteringly, she let it all out; well, most of it. He listened in amazement as her tale of woe developed, tried to reason with her, calm her, but that infuriated her. Her voice became so shrill at one point he had to put his hands over his ears. And then she quietened down and stood by the window looking out at the river. Did he realise how difficult he was to live with? He was so bloody self-contained. Butter wouldn't melt. Always on the side of the angels, so it seemed. A paragon of virtue and good sense and never out of line. Did he realise how maddening that could be?

"There isn't much I can do about my personality," he replied, feeling the spirit drain out of him.

"You're so damned superior!"

"It's all my fault?" he said back. "It's my fault our sex life is a shambles. It's my fault you're bored out of your mind here and at work. It's my fault I don't fly off the handle at the slightest provocation."

She raised a hand in self-defence. Okay, so she was in a mess over her job, she admitted that. But he knew damn well that that was not the root of the problem. His morose silences were deadly. He went off into that little world of his for days on end and could not be reached. His inner world appeared to be more important to him than the real one.

"Sometimes it is."

"Well, then."

"Well then what? You know what it takes to write something. If anyone should know, *you* should know."

"Yes, but—"

"What you're criticising now is not what you were criticising a moment ago. You're running two separate arguments and I can't let you get away with that."

"I can't criticise your behaviour?"

"You're not listening. You can say whatever you like about my behaviour, but you do not have the right to criticise my space. That is to go too far."

"Now you're a law unto yourself?"

"I'm suggesting no such thing. I'm saying that when things are *a-cookin'-there-aint-nuthing-I-can-do-about-it-baby*." His fake American accent almost made her laugh. "That's what I mean, and you ought to know that without being told."

"Now I'm a dolt?"

"Hardly," he said, tired of her halfway logic. Then, changing tack, he said, "All I've heard from you for God knows how long is Tuffnell, Tuffnell, bloody Tuffnell, so I'm actually glad to see this out in the open."

She did not respond immediately; she stood blinking at him. Then she said, "It's more than Tuffnell, John. It's us. We've run out of steam."

"You don't really believe that."

"I know what I feel."

"You're allowing Tuffnell to colour everything. That isn't fair."

"It isn't just Tuffnell."

He acknowledged the point by jutting his chin at her. "So, what are you saying?"

She twisted her mouth to one side, then the other; it was as if the words she was forming were fighting one another. "I need time to myself."

"So, you keep saying, but what does that mean?"

"I want a trial separation."

Dumbfounded, he stared at her.

"I'll move out for a bit, get a room in town."

"How long is a while?"

"I've no idea."

She would take a few overnight things and come back later for some clothes, she said in a small, determined voice. She would stay in a hotel for starters.

"I can't believe you're doing this."

"I've been thinking about it for weeks."

"Is there someone else?"

Her reply was chastening. "Don't shift the baseline, John. It's *us* that's the problem."

An hour later she was gone, and the house echoed with the lack of her. He stood in the hallway and contemplated that fact, the sensation of her parting kiss flaring on his cheek

7
Short-changed

A handful of words had changed everything; it was as if she had slapped him hard across the face without warning. And now here they were, she in her too expensive hotel room with its single bed and fake marble en suite, he amidst the bits and pieces that up until an hour before had constituted their home, their life. The basic problem was out in the open like a wound with the bandages removed, and she suspected there was little chance of it healing.

She bent forward and rested her head on her arms, the warmth of her breath returning to bathe her face. So, what to do? Ring Mark and have him come over to comfort her? Take a sleeping pill and drop into oblivion? A deep breath and she was straight again. She would arrange to meet Mark in the bar downstairs — seeing him would push things into perspective.

Unpacking her overnight case, she tidied everything away and returned to sit on the single bed. A smile. John would be at the whisky by now, his Irishness would demand it. The image in her mind sparked off a similar need. Getting up, she availed herself of a brandy from the mini bar. When Mark arrived, she was nursing her second brandy in the high-vaulted space downstairs. She signalled, and he came over. Proffering a cheek, she said that a couple of brandies had steadied her.

"You told him?"

She shook her head. He stood looking down at her for a second or two, then went off to get a drink for himself. She watched him order. When he returned, she said, "The barmaid watched you all the way back."

He returned an inconsequential smile. "What happened?"

"It started with him wanting to take me to Sydney. I said I couldn't just float off like that. He persisted and things got out of hand."

"Why didn't you tell him then?"

"It wasn't a confession; it was an argument." She remembered how she had screamed, how John had winced. "I'm not as nice a person as you think I am."

"We all have our dark side, Laura."

"I've never seen yours."

"I've got a bit of a temper." He looked across at the bar, back again. "So, what did you say to bring this about?"

"I told him he was too wrapped up in himself. I told him he was smug. I told him we had run out of steam." She gave a little laugh. "I told him he was a paragon of virtue and good sense and that I found that maddening at times."

"Not exactly an indictment."

"It got more complicated after that." Draining her glass, she placed it a little too carefully on the mat. "He can be infuriating, Mark. "

"What else did you say?"

"I said I needed to be on my own for a bit." She made a face. "I said some pretty hurtful things by the time I'd finished."

"How did he react?"

"He had a go at me. I've never seen him quite that angry before. I didn't know he could get that angry."

Mark was frowning. "So, what happens now? Are you going to stay on here?"

"I'll get an apartment."

"You're saying it's over."

"We've agreed on a trial separation."

His frown became a twisted smile. "Trial?"

"A trial separation was difficult enough for him to digest; it came out of the blue as far as he was concerned."

"He must have known it was more serious than you were letting on."

"He knew; he didn't know."

Mark, too, was finding the situation difficult to digest. "I'm going up the island for a couple of days. Come with me."

A quick shake of the head. She preferred to stay put. A big impersonal hotel was just what she needed.

He looked away, and up. "We won an architectural award for this place."

She followed his gaze up into the desolate heights above the bar. "You must have built it with the likes of me in mind."

"Come with me, Laura."

She shook her head again, smiled at him.

"So why am I here?"

"Support?" Tears welled. "I feel so *awful*, Mark."

"It would have been a good time to end it, Laura."

"It would have confused the issue."

"That being?"

"That something has failed that wasn't supposed to." She took a breath and struggled on. "If I can get out of this without telling him, I will."

"Why, for God's sake?"

"Because I don't want him to think he has an excuse to not bother thinking about what has happened — it's as much his fault as it is mine. He has to realise that." Her tears had not come to anything. "I didn't tell him because he would have used the information to close shop. It would have been shutters down and good night, Laura. I did not want it to end like that."

"It would've been kinder."

"He asked me outright if there was someone else."

"And still, you didn't tell him?"

"It was too easy."

"Too final?"

"Too quick."

"What did you say?"

"I told him the baseline was *us*, not some other dredged up notion. I'm paraphrasing."

"He left it at that?"

"He responds to subtlety."

"I think all you've done is postpone the inevitable. You should have put the poor bastard out of his misery." The twisted grin returned. "If he finds out you've been screwing around—"

"Pardon?"

"You know what I mean."

"I do *not* know what you mean!"

"Us?"

"That's not how that sounded." Her eyes were alight with a mixture of chagrin and brandy. "It sounded like an accusation."

"It was nothing of the kind."

"I am *not* screwing around, Mark!"

"Of course not; that's not what I meant."

Tears welled again. "Sorry, I'm not at my best right this minute."

"Of course, you aren't."

"I just want to sleep, and sleep…"

Getting up, he came round to her, attempted to comfort her, but she very gently pushed him away. The barmaid was watching, she said.

"Shall we go upstairs?"

A shake of the head; she needed to be alone.

"I won't be back in Hobart for a couple of days."

"I'll survive. Being alone is what I need."

"We could eat here this evening."

Another shake of the head. She was too upset to eat anything.

"I'll ring you the moment I get back."

"Yes, do that," she said.

***

Hennessey made himself a mug of tea and sat sipping at it; his second glass of whisky was on the lounge room table untouched. He could smell it. The tea was bitter on his tongue; he'd forgotten to add sugar. He sipped slowly, the hot liquid pacifying him. For a brief moment he forgot that anything was wrong, then the feeling of dread came back like a weight. She was gone and he was alone; time had been suspended. His mind slipped a gear, and he started thinking about Gavin Dean. What was he going to do about that bastard? Dean and Laura, Laura and Dean — it was all too damned much. Tears formed in his eyes, but he brushed them aside. How was he going to work while in such a mess? He exchanged his empty mug for the glass of discarded whisky and downed it. God how he wished he still smoked; he'd give anything to light a cigarette and feel it flush the tension out of him. He closed his eyes. He could smoke if he wanted to. She was gone. The tears started again, and he did nothing to stop them.

He ate out that evening, at his favourite Thai restaurant, read a little to evade his thoughts, and was accosted by a friend of Laura's that he did not like. She was effusive; he was evasive. Laura was... visiting. He smiled, willing Laura's friend to go away, but she persisted. He was to join her party of two women and a man since he was on his own. He continued to resist; she continued to persist. She said that he just had to join them because he could not sit there by himself reading. He said that he did not mind being by himself and that reading in restaurants was something he enjoyed doing. She said that he'd find the people with her really interesting and that he just had to come over and join them. He declined for a third time. She started in on him again and he told her to fuck off. Quietly and looking right into her face he said, "Fuck off." She stared at him and blinked. He kept his eyes on her face until the penny dropped. She turned and walked back to her table without a word. It was the first time he had ever done anything like that, and it exhausted him.

He sat staring at the page he had been reading without taking anything in; it was as if he had changed dimensions. The light seemed yellower; the book seemed to float in his hand. And when his meal of sizzling chilli fish came, it looked positively psychedelic. Was he developing a migraine, he wondered. He was one of the lucky ones, he got migraine without the pain. Jagged strings of emerald, green light and a feeling of vertigo would herald their approach, but there was never ever any pain. Bits of light, like teeth, or the filament in an electric bulb, would burst into his visual field along with a metallic taste in his mouth, but the pain never came. Someone had suggested that he might be an epileptic without fits. Migraine without pain? Epilepsy without fits? What else did he lack? The usual emotional responses, Laura had suggested.

He ate slowly, savouring each mouthful. The woman he had rebuffed turned to glance at him a couple of times, but he pretended not to notice. His name would be mud within a few days, but that did not bother him. In fact, it pleased him to think that he had finally got this fawning female out of his life. He had put up with her imbecilic attention on a number of occasions, on the street and elsewhere, and it was only Laura who had stopped him from dropping some acid remark. Laura would give him one of her looks and he'd stand under an avalanche of praise and appreciation. She was not a bad sort, Laura would say. Her heart was in the right place. But there was a limit to how much fawning and scraping and cajoling one human being could take, and for reasons that he could never quite understand she had always stood too close. It was as if she were trying to crawl inside your skin as she lavished you with praise.

He finished off his meal with a strong black coffee, something he did not generally do, paid his bill and made to leave, but it was not to be. She of the overflowing sensibilities got up and headed for him as he headed for the door. They triangulated at the door handle.

"Yes?" he said.

"I've got to say something.".

"You surprise me," he replied.

"That was the rudest thing anyone has ever said to me. I think you should apologise."

"Why?"

"I've just told you why."

"No. You've stated a simple truth."

"I'm sorry?"

"What I said to you was the rudest thing anyone has ever said to you. So, the real question is, why?"

"You owe me an apology."

"No, it is you who owe me an apology." He opened the glass door to let someone in. "I've never ever spoken to anyone the way I just spoke to you, and it was you who caused me to do so." Her mouth sagged open. "You just don't get it, do you? I did not tell a nice, kind, helpful woman to fuck off, I told you to fuck off because you are a pain in the arse. You don't know you're a pain in the arse, but that is what you are, and telling you was my way of letting you in on a secret. Now if you would like to discuss this further, I'll stand you a coffee and we can sit over there in the corner and discuss it. If not, I'm going home to bed."

She looked round involuntarily at the corner he indicated. Then, looking back at him, she said, "You're raving mad!"

"You're absolutely right," he replied, "I'm mad as all hell and you had better believe it!"

8
Birds of a Feather

Gavin Dean and Gunther Harrenstein approached Rosie's Steak Bar around eleven-thirty in the evening. It was a warm, breathless night and Sydney's red-light district was abuzz with life and drama. So much so that a white paddy wagon outside one of the many neon-lit clubs was already full of customers. Dean stopped to watch the officers — one of them an attractive brunette — go about their business. He was in such a good mood even their antics seemed to please him. Engaging the female in banter, he let it drop that he had been with the Victoria force, district something-or-other, plain clothes, but that he had had to leave for health reasons. So, what was going on? All done with an insider's knowledge of the lingo and the attitude; an insider on the wrong side of the law who collected experiences like an entomologist collects insects. And when asked by Harrenstein why he had taken such a risk, informed by Dean that that was what made life interesting — people wanted to believe what they were told, even policewomen. A guffaw from Dean as they entered the air-conditioned bar and headed for the open plan balustraded restaurant with its pink-shaded lights and matching starched tablecloths. The bitch had been wide open and off guard and given another half an hour he could have got into her knickers.

What was left of the evening became progressively more bizarre. Dean was charming and civilised one minute, argumentative the next, brash and alternately withdrawn. Nothing about his personality seemed fixed. It wavered like a candle in a draughty room. His strong, bony hands clenched and unclenched as he spoke, his eyes darting this way and that as patrons poured in to eat and drink and listen to the jazz quartet that played into the early hours. When the music started up it was as if he were feeding off the energy of the sound. By the time their meal arrived, he was high and talking excitedly about some CD he had bought.

"You like music?" asked Harrenstein, fascinated by Dean's catlike attention to everything; there was even something catlike about his eyes.

"Yeah. You?"

"Very much. My daughter is a very fine musician. She's at the conservatorium."

"No shit."

"My father played the violin."

"My old man played the mouth organ."

Harrenstein was at a loss; Dean was not smiling, and he did not know how to react. "My father died of a heart attack some years ago," he said, not knowing what else to say. "My mother died soon after."

"Mine too," said Dean. "They fell off the perch in the same week. Left a house and a car and about twenty grand in cash.

"You were close?"

"Nah. My old man was bonkers, and she wasn't far behind."

"Siblings?"

A look of distaste formed on Dean's face. He had a younger brother, a non-entity and proud of it, he said. Chalk and cheese, they were. Lived in Tasmania with some bird he'd picked up in Sydney. Neither of them could read. Not a word. But Christ he could draw. Anything. Birds. Animals. Especially rearing horses. Bloody brilliant at drawing horses. He made his living selling drawings in Salamanca Market on a Saturday morning. A wizard with the brush as well. Got it from his old man.

"Your father was an artist?"

"Yeah, a piss artist." Dean exploded into laugher. "Couldn't hold a fucking pencil most of the time."

The first two hours passed. Dean drank heavily, Harrenstein circumspectly. A singer appeared, a tall blonde with a deep voice and an even deeper cleavage. She seemed to know Dean and it soon became obvious that she was the reason they were there.

"Beautiful tits," he kept saying.

Harrenstein's eyes rested on the heaving bosom, then moved back to Dean's face. It was a remarkably smooth face for a man of his age, the teeth small and even, the nose straight, the eyes grey green, the hair sandy, but thinning. An intelligent face but twisted at the jaw.

"What's her name?" asked Harrenstein.

"Milly. You like?"

"She's got a good range."

"More than you'll ever know."

"You've slept with her?"

"You don't sleep with a woman like Milly."

When her bracket ended, Dean made his way to where she was standing, and as Harrenstein watched, all hell broke loose. Kissing the singer on the cheek, Dean was on the point of saying something when a big man in a checked shirt rolled out of the crowd and landed him one on the side of the head. It was a heavy blow, and a second and third to the body brought Dean to his knees. But although down, Dean was not out; he caught his attacker off guard with a jab to the genitals, and as the man bellowed and doubled over, an uppercut sent him sprawling back into the crowd. On his feet again, Dean dived at a very drunk Norman Giffard. Seconds later, spitting invective at one another, they were hauled apart by a couple of bouncers. The police arrived: a burly sergeant and a diminutive brunette. Saying something to the sergeant, the policewoman turned to Dean while Giffard shouted obscenities.

"Don't ask me what happened." He waved a hand at the crowd. "Anyone'll tell you he came at me without warning."

A chorus of voices confirmed that that was true.

"Are you okay?"

"Couple of bruises. Nothing to cry about."

"You know him?"

"Never saw 'im in my life."

"You want him charged?"

"What's the point? He's drunk as a skunk. Must have had a crush on Milly." Turning, Dean put an arm round Milly's waist and drew her in tight; her bosom bulged ominously.

The young constable smiled. "We'll take him off the street. Might have another go."

Giving her a knowing look, Dean said, "For the best, I think."

And that was that. He returned to his table and stood watching as Giffard was led from the premises, both bouncers walking behind just in case. Harrenstein mimicked applause as Dean seated himself. No reaction from Dean; the bruise on the side of his head was beating out a pulse in time with the music, which had started up again.

"She was working on the assumption you really had been in the force. I could see it in her face."

A winded Dean smirked, but he was shaking slightly and hid his hands from view.

"That was some wallop you took."

Dean touched the side of his head gingerly.

"Someone with a grudge?"

"Must have thought I was someone else."

Harrenstein said nothing for a second or two, then quite pointedly he said, "You don't have to lie to me."

"I don't have to do *anything* for you," said Dean, his tone flat and menacing.

"We have to be careful, Gavin. *You* have to be careful. You should only use your talents when they're required."

"I like to keep my hand in." Dean grinned. "Or up."

"Yes, but—"

"If I hadn't told that bitch, I'd been in the force I might still be trying to talk my way out of what just happened."

"That's hardly likely; there were plenty of witnesses."

"If they'd checked my ID things would have been different."

"Then it was a chancy thing to do."

"Not when you're awake. When you're awake you see what other people don't see, do what other people don't do."

"What do you see?"

"That everyone's telling everyone else stories, and that they never stop." Dean laughed at Harrenstein's incomprehension. "They're all dreaming, mate. All of them. Dreaming with their eyes wide open. The young cop I talked to was dreaming. You're dreaming."

"I'm wide awake."

"You're asleep with your fucking eyes open!"

Harrenstein had no idea what Dean was on about; he began to argue with him but was told to shut up. Becoming belligerent, Dean said that everything was a story. What he did was run his story into someone else's until his story took over.

"That doesn't mean other people are idiots."

"It does if they don't ever wake up to what's going on."

A glimmer of what Dean was getting at began to register on Harrenstein, and Dean's smile, thin and lopsided when it came, gave Harrenstein's glimmer of enlightenment recognition.

***

Laura's clothes were still in the wardrobe when Hennessey returned from the shops. He stared at them for a moment, then slammed the wardrobe door. Going back into the lounge he wandered about distractedly, then went into the kitchen, then, for no other reason than that he was in the kitchen, out into the garden. The nectarine tree, he noticed, was laden with fruit, so he pulled one and bit into it, but it was not quite ready. His temper flared. How he hated this so-English garden with its endless rose beds and its big backgrounding wall of sandstone. It was an old woman's garden. Everything about it stank of age and another time. The old rose bushes. The old fruit trees. The old wall linking it to Secheron House. He stamped back inside and slammed the backdoor behind him with such force the whole house trembled, and the key fell out of the lock. Grimacing, he headed back down the hallway. He'd call Emma and have a chat; she'd talk some sense into him. Into Laura, too, perhaps.

That was when he remembered how cold he had been during the night. Lying wide-eyed in the dark he had contemplated their argument and concluded that she had been not a little dishonest. Yes, he had some funny little ways, but she was no different in that respect. Her obsession with literature and the department were just as idiosyncratic as any aspect of his creative life. They were workaholics both who had lost touch with one another, that's all there was to it. He could not remember falling asleep, but it must have been an age afterwards. Later, when he had got things back into perspective, he phoned his Sydney friends and got a very surprised Laura instead.

"You're at Emma's?"

"I caught an early morning flight."

"How are you?"

"Does it matter?"

A normal kind of question, but not on this occasion; it left him further deflated. "This is silly, Laura."

"I need time to find my feet, John."

"Yes, but—"

"I don't much feel like another argument."

And that was that. She said bye and hung up, leaving him wondering what the hell she had told Emma and Michael. He groaned at the thought of that. Another argument? He could not remember arguing with her the first time. Yes, he had made a point or two, but he had not argued with her in any real sense. There were lots of things he had wanted to say, but he had not been given the chance. And when she fell silent, he had felt that anything he had to say was no longer relevant — except for the question she had so neatly avoided. Out of all the replies she could have come up with the one delivered had left him outflanked.

The phone rang ten minutes later; it was Michael. He talked freely, so Hennessey guessed he was in his study. Laura was now in a better space, but she had been pretty ragged when she arrived. And he should not bank on seeing her any time soon; Emma was trying to keep her in Sydney for at least a week. Maybe longer. Hennessey asked what had been said about their situation. Not all that much, according to Michael. At least not in his company.

***

Palfreyman spoke into the receiver with an almost exaggerated precision. There was nothing to be had from Dean's brother. The man was an innocent with no knowledge of Dean's trafficking. He should have another crack at Giffard; he was the key to finding Dean.

"Why are you so interested in Dean?"

"Because it's rumoured, he's moving large quantities of drugs and we want to know for whom."

"So?"

"They're being used to generate income on a large scale."

"If you know that much—"

"Rumours, John. A word here, a word there. Nothing substantial. It's a ghost town out there except for small fish plying their wares. We *all* want to know why. You'll be doing the Giffard's a favour. Dean must be aware by now of Giffard's blundering attempts to find out where he is, so the faster we find Dean the faster any threat to Giffard and his wife will be removed."

"He's married?"

"Didn't I say?"

"Hennessey shook his head.

"Quite touching, really. Aboriginal. Her name's Mary."

"He'll probably clam up on me like he did the last time."

"I get the impression you like him."

"He's brighter than you give him credit."

"Perhaps."

A sigh from Hennessey, then, "Explain to me how Dean managed to escape from police custody twice? How is that possible?"

"He may have had an arrangement with the squad. It's not unheard of. Could be he had immunity in New South Wales at some point for dropping a hint or two."

Having opened a crack for Hennessey, Palfreyman opened it further still. "Giffard may have been a present by way of that arrangement."

"I find that disturbing."

"You don't know the half of it."

Hennessey hesitated. "If his resistance is too great, I'll withdraw."

"I trust your judgement."

"Perhaps more than I do," said Hennessey.

9
Mad as all Hell

Laura found herself having to justify her actions to Michael, and that annoyed her. So much so that at one point, as all three wandered around Sydney's sparkling Circular Quay, she attacked him and said that his being a man was distorting his perspective. That did not go down well. Michael came straight back at her, and Emma was forced to intervene. Not a pleasant moment, and one that rankled for the rest of the afternoon in spite of the beautiful weather and Michael's rather obvious attempts at atonement.

A rather cardboardish submarine tethered next to a frigate held their attention for a moment; the submarine looked like something out of an old Flash Gordon movie. Emma suggested they grab a coffee and they wound their way back the way they had come, the 3-D super-screen cinema's cafeteria being where they ended up.

"How serious is it, Laura?" asked Michael, daring to broach what had become the unbroachable when he was around. The two women had talked long and hard in the privacy of the garden, and that signalled stuff said beyond his knowing.

Laura's reply was off centre; it jumped the rails. Looking out at the quay where the water glistened almost blindingly, she said what she believed to be true: she would rent a small apartment and settle down to write. Probably in Sydney. Most likely in Sydney. When she gave up her job all sorts of things would be possible.

"You're resigning?"

"I want to *write*, Michael; he isn't the only one with that bug. I've been thinking about it for years. He's amenable to the idea but doesn't really believe I've got it in me. I'm talking fiction, of course." A looking away, then back. "My being an academic apparently debars me from having an imagination. The imagination is sacred territory for John. A fetish, almost. He talks about it as if it's another bloody brain."

"I've never ever detected what you're describing."

"Let's just say that he'd much prefer that I kept doing what I'm doing." Laura grimaced. "It's not so much in what he says, but in how he says it."

"He may not like the idea of someone trying to write fiction in the same space as himself." Laura was reminded annoyingly of Mark having made the same point. "You know, she's working and I'm not and I've got to work because she's working kind of thing. More a fear of being driven to compete when all he wants to do, say, is sit in the garden, or go for a walk. It could be as simple as that."

Laura's reply was again off centre. "When things aren't *cookin'*, he goes to a café and reads. Waits." A frown. "He spends a lot of time *waiting*."

"What do you do?"

Laura found Michael's question disturbing; it made her stomach contract. Looking straight at him, she said that her attempts at the novel were done in secret and always ended up in the bin because she didn't have the *necessary* time to develop her thoughts, the *freedom* to develop her thoughts. Novels were tricky things; they demanded endless skill in composition and her job simply didn't allow for that kind of concentration. Sensing continuing resistance, she said that she never got the time to cook the way he cooked. She grabbed an hour here or there; he, on the other hand, spent whole days, sometimes a whole week, trying to find out what it was he wanted to say.

"That's why you left?"

"It's complicated, Michael. Let's leave it at that."

"Complicated?" He frowned back at her. "What aren't you telling us, Laura?"

Emma's expression signalled that Michael should desist, for what Laura was saying without saying it was that she had had an affair as a result of creative frustration and not much else, and that it had become a catalyst for change. It was not that she had fallen out of love with one man and into love with another, it was that an affair had been her way out of an impasse.

There was a silence. Laura broke it with yet another off-centre truth. She was afraid of failure, she said. She spent most of her time lecturing about writing and the madness of writers and knew how difficult writing could get.

"You envy them the battle?"

"Yes, I do. Why should *he* have all the fun?"

It was a ridiculous statement, and they laughed, but it was nervous laughter, for at the back of Laura's mind, and Emma's, was the glaring fact of betrayal. Shocked by the starkness of that fact, Laura sat forlorn and momentarily mute. Then she said, "I think we've had it, Michael."

The anguish in her voice was such that neither Emma nor Michael felt able to reply, the ensuing silence dummying and flattening the atmosphere like a withdrawal of breath.

"It doesn't have to be like that," Emma said, touching Laura's arm. "What happens next is up to you."

"What happens next is anyone's guess," Laura replied.

***

Michael rang the following morning to confirm that Laura had been talked into staying on in Sydney. Hennessey said he would be there himself later that day; could they meet for lunch. Michael was enthusiastic, then apologetic. Where would he stay? A hotel, Hennessey said. He rang off soon after and managed to get a cancellation on a packed flight, but not a return.

Another hated flight to try his nerves.

He arrived in Sydney fifteen minutes late. An animal of some sort had escaped its pen and was roaming around the disembarkation area. By the time they landed there was almost a carnival atmosphere on the plane, the pilot having kept everyone informed of developments. Pensively trying to ignore the plane's internal rumblings, Hennessey thought about what he might say to Giffard. Or to his wife if he weren't there. That realisation stopped him in his tracks; he had never spoken to an Aboriginal person before.

Michael, too, was late. When he arrived, Hennessey was tucking into a plateful of onion bhaji, an ice-cold lager already drained and replaced. The journey in from the airport had been hell due to a breakdown in the bus's air-conditioning system.

"You've got a head start."

"I was famished."

Lifting the menu, Michael said, "Emma sends her love."

"And Laura?" asked Hennessey.

"I didn't mention your being here."

"How is she?"

"Wretched."

Hennessey looked down into his plate. "She's been winding up to this for months, Michael."

"You didn't say anything?"

"I didn't know what to say. She was too prickly to tackle."

"She still is."

"You've had a run in?"

"Several. I think journalists are below her dignity."

"Emma?"

"Emma knows how to handle Laura."

"God bless Saint Emma."

A waiter came and took Michael's order.

Omitting to say that he was working alongside the police, Hennessey filled in the blanks.

"Is doing what you're doing advisable given what you've told me about Dean?"

"I'm looking after my own interests. The police are only interested in the supposed drug connection."

Michael began to probe, but Hennessey kept him at bay. It was too soon to say what was going on, but it was getting interesting. He returned to Laura and her intentions, to what she had said and not said, to how Michael was reading her *not* said.

"She's hurting, John."

"I'm aware of that."

"Are you? Really? She doesn't think you are."

"Did she talk about wanting to write?"

"That's when I got it in the neck."

Leaning on the table, Hennessey stopped eating. Laura's declared wish to write was one of the great imponderables he had had to deal with, he said. She kept talking about wanting to write, but nothing ever happened, at least not to his knowledge. In saying continually that she wanted to write she had found a foil to parry with, a sharpened tool with which to inflict passing pain. She didn't talk about wanting to write a novel; she talked about wanting to write *novels*. She was, in her head, far too far ahead of herself because she was full of other people's novels and unable to decide what kind of novel she wanted to write. There was this kind of novel and that kind of novel, there was this style and that style, this tense and that tense. Stuff like that; endless stuff like that. All legitimate questions, of course, but way down the track from sitting in an empty room staring at a sheet of blank paper. *That,* she had not yet properly addressed.

"Imagination?" ventured Michael, remembering Laura's remark about imagination being sacred to Hennessey.

"Imagination is *descent*, not *ascent*," said Hennessey, past conversations with Laura surfacing. "Imagination, as Coleridge rightly inferred, is not *fabrication*. Fabrication is taking characters or ideas and twisting them to your own meagre conscious purpose; imagination is the exact opposite of that. One does not write a novel; one is written *by* a novel."

"That's—"

"Shite? A lot of people would say so." Hennessey's smile was enigmatic. "Laura thinks I'm talking shite when I talk like that."

"You can surely understand why."

"Yes, I can; but that doesn't mean that I am."

"Books don't write themselves, John."

"That's not what I'm saying. I'm saying that writing a novel requires a form of honesty that changes the writer. If it doesn't, then there's something wrong with the writer."

"She's afraid of failing, John. Said so herself."

"Laura's problem is that she knows too damned much about writing, and writers." Hennessey spoke between mouthfuls of hot curry. "She's a walking bloody encyclopaedia of who wrote what, when and why."

"Why is that a problem?"

"It's a problem because she knows instinctively that writing is about more than stringing words together. A damned sight more." Hennessey put his spoon and fork down; he never used a knife when eating curry. "She knows that as surely as you know it as a journalist. She's bright. In fact, I sometimes think she's too bright to be a novelist. Laura's problem is that she's caught up in her own subjectivity; she thinks that registering things subjectively equals being sensitive. It isn't. Feeling is evaluative; emotion is reactive. Feeling is what allows us to penetrate the surface of reality to the point of revelation. She hasn't learned that yet, and that's what's bugging her."

Michael stared at Hennessey. Then, quite without malice, he said, "Maybe she's afraid of you."

It was an astute observation; it made Hennessey flinch. "Passively aggressive was how she put it." By way of self-mitigation, he added, "I tend to bottle things up; that can charge the atmosphere."

"The novelist as electric battery?"

"I prefer to think of myself as a thief in the night." It was an unusual description; Michael waited for Hennessey to continue. "When we're working properly, we're like Prometheus, Michael; we steal fire from heaven."

"The artist as romantic hero?"

"Try archetypal dupe."

"Tricked? By what?"

"*Enticed* would be a better word. We don't know what's happening to us until it happens, then it's too late. We're in the spider's web and there's no escape." Hennessey's laugh was derisive. "What we get mostly these days is excursions into nothingness, language, languaging its way down into a kind of postmodern darkness leavened by metaphors. Fiction is reeling with fatigue in its attempt to stay relevant to the human condition. There's seldom a moment *under* the moment with which to grapple." Another mouthful of curry and an abrupt change in direction. "Has she taken a lover, Michael? I need to know."

"I'm out of the loop."

"Emma?"

"Nothing. They go back a long way, John."

Hennessey watched the waiter approach with Michael's meal. "I'm unable to supply what she needs, Michael. What she *want*s. I don't know what she wants, and I don't think she does either."

"Ah," said Michael. And when he had been served, "She envies you your creative space, John. Said so."

"Creative spaces don't come wrapped in Christmas paper."

"She envies you the battle."

"Well, that's something."

"She's afraid of failure."

"No, not failure, Michael. She's afraid of *not* succeeding; there's a difference." A wave of the hand from Hennessey; he wanted to talk about something else. "I'm to have another chat with Giffard."

"Have?"

"They got into my military file and thought I might be useful. That cuts two ways, of course."

"Cheeky buggers!"

"He's a professional liar and so am I. It's one liar against another."

"That's to twist things somewhat, isn't it?"

"Not really. The Egyptian god of the arts was Thoth Hermes; he was also the god of thieves. We're a matching pair, Michael." A smile that was a question. "So how do I avoid sounding like a right phony?"

"By being yourself?"

'I'm beginning to wonder who that might be."

10
Ubermensch

She was around thirty, small, more brown than black, and not at all what Hennessey had expected. Her dark eyes spoke of caution; but she was not afraid of him. Her look was straight, quizzical and intelligent. She asked him what he wanted, and he told her that he wanted to talk to her husband. Was he about? She said he was not and that she did not know when he would return. Then perhaps she could help him, he suggested. They had been working separately to find someone, a man by the name of Gavin Dean, and it was his hope that Norman had had more success than himself. She stared at him for a long moment, then with a look verging on amusement asked him what the hell he thought he was up to.

"What do you mean?"

"You know fine what I mean."

Hennessey withered under her stare.

"Norman said you'd be back."

"So here I am," he said.

"He also said I was to tell you nothing."

"I was under the impression we had an arrangement."

She continued to stare at him; then, in a gesture of defiance, she leaned against the doorpost and folded her arms.

"It's important to me," said Hennessey.

She shrugged; made to turn away.

"When do you expect him back?"

"Sometime. Who knows?"

"Will you pass on a message for me?"

"He doesn't want to speak to you."

"He's heading for trouble."

"Why should you care?"

"Because I don't like to see anyone get done like a dog's dinner. The situation's much more complicated than he thinks, much more dangerous."

"What would you know?"

"I know more than you think. I'm a journalist; I've got contacts. Good contacts. Did he tell you that?"

"He said you wrote books."

"That too."

She was suddenly less confident; it showed in her eyes.

"What's your name?" he asked, pretending not to know. "I'm John Hennessey."

"Norman said you were Irish. You don't sound Irish."

"I haven't lived in Ireland for a very long time."

"I'm half Irish," she said, astonishing Hennessey. There was no hint of irony in her voice. "My father was a Dubliner."

Bemused, he waited for her to continue.

"Straight nose?" she said, pointing at her nose. "Didn't you notice?"

That was when Hennessey really looked at her. She was slim, but not skinny, her hair bushy and tied back, her dress simple, her feet bare. A classical urchin with small breasts and big eyes. But not a child. Very definitely a woman, an adult, someone who had seen a thing or two. He thought of Giffard and wondered how the two of them had come to meet.

"How did you know we were married?"

"I was just being polite. I didn't know whether you were or not."

"Are you?"

"Married? No. I live with someone."

She kept her eyes on his face. "I don't want to see him get hurt."

"Nor I."

"He's a good man."

"Tell him to ring me."

"Why should he trust you?"

"Because I'm the best bet he has to stay out of trouble."

"You're a funny bloke," she said, tilting her head to the side.

"I'm Irish; we're all funny," he said back, and she laughed a little. He added quickly, truthfully, that he needed her husband's help as much as he needed his.

Her bravado gave way a little, but her frown returned.

"You know he can't handle this on his own; he'll need help to bring Dean down. You've got to make him see that."

"He doesn't listen to the likes of me."

"Yes, he does, I can tell."

"How can you tell?"

"By the way you talk about him."

After a pause, she said, "It won't work. Dean's got a thing going with the police. Norman bumped into him in a bar at the Cross the other night and a fight broke out; he was with someone. Norman said they were arguing. The police let Dean go. Norman ended up in a cell because he was drunk."

"Who was he with?"

"Norman didn't say."

"The police knew Dean?"

"The girl cop was all smiles."

"Where's Norman now?"

"Out trying to make a dollar. We're stony."

Digging out a fifty-dollar bill, Hennessey proffered it. Mary hesitated, then with a 'what-the-hell' look took the note from him.

"Tell him to ring me. Tell him I know about the fight at Rosie's."

"How can you know about that?"

"Because Dean's not the only one with friends in the force." He let that sink in, then he said, "By the way, you don't sound very Irish either.

She turned back into the gloom of the corridor smiling and he knew he had made his mark.

***

Hennessey phoned Palfreyman with news of the female officer's reaction to Dean and they agreed to meet around six in the bar of the Belvedere Hotel, a favourite watering hole of Palfreyman's. Hennessey arrived first, chose a corner window with a view of the street and ordered a whisky. He nursed it until Palfreyman showed up. Sitting there among relative splendour, his mind turned again and again to the fact that Dean had been arguing with someone. When Palfreyman appeared, they got straight down to business.

"You've opened a door, John. Well done." Two young women in tight-fitting dresses wiggled by. Palfreyman looked them up and down as they passed. Still looking, he said, "Would Harrenstein be so foolish, do you think?" His gaze swivelled back to Hennessey. "If it was him, he'll argue coercion. He'll say he was too afraid to resist. It's the kind of thing Dean would do."

"The female officer?"

"Thereby hangs a tale. He'd spun her a yarn earlier about having been in the force. When she and her partner were called in, she recognised Dean. That's all.

The kind of arrangement I was referring to was collusion with the squad for the sake of information. Relationships between crims and the police can get complicated."

"Harrenstein's not under surveillance?"

"Aranda's under surveillance, not Harrenstein; at least they were. Time is money, John. We're all fighting for resources."

"Escaping twice from police custody goes well beyond any kind of arrangement I can envisage. How thorough was the check on Harrenstein?"

"Not exhaustive. A full check would have entailed gathering information on his friends, his business associates and banking transactions. You have to be very careful how you handle that kind of thing. Civil liberties and all that. And you have to have funds. And warrants. You can't just bill the department afterwards for thousands of dollars. We're a bureaucracy, hence the chitties I expect you to come up with."

"Where I'm staying won't exactly break the bank."

Palfreyman laughed and one of the girls who had wiggled by looked across at him and smiled.

"I think you've got an admirer."

"Too brassy. Another? No, these are on me."

When Palfreyman was seated again, Hennessey said, "Does two drinks mean you've got more on your mind?"

Extracting his wallet, Palfreyman handed over the photostat of a newspaper cutting. It was a Reuters pickup of about five hundred words, and it quoted the reviewer of a recent book as saying that underneath National Socialism's brutal policies had lain a vision that no commentator then or now had managed to properly decipher. The reviewer's hope was that modern scholars would take a closer look at the thinking which lay behind the Third Reich's bizarre offering, for it was his belief that it concealed ideas that had been bastardised and literalised into an elitist nightmare. Modern scholars had an important task ahead of them, and that was to understand how and why an intelligent nation like the Germans had succumbed to the phenomenon of Nazism. What was it that Germans and many non-Germans had sensed behind the general rhetoric of the Nazis that had made them vulnerable to Hitler's excesses? What was it that made the writer of this new book willing to put his head on the chopping block and suggest another approach?

"Extraordinary," said Hennessey. "Can I keep this?"

"Of course."

"Your reason for showing it to me?"

"More the reasoning of our senior analyst; he's earmarked it as socially significant and relevant to Australia. I'll get you together with Frank some time. Bright fella. Oxford. Speaks God knows how many languages."

Hennessey stared at Palfreyman, then he said, "According to Goebbels a good socialist was someone who submitted the I to the thou, which meant sacrificing the individual to the whole. That's a religious statement of sorts."

"Our society is built on Mill's premise of individual rights."

"Theoretically, yes, but Mill is misquoted on that point. He argued that society should leave men free, but his ultimate premise was that it is the group that permits such freedom, and that freedom should be used on behalf of the group. That suggests to me that he saw the right to freedom as ultimately the property of the collective."

Palfreyman's expression remained blank; he opened a hand to indicate that Hennessey should continue.

"All I'm saying is that he ended up believing that society is the source of all morality, not God or the individual. That, with a Third Reichian twist, is what Joseph Goebbels believed." Palfreyman remained mute, so Hennessey continued. "I'm not saying that Mill and Goebbels believed the same thing. I'm saying that the Nazis took the idea of society as the fundamental source and justification of morality and so messed it up we've been struggling to understand ourselves and society ever since. The Third Reich picked up on certain movements of thought within society at the turn of the last century, got them arse about elbow, and all but disallowed anyone from ever seriously considering them again. That's our legacy, and that's what the reviewer of this book is getting at. He's saying we've been conned into dropping certain kinds of thinking and experience simply because they're associated with Nazism."

"This obviously isn't new territory for you."

"I studied German literature at university. I speak German. I've discussed these problems with all kinds of people in the past. I sometimes dream in bloody German!"

They sat looking at one another for a moment or two; it was as if the conversation were continuing on some other level. Hennessy could feel the whisky acting on him, warming him, loosening him. He smiled at Palfreyman and looked away, observed the bar area and the different kinds of people who had taken up residence. Young. Old. The ordinary and the exotic. The lone drinker. The duo. The girls who had wiggled past were hard at it, talking, their cigarettes held expertly, their lips stark red against pale, powdered skin. He took it all in, stored it away and asked Palfreyman to define the context of the conversation they were having.

Palfreyman's reply was precise and to the point. Political and religious extremists were crossing international boundaries every minute. A brain wasn't a suitcase; it couldn't be opened and have its contents checked. But there had been arrests. ASIO had refused around twenty people permission to enter Australia the previous year because of links with terrorism. Others had been identified as spies. Some were known to harbour racists beliefs. A bitter laugh from Palfreyman. Most people would be amazed to learn that there were two hundred and forty far right groups in Australia with an estimated one hundred members each — an estimate that was conservative and provisional. That added up to thousands of like-minded individuals mixing with a population of around twenty million. He was not saying that these people were all radicals of a Nazi variety, which would be plain silly. But it would not be silly to say that not a few believed in stuff so bizarre they were vulnerable to that kind of extremism. Okay, so almost everyone felt, from time to time, that the government of the day was hiding something, that it had Big Brother tendencies; but when that feeling was cultivated and became the main focus of one's life, then watch out. That was where Dean was at, and he was known to be in cahoots with others tainted in the same way.

"I can't help but think of the McCarthy era when I hear someone talk like that."

"There's a difference, John. The paranoia you're referring to belonged to the investigators; that's not how it is here. The Australian Government is bending over backwards to avoid that kind of reaction. How else could so many groups continue to exist? Yes, they're being monitored, even infiltrated on occasions, but they are not being closed down. If some of them want to dress up in funny uniforms and strut around in the privacy of their homes listening to military music, that's their affair. It's only when they translate their obsessions into unlawful acts that the law has to step in."

"Democracy triumphs."

"Yes, I would say so."

"So, what exactly is it your analyst thinks Australia has to learn from that review?"

Palfreyman's response was again precise. The Third Reich, he said, had attempted to exploit something fundamental to all of us — our desire to overcome the limitations of our own nature. The Nazis had translated this basic instinct into the idea of self-mastery through the development of the will, and that, in essence, was what all the butchery had been about. Self-mastery had been conceived to be of the mind; it was the mind that had to be brought to heel, the emotions made to follow. The nineteenth century had had an obsession with the idea of hereditary degeneration — social theories had stated that 'bad blood' could be passed on — and this idea had come to underpin all of the Reich's policy decisions. A common theme at the time had been that European culture was decaying and dying. In his music, and in his critical writings, Wagner had captured this theme and expanded it into a grand play of cosmic forces working in and through the individual, and Nietzsche had reinforced this notion through his rejection of everything modern. Condemning his own times, Nietzsche had set the pace for other writers and thinkers — in particular the philosopher Martin Heidegger. By the end of the nineteenth century the idea of society's collapse had become wedded to the equally powerful idea of an awakening, and it was this glimmer of hope that the Third Reich had exploited.

"That's a neat summation."

"Frank thinks the Dracula myth is about degeneration in this sense. Ultimate degeneration. Dracula was seen as something that drained the vitality out of living things."

"And so, the aesthete Dorian Gray degenerates on canvas."

"Exactly."

"And Bernard Shaw can wax poetic over Wagner's Siegfried."

"Really? I didn't know that."

"He saw Siegfried as a naive hero with the capacity to overturn religion and law and replace them with… unfettered action. And all for the good of the race, I might add."

Palfreyman returned to his thesis. "Frank says we're in much the same position as the Europeans at the turn of the last century. We're in the clutches of a mania for self-improvement that has spilled over into things like conspiracy theory and the belief that human beings are being abducted by aliens. The far right isn't far behind with notions of a strengthened conservatism. The people in some of these groups believe in that kind of stuff without question. They're hooked on it. Some believe the Earth is hollow with openings at the poles.

Some have put the whole lot together and are selling the notion that western governments are involved in a grand conspiracy. And that's only the iceberg's tip. There are also links to the Christian right. Some Christians believe aliens are demons and that Christ will return on the stroke of midnight as the century ends.

"Frank's diagnosis?"

"That we have to home in on the underlying reason for it all — our desire to overcome the limitations of our own nature — and try as best we can to redirect the traffic."

"A tall order, surely."

"At least it's a focus."

"I'm surprised anyone's interested."

"The public pulse is always of interest,"

"To the extent of trying to regulate it?"

"Someone had better, don't you think?"

"Who's paranoid now?"

Palfreyman paused, then he said, "Human beings crave transcendence, John."

"Ubermensch," said Hennessey.

"Ubermensch mistranslated as 'superman'," said Palfreyman.

"Overman," said Hennessey.

"Exactly. Nietzsche's creature of the imagination was transformed by the Nazis into a super being purged of all emotion. When Wagner's *Ring Cycle* was performed at Bayreuth, it's said the town took on a sacred aura."

"Which is the religious element," said Hennessey, intrigued by the direction their conversation had taken. "There were Wagner associations in all of the major German universities; it became a worldwide phenomenon with chapters throughout Europe."

"Then came the essays on Pan-Germanism and anti-Semitism followed by Hitler's elevation to power in 1933." They stopped talking for a moment; it was as if something indecent had reached out and touched them. "It must all have seemed so... so innocent; so right." Palfreyman pondered his own statement. "What a shock it must have been to wake up."

"It's always a shock to wake up," said Hennessey. Before Palfreyman could reply, he added, "And again there's something you're not telling me."

Palfreyman gave a little laugh, lifted his whisky and drained it. Then in response to Hennessey's question, he said, "I was not telling you that a third force is about to enter the Australian political arena, and I'm not referring to One Nation."

Hennessey toyed with his glass, then he looked up and said, "The German chancellor said yesterday that Europe could risk a repeat of the horrors of the past century if member states didn't subordinate national self-interest to a higher European ideal. He spoke of a revival of local prejudices and grassroots racism that could see all of us at each other's throats."

"It's not impossible. There's a lot of buried resentment out there."

"Governments are seldom in step with what people want."

"Governments are expected to stay ahead, John."

"Only by the cultural elite."

"Which leaves most people wondering what the hell's going on."

"Which brings us back to what it is you think you're measuring out there in the community."

"Gullibility," said Palfreyman. "The inability to detect when reality has been falsified."

Hennessey was impressed. "That's well put," he said.

11
Descending into Nothingness

Hennessey was asleep when reception put the call through. Within seconds he was wide awake, Norman Giffard's voice saying gruffly that they should meet at some café or other. "Where again?" he asked. Giffard repeated the café's name and location, gave a time and hung up. When Hennessey checked his watch, it had just gone seven-thirty in the morning. He lay back and drifted again towards sleep knowing that there was no rush, but after a couple of minutes decided to get up anyway.

It had been quite a night. Palfreyman had fed him single malts for an hour, then suggested that they go upstairs and sample the *à la carte* menu. It was on the house, he was told. He should try the so-an-so, he was told. If he did, they would have a bottle of the nineteen-blah blah. Or maybe the… Hennessey had said little in reply. Palfreyman's suit, he had decided, after his fifth whisky, was too blue, his shirt too white, his shoes too polished, his use of information too studied. He was obviously highly intelligent, but too showy; handsome, but too tanned; a little rich kid to whom education had been no more than a game. Yet he could not help liking him. There was something about the man that made one want to shield him from himself, something oddly genuine but buried that surfaced from time to time in a look, or a smile. And a sadness. After a sumptuous meal and a good bottle of wine the gory facts behind Palfreyman's sadness spilled out across the table in the same offhand manner as everything else. His wife, he revealed, had died in a horrendous car accident.

As the steaming water cleansed his pores and eased the stiffness in his joints, Hennessey pondered that moment and marvelled at Palfreyman's control. There had been no self-pity in his statement, no canvassing for sympathy. Underneath that lazy exterior lay a will of iron, and as he turned off his shower and stepped out into the tiny bathroom with its equally tiny prison cell window high up, he wondered how such resolve had come about.

Later, facing Giffard's bulk across a narrow table in what turned out to be a crowded sandwich bar on King Street, he was left marvelling at how different human beings could be — intelligence had so many faces. Nursing a mug of black coffee, Giffard barely acknowledged his arrival. Hennessey remained equally offhand and silent.

"So, what did you find out?" Giffard asked.

Hennessey signalled to a passing waitress, but she raced by without a glance. He looked back at Giffard. "Dean didn't know that female officer. There had been a raid further up the strip and he'd chatted her up on the street. Spun her a yarn about having been in the Victoria force. "

Giffard's sigh contained despair. Losing Dean and hearing yet again how lucky the bastard was seemed to demoralise him. But he still had the presence of mind to hold up a hand and stop the waitress who had not stopped for Hennessey.

"You couldn't have picked a busier place."

"I like it this way."

"So, what changed your mind?

"Mary talked me into it."

"I tried to con her."

"Yeah, she said." Giffard laughed. "You picked the wrong one there." Their eyes met and held. "She says you're okay."

"Return the compliment."

A pause before Giffard spoke again. "Dean wants to get even."

"With whom?"

"Everybody?"

The waitress appeared with Hennessey's coffee. He smiled at her, but she did not respond.

Giffard elaborated. "His job is to set up drug deals," he said, toying with a paper serviette. "He's been given permission to do that."

"Permission?"

"Ordered?" Giffard bent in towards Hennessey. "There are a *lot* of drugs involved."

Hennessey did not reply.

"Dean isn't top of the heap; isn't even near the top."

"You have names?"

A shake of the head.

"I need names," said Hennessey.

"Don't know any," said Giffard. A pause as he debated something with himself. "There's even training. I was part of that until I fell out with Dean. Told me to get rid of my Aboriginal slut and I told him to stick his head up his arse."

"That's why he set you up?"

"Nah." A smile. "I tried to rip him off. There were two of us handling a consignment and I tried to skim it. The other guy got cold feet and blabbed. Dean was so fucking angry he set me up for a fall." A shake of the head. "He sent me across town with enough uncut heroin to knock off a whole fucking suburb. I was picked up at the delivery point neat as you like."

"You could have dobbed him in."

"I thought it was just bad luck." Giffard's smile was disconsolate. "I was a year into a three-year stint before I found out. An inmate walked up to me in the exercise yard all smiles and said that he had a message from Gavin. The message was that I was a fucking bastard for having tried to rip him off."

"Tried?"

"He got the stuff I'd taken back; gave Mary a black eye while doing it."

"You could have dobbed him in then."

"He'd have gone straight back after her and I wouldn't have got out of prison alive." Giffard looked away. When he looked back, Hennessey found himself looking at a different man. "He likes to bash women; he enjoys it."

Hennessey paused. "You and Dean were mates?"

"He treated me like a pet dog."

"But he liked you."

A shrug from Giffard. And then, "I can't believe I had the bastard and he got away."

"You were drunk."

"I hit him hard. Twice. And still he came back at me."

"Maybe you didn't hit him as hard as you think you did."

"I hit him hard." A look. "What would you know?"

"I've boxed."

"Where?"

"University."

The big man's expression was one of dismissal.

"I *know*," Hennessey said again.

Giffard digested that and withdrew into himself. "I had him," he said again.

"And if he hadn't come back at you?"

"I'd probably have killed the fucker." A look. "I wasn't thinking straight, was I?"

"Have you told anyone else about Dean's backers?"

"I tried to while in prison, but they didn't believe me. They thought I was bonkers."

"You told them what you've just told me?"

"More or less." Giffard's smile was without guile, and for a moment Hennessey saw what Mary saw in the big man. Then he said, "You sure are cosy with the police."

"I'm playing the Hobart mob off the Bondi mob."

"They'd only do that for the likes of you."

"Don't knock it," said Hennessey. Then, "What exactly is Dean's role in all of this?"

"He's good at organising things. Got a fucking amazing memory."

"But takes orders."

"There's a good buck in it. He'll do *anything* for money."

"Seems to be more in it than that from what you've said. What did you have to do?"

"I was part of the delivery service."

"Why try to rip Dean off? You must have realised it was a dodgy thing to do."

"I saw the chance to solve our problems in one hit." A grimace. "With that kind of money, we could have disappeared for a long time. It was a real big assignment; didn't think anyone would notice a missing bag or six."

"You kept what you'd taken at home?"

"I'd made up the weight, didn't think they'd notice."

Hennessey shook his head, finished off his coffee and asked if Giffard had considered going directly to the police with what he knew. The police were always trouble for someone like him, he said. Nothing ever worked out the way it was supposed to. Then why had he tried to speak to the authorities in prison? Because he wanted to get the hell out of prison, was the reply. Or at least shorten his stretch. That no longer applied.

"But you want to see Dean go down, right?"

"Yeah, and that's where you come in." Giffard's eyes brightened "Mary will leave me if I end up in prison again."

"I'll have to pass on what you've told me."

"Keep my name out of it.".

"I won't be able to do that."

Giffard's fingers spread in protest; they looked like sausages. He would not talk to the police, he said. It was between Hennessey and himself. Once tarred? Hennessey's response was equally adamant. He'd have to get used to the police being in the background. He was now on the opposite side whether he liked it or not."

"I'm on no one's *fucking* side!"

"Not for yourself, for Mary," said Hennessey. "We can get you out of this mess." He hoped that were true.

Giffard's stare was intense.

"They'll want dates, locations, stuff like that. Can you do that? Can we start now?"

"I need a drink first," said Giffard.

"Is that a, yes?"

Giffard stood up.

Hennessey got up, pleased to escape the sandwich bar's fluorescent glare.

"They'll want paying," said Giffard.

"Who will?" said Hennessey.

"Her," said Giffard, thumbing at the waitress.

***

Laura was looking across the room at the French doors, which were open an inch or two. The curtains were billowing slightly, and she could hear birdsong and feel a warm draught coming to where she stood. It was as if a gauze screen had been placed between her and reality. She was reminded of Gogol's notion of descending into nothingness, of descending into the devil.

"I'm spinning, Emma. I didn't think it would be like this."

"What did you expect?"

"I don't know. Not this."

"Have you phoned Mark?"

"No."

"Do you intend to?"

After a pause, "No." A shaky breath and the words she was afraid to articulate toppling out into the room. "I think I may be having a breakdown." As if to prove her point, her jaw began to judder. The two women came together in that moment, Emma holding, Laura gripping, Emma saying that it was just overload, that the feeling would pass, Laura, her chest heaving, that she had really messed up.

"You did what you felt had to be done."

Not knowing how to disengage, they parted awkwardly. Mark Bishop and Tuffnell and John were all knotted up inside of her, Laura said. They would have to be teased apart somehow; she would have to make sense of them, deal with them.

"John's in Sydney," Emma said. "He's at the Lancaster. Michael and he had lunch together yesterday."

"And?"

"John kept asking about you. He's worried sick." Emma made a face. "Michael said not to tell you, but it's time you two talked."

"It's too soon."

"It'll get more difficult the longer you leave it."

"He unnerves me." A look. "He sometimes makes me feel like a child."

"Do you act like one?"

It was a very confronting thing to say; it took the breath out of Laura. When she recovered, she said, "Is that how you see me?"

"We're all children pretending to be grown-ups." Emma's smile was kindly, but her eyes carried a different message. "John's just a little boy at times. I'm sure you've noticed."

"That's not quite how he comes across to me."

"That's what he's shielding, Laura."

"You think so?"

Emma paused. "The jump from Belfast to London must have been traumatic for him. What was he, fifteen? He must have stood out like a sore thumb."

"He's said as much?"

"You have to read between the lines with John."

Laura's stare was quizzical.

"Yes, we've talked. A descent whisky helped." Laura returned to her chair. "Look, you're not the only woman to have ever had an affair, and you won't be the last. Michael and I have had own difficulties; you can't be married as long as we've been and avoid the odd hiccup or two. It goes with the territory."

"You had an affair?"

"No, but I did get emotionally involved with someone. It happens."

"Michael found out?"

"He knew something wasn't right, that's all."

Laura was staring at Emma with interest.

"You kept it from him?"

"I kept it from myself, for ages. It's the kind of thing that can creep up on you."

"Then you told him?" Emma's look was enough to make her add, "You didn't tell him?"

"What would have been the good of that? It was an infatuation, no more than that."

"I've gone further than that."

"Yes, you have."

"What do you suggest?"

"A *holiday*," said Emma. "Put you head down somewhere nice and take a rest from yourself."

Unable to fathom what that Emma meant by that; Laura did not reply.

***

Norman Giffard was easier to deal with after a few beers; he became quite talkative. Hennessey asked questions and took notes. Some of the stuff that came out astonished him. There were descriptions of training sessions in the bush, drug runs worth hundreds of thousands of dollars, even meetings with members of Sydney's old guard underworld. But to what end, Hennessey wanted to know. Giffard was vague on that; he seemed to think social disruption was the aim. One highly respected crook — he had been to university — had said that the society was just fine the way it was. Disable the system and business might fall off; they might all end up on the dole. Others had seemingly liked the idea; it had been enough for them to think that ordinary blokes might at last get a crack at the whip. Hennessey could hear the voices of these ordinary blokes trying to make sense out of their lives, angry voices trying to channel feelings of inadequacy and perplexity into something vaguely constructive. But it was all nonsense, of course, a hotchpotch of absurd notions cobbled together into a manifesto that read:

You've done your dash; we're coming to get you. But what did that mean?

More questions failed to elicit an answer; Giffard was already on the downward spiral to oblivion. Then, when least expected, a glimmer of light: independents were being primed to contest carefully chosen marginal seats at the upcoming general election. Not quite phrased like that, but that was the gist. Hennessey dug deeper, but to no avail. Giffard's three-year stint in prison had robbed him of his capacity to hold his liquor. Eyelids drooping, he slurred his way towards a final incomprehension.

"Com'on, Norman," urged Hennessey, but it was all over. "I'll get a taxi," he said.

It was an expensive ride. Locked together, they rushed down the path towards the veranda and the door that did not fit properly. When Mary opened it, she gave Hennessey a dirty look and helped him steer her husband down the hallway. "In here," she said, guiding them expertly round and into their front room. She nodded towards an armchair and Hennessey tumbled Giffard into it. He looked up grinning and said something about a safe landing.

The room was unlit, the curtains closed, a television screen the only source of light. A punch-drunk couch and matching armchairs — Giffard was in one of them — were the only concession to comfort, a low table with a scattering of woman's magazines the only sign of mental involvement. On the floor, a dark rug from which the colour had fled stared up hard and ungiving. The television was tuned to a particularly nauseating quiz program.

"It's my fault," Hennessey admitted. "I should have tried to slow him down."

"Not a chance," she replied. "Once he's into it…"

"This-is-a-good-man," Giffard said with great concentration. Reaching out, he clutched at Mary's elbow. "Get him a beer!"

"No beer for me," said Hennessey.

"*Fucking* good man," said Giffard, trying to get up, but he failed and fell back heavily. His eyes closed and his breathing became heavy in the same moment. He was suddenly asleep.

Thunderous applause from across the room caused Mary to look round at the television. Hennessey turned to leave, but she barred his way, wanting to know what they had talked about. Every word. Going into the kitchen, they left Giffard to his dreams.

If the front room had been depressing, the kitchen was a full-blown pathology. It was ramshackle. A window with broken astragals and cracked panes looked out onto a garden of long grass, weeds and debris where a nectarine tree with diseased leaves struggled to bear fruit. Clothes of all sorts littered the floor. The strapped, Masonite walls that had once been cream in colour were now all but stripped of that through dampness and neglect.

"How long have you lived like this?"

"A year. A year and a bit. A friend tipped us off and we moved in." Mary gave a little laugh. "We didn't decorate."

It was a terribly middle-class thing to say.

"Norman's been very helpful, Mary."

"They'll kill him if they find out." Her tone was matter of fact, her dark eyes steady and penetrating. "It'll be your fault if that happens."

"*He* rang me, Mary," he said back, avoiding the fact that it was she who had talked her husband into ringing him. "He won't be going after Dean any more. Isn't that what you wanted?"

"You've changed his mind on that?"

"I think so. Better that he helps us than try to do it by himself."

She stood, arms folded, and stared at him, then with a look that was also a warning, she said, "I'm counting on you."

12
A Terrifying Moment

Hennessey thought about what he had seen and heard in Marrickville all the way back to central Sydney. As he alighted at Town Hall and climbed out of the subway into the brilliant sunshine, he realised, yet again, how lucky he was. It was true he had very little money, but he was not poverty-stricken, and in comparison, with what he had seen in Norman Giffard's eyes, his own dislike for Dean and what he stood for was as nothing. These people had been daggered by reality, he no more than irritated by the fact that Dean had pulled a fast one on him. A call from his lawyer deepened that sense of irritation. A Brisbane newspaper was lauding Dean for being a writer of perception. Although not born in Ireland, Dean apparently felt Irish because his mother had come from County Clare. It was, he believed, the Irish in him that had made him want to write in the first place — storytelling was in his blood.

"You've talked to the reviewer?"

"We had a chat; he sends his condolences."

"How was it set up?"

"The usual visit plus a press release."

"Patricia Dyson?"

"Ryson, on this occasion." Balchin laughed, he had also spoken to Rose Munroe at *the Sun-Herald*. She had asked him to put what he believed to be the case in writing.

"Is it possible to forewarn other newspapers?"

Balchin said it was not. His firm did what it could to help artists, but there was a limit to how much time they could afford each client.

"What have the police come up with?"

"Nothing."

"Harrenstein?"

"He's complied to the letter. The books have been withdrawn and are ready to be picked up."

"I said I'd arrange that and promptly forgot."

"I'd get onto that if I were you."

Hennessey decided to ring Emma and take the chance of getting Laura, but it was Emma's voice that sounded in his ear. She said immediately that Laura was out.

"I need to talk."

"Any time."

"Now?"

"Any time but now," she said back. "Alix'll be home in half an hour from school. Laura went over to Chatswood to do some shopping and have her hair done. She'll be back any minute."

"Tomorrow?"

"I could do lunch."

He said lunch would be fine and they agreed on a meeting place. When he rang off, he had no idea what to do with what remained of the afternoon. Out on the street again, he hailed a taxi and returned to his hotel. As he entered his room and closed its ever-so-thin door he wondered what Laura had had done to her hair. Shopping? He stood perfectly still and took in his surroundings. The single bed, the window looking out into a brick wall, the framed picture of the tall ships entering Sydney Harbour. Shopping? For what? he wondered.

After a sleep he went looking for a quiet place in which to read, but it was not that kind of area. One pub was quite empty, but he knew by the look of it that a reader of books would not be popular. Another served counter meals and the smell of cooked food put him off. A coffee shop looked just right, but it was packed with youngsters and too noisy. A darkening sky suggested rain, so he turned back. Why could she not have said what was on her mind weeks before and saved them both such heartache? Two adults stranded in the same city and unable to talk to one another was childish. His pace quickened as the sky darkened. Resentment was insidious; it crept up on you unnoticed. Avoiding confrontation, we withdrew into dull silence and slowly lost interest in the other's existence.

It seemed to Hennessey that human beings were incapable of shaking off the lies and half-truths that made up their lives. We were all liars, he reasoned. We were all in some sense dishonest. We were all prisoners of our own narrow subjectivity. We carried, secretly, all sorts of strange notions and beliefs. Being from a nominally Christian Protestant family Laura had never had to contend with religion. He, on the other hand, had been brought up conservative Catholic in spite of having a Protestant father, and had had to wrestle with religion as far back as he could remember. There were times when he envied her simplicity of approach, her casual disregard, but there were also times when her unthinking dismissal of the religious viewpoint infuriated him. It made as nothing, what it had cost him and others to escape its clutches. Like Jacob he had wrestled with an angel and emerged from the contest lame. Laura had never had to face any such challenge.

It started to rain heavily, and he ducked into a shop doorway to shelter. Emma would be able to advise him; she would have determined where Laura was at in herself by now. Hennessey smiled. Michael was lucky having someone like Emma, she was so cluey. The rain eased and he made a dash for it but was soon sheltering again. His thoughts rattled around the problem of Laura's dissatisfaction, and his own. The two women were so different. Laura was highly intelligent, but brittle, Emma equally intelligent, but somehow able to accommodate the world without fuss or bother. Maybe having kids was the answer; or was it just a matter of personality? There was no doubting Laura's sophistication, but it was a sophistication laced with pomposity.

He had already decided what he would do when he got back to the hotel; he would take a trip across town and visit Rosie's Steak Bar — that would give what remained of his day focus. Later, sitting in the big red sofa that decorated the hotel foyer, he read a few pages of his book and waited for the taxi to arrive, his mind divided on the question of how Laura perceived him as a person. Was her biting evaluation of his character in any real sense accurate? When the taxi turned up, he was glad to swap her unflattering portrait of his traits for the driver's folksy chit-chat.

Rosie's Steak Bar was tastefully decorated. There was a long mahogany bar with brass foot rail on the left, on the right an all but empty balustraded restaurant with stiff pink tablecloths and pink-shaded wall lights. Straight ahead, on an elevated platform, sat an immaculate grand piano with open lid. On the other side of the bar a vast figured mirror reflected the entire interior back on itself. John Hennessey looking at John Hennessey. A thinnish body and thinning grey-black hair. A tired-looking summer jacket and open-necked white shirt. Not a bad jaw surmounted by a thin-lipped mouth, straight nose and blue eyes. No beauty but hanging together reasonably well.

The barman's gelled hair was sleeked straight back; he was a picture of health and Italian good looks.

"Whisky, Irish," said Hennessey, with a touch of Irish. Then, "When do things liven up?"

"Around ten. The jazz quartet starts up about then."

Lifting his drink, Hennessey walked the length of the bar and stopped next to the piano. Turning, he looked back towards the entrance and tried to imagine the place full of people. Then, sitting down at a nearby table, he took out his notebook and began to write a detailed description of his surroundings.

***

Gunther Harrenstein's reaction to Hennessey turning up the following morning was cool, but polite, Hennessey's apology for the books not having been picked up accepted without fuss. But there was a tension in the little man, and Hennessey exploited it.

"He hasn't been in contact?"

"Not a peep."

"He's in Sydney."

"Who told you that?"

"The police were tipped off."

"And?"

"They'll let me know when they nab him."

A slow nod from Harrenstein. He was behind his desk and Hennessey was seated in a chair opposite. "What about, eh, Giffard? You said he had given you a lead."

"Didn't work out. He was just trying to get money out of me."

Another nod from Harrenstein, and a smile. "I very quickly learned not to trust anyone associated with Dean." His look was suddenly keen edged. "So, what are you going to do now?"

"Hang around until he's caught."

"Sydney's a big place."

"They sounded confident."

"A tip-off?"

"That's what they said." Hennessey changed tack. "You're... Austrian?"

"How could you tell?"

"Just a guess. I spent some time in Germany way back. British Army. National Service."

"Where were you stationed?"

"Westphalia. Bielefeld. Moved around quite a bit. Got up to Berlin a couple of times."

"I was born in Vien." Harrenstein corrected himself. "Vienna. My father was from Munich. My mother was Viennese."

"I spent three glorious weeks in Vienna when I was demobbed. It was spring. I had a wonderful time there."

"You've been back?"

"Twice. Years ago."

"You speak German?"

"Just a few words. Enough to buy a cup of coffee. I was never any good at languages."

"I already spoke English when I arrived here in '47. I was seventeen. I didn't like Australia. All I could think of was Innschbruck."

"I know the feeling. I arrived in England from Belfast at the age of fifteen and felt much the same. I couldn't believe my parents had chosen to live among the English."

"I would never have guessed you were Irish."

"I thought at first you were German. German-German, that is."

They laughed at the distinction and Harrenstein asked which mob Hennessey had been with.

"Infantry."

"Commissioned?"

"Scraped in by the skin of my teeth."

"My father's brother was in the infantry. He died on the Russian front."

"And your father?" asked Hennessey.

"He was exempt from military service; he had flat feet." A smile. "A flat-footed doctor."

"Medical?"

"Yes."

"In Munich?"

"Mostly in Vienna; he settled there after he married my mother."

"What brought him to Australia?"

"Employment. Money. Us. Australia was the land of opportunity." He gave a little laugh. "The land of the free."

"You go back?"

"Yes, of course. I have relatives there. I have a house there." He was suddenly expansive. "I've thought more than once of packing up and going back for good."

"What's stopped you?"

"Family. My children are Aussie through and through. Austria is for holidays. Do you have kids?"

"No."

It was Harrenstein's turn to surprise. "I read that book of yours. Have you written much?"

"A few novels."

"I didn't mean to read it; I read a few lines and got hooked."

"The same thing happened to Dean."

"Well. There you are. Even Gavin's got good taste."

"Has he?" said Hennessey.

Harrenstein smiled. "Gavin's bright enough, but I wouldn't say he had taste. He's a maverick. You should have seen him selling advertising. Amazing. He hypnotised them. His problem is boredom; he gets bored quickly." Another smile. "That's why things fell apart."

"That plus the strangers, the parcels," said Hennessey, by way of a reminder.

"Exactly. Place became a bloody post office for crooks."

They laughed again and Hennessey asked another question, then another; then quite suddenly Harrenstein clammed up; it was as if a switch had been thrown. He was in the process of describing Dean's habits and proclivities when it must have dawned on him that he was going too far. Looking at his watch, he said he would have to terminate their little chat, that he had an appointment with a client.

Hennessey rang David Palfreyman soon after and filled him in on Harrenstein and Giffard. What Giffard had had to say was not for the telephone; they would have to meet. To Palfreyman's chagrin, he found himself eating curry that evening in an almost empty restaurant. Hennessey ordered a beer; Palfreyman ordered the most expensive bottle of wine on the menu. He was not in a good mood, it seemed; he was having problems with a superior. When handed Hennessey's notes on Giffard, however, he brightened.

Scanning the material, he asked if Hennessey thought Giffard was on the level. Hennessey said that he had no reason to doubt him, that he had been pretty drunk by the end, but had not contradicted himself. He had also given much the same information to the prison authorities. That could be checked. And anyway, how could a man like Giffard make up such a story; it was so improbable it had to be true.

"The bit about independents contesting marginal seats is *very* interesting. What do you make of it?"

"What do you make of it?"

Palfreyman lifted his glass of wine and sipped at it, then, with a shrug, he said, "Tell me what he said about the camps."

"It's all in there."

"As you remember it, please."

Hennessey registered the sudden formalism and reiterated, as best he could, Giffard's exact description.

"Murchinson will have a fit if all of this turns out to be true."

"Why? Isn't really your province, is it?"

"It's messy, John," Palfreyman said, re-establishing familiarity.

"At least Giffard's out of the firing line now; that'll please his wife."

Palfreyman said he preferred the big man on the loose; with Giffard on the loose there was the possibility of Dean being forced to the surface.

"You can't blame his wife for wanting him out of it," said Hennessey. "She knows firsthand what Dean is capable of. He gave her a black eye."

"She can't have it both ways," said Palfreyman. "He either cooperates and benefits, or he doesn't and is left to Dean's tender mercies."

"That's unfair."

"It's the way of the world; *our* world." Palfreyman returned to Hennessey's notes. "He hasn't given much information on locations."

"They seldom use the same place twice."

"I'm thinking more in terms of evidence left behind. Spent ammunition, discarded bits and pieces. A possible fingerprint or two. We have to build a profile of these people. Pity he got so drunk."

"It helped loosen him up." A shake of the head from Hennessy. "You should see how they live."

"Don't get too close, John."

"I can't ignore what's under my nose. They're all but destitute." Hennessey paused. "You don't give a damn, do you?"

"I'm not a welfare worker, John." A sigh. "If I could wave a magic wand I would."

"I sat where they sat, and I was astonished," said Hennessey.

Palfreyman frowned.

"Isaiah."

"You read the Bible?"

"Doesn't everyone?" said Hennessey.

"Harrenstein?"

"He opened up a little about his father, and his brother. Said that his father was exempt from military service, and that his father's brother had died on the Russian front. The father was from Munich, the mother was Viennese."

Palfreyman hesitated, then conspiratorially he said, "What I'm about to tell you can't go any further, John." His stare was steady. "Harrenstein's father wasn't a medical doctor; he was a physicist. He ended up working for the Australian government in '48. Between

'46 and '51 around one hundred and thirty German scientists were spirited out of Germany and into Australia via Britain and the States. Herr Doctor Victor Harrenstein was a late pick up. He was recruited to work at a senior level in a government research laboratory in Melbourne. The fledgling OSI and the federal security agency had no say in the matter; their requests to run security checks were rejected by the government of the day. Hence the one year delay before his family came out to Australia; they had to find out if he was any good at his job."

"When did this surface?"

"A day or two ago. Our initial enquiries ran into a wall of obfuscation."

"From whom?"

"Government."

"What made them back down?"

"Our cousins in ASIO do not like to be knocked back. The embargo on certain files was broken when our separate department heads backed each other." A smile that was not a smile. "There's more to what's going on that I can divulge at the moment. The file behind the file shows that the father was a hard-line Nazi who sidestepped the de-Nazification process. It's on record that he caused problems with foreign workers from the moment he arrived, and that these problems continued. He was an arrogant bastard, and he stayed that way." Palfreyman stopped talking for a moment and stared across the empty restaurant, then with a touch of weariness he said, "Special tribunals were set up in the Western zones of occupied Germany after the war to weed out people like Victor, but if they had something tasty to offer a blind eye was turned regarding Nazi associations."

"ASIO had no access to that file?"

"They complained as far back as '48 that they hadn't been allowed to run checks on any of the arriving German scientists. The acronym was CIS in those days — the *Commonwealth Investigation Service.*"

"The *greater* good." said Hennessey.

"Exactly. Done so that we wouldn't fall behind the Russians. Hundreds of German scientists and technicians were available as early as '45. Some countries resorted to kidnapping. The Western democracies were afraid Russia would get an edge and use it."

"The ones here must have formed a pretty tight-knit community."

"They worked together side by side on a whole range of projects for years — some of those projects were top secret. Our man ended up at Woomera."

"Intelligent *and* deadly."

"Intelligence has never been much of a safeguard against bastardry. About half of those who put together the Final Solution had doctorates."

"So, what happens now?"

"We move carefully; we don't want to frighten the chickens and have them scatter."

Hennessey spooned the last of his curry onto his plate. "What does one do with old Nazis when they've served their purpose?" He looked up from his plate. "You can't prosecute them."

"That's why we've never been any good at it; the nasty ones were, and still are, under wraps. Not that there's many of them left."

"Not a single prosecution," said Hennessey, remembering.

"That's a different story. It's almost impossible to prosecute alleged war criminals when the events in question took place more than fifty years ago. Evidence is difficult to come by. It's expensive and all but impossible to pursue a case to finality."

"Did any of them return to Germany?"

"A few. Others headed for America or Britain where they got plum jobs without being screened."

"Didn't anyone object? "

"They were silenced, national interest. High-ranking technicians were brought in from Europe. They escaped investigation by the federal war crimes unit, which was *us* way back then. The codename used by the Americans and the Brits was Operation Matchbox. To cash in, the Federal Cabinet set up ESTEA — the Employment of Scientific and Technical Enemy Alien*s* — to make deals. Australia had to bid for her Nazi scientists."

"They must have thought all their Christmases had come at once."

"While their buddies were being sentenced at Nuremberg, they were being carted off to take up posts in the most sensitive areas of research. And there were rewards. Bank loans were arranged. Monthly payments were even sent to families still in Germany. And not a whiff of it in the press."

"Extraordinary."

They sat contemplating that fact. Then Palfreyman said, "Giffard has agreed talk to us?"

"He wants to do everything through me."

"Not possible, John. Get Mary to talk to him?"

"She likes the police as much as he does."

"Look, Giffard's probably dealing around the Cross most nights; that's his style. Or a bit of break and entry. If he's picked up, he'll be back inside in a flash. We don't want that to happen; he's valuable."

"They have no regular income."

"All the more reason for him to talk to us direct."

"He's already talking to me. What's the difference?"

"Tell him we'll give them protection if they cooperate."

"They're already cooperating."

"He has to be willing to testify against Dean and whoever."

"That's a big ask."

"Tell him he'll make good money out of the media when it all blows up. Lay it on a bit."

"Will you meet with him personally?"

"Of course. Set it up."

"He'll take a bit of persuading; he doesn't like the men in blue. Doesn't trust any of you."

"If anyone can persuade him, you can, John."

"That's what bothers me," said Hennessey.

***

At twelve-thirty sharp, Hennessey entered the Burlington Arcade, made his way up to the top tier and found Emma already there sipping coffee. They embraced. She said immediately that Michael would be happy to collect the books from Aranda. He passed on the address and gave her an edited version of his meeting with Norman and Mary Giffard. She listened attentively, asked a question or two, then with a worried look said that Michael had tried to explain what was going on, but had only succeeded in making the situation sound utterly bizarre. Hennessey said it was bizarre, that he had stumbled into a hornet's nest and had no idea where it was going to end up. Dean was involved in something nasty, and the police were trying to fathom the extent of that nastiness. Emma wanted to know if the people he was dealing with were connected to ASIO, for if they were, then he should watch his step. His assurances were met with scepticism.

"It doesn't sound normal to me, John."

"It's a special unit set up to look into crime syndicates."

"Laura thinks you're headed for trouble."

"Michael told me."

"She's really worried."

"That's nice."

His tone made Emma hesitate. "She's hurting, John. She blames herself for what's happened."

"That's not the impression I get."

"She's had time to think."

He looked away, looked back and said that he'd all but given up trying to fathom Laura's thought processes. She was a law unto herself. Grappling with her temperament was difficult.

"She says much the same about you."

"I'll bet."

"You *are* very taken up with your work."

"So, what if I am?"

"She says you cut her out."

He lifted the menu and glanced at it, put it down again. "She blunders in and out of my creative space as if it's the lobby of a bloody hotel. I won't put up with that. She ought to know better."

"You're doing what she wants to do."

"She's the one who chose academia."

"She wants to give up her job."

"And I'm stopping her? Is that it?" He shook his head. "No, sorry, I don't buy that. She's got enough money in the bank to leave whenever she likes."

"Then what's the matter? Really the matter?"

"I *don't* know. I wish I did."

The waitress came and they ordered.

"She thinks she's having a nervous breakdown."

"What do you think?"

A grimace from Emma. "I don't think so."

"It's got to the point that no matter what I do, or say, I'm in the wrong. I don't know how to respond any longer."

Emma sat back into her chair, then with a little smile of apology, she said, "Life wasn't meant to be easy."

He had always thought Emma attractive, and intelligent, but as they talked and drank coffee, he became conscious of being a little more attracted to her than he had first realised. The feeling had always been there, he supposed, but as they shared their thoughts on life and love and just about everything else, his feelings for her underwent a subtle change. One side of a particular moment he was seeing her as usual, the next he was aware that he had crossed some kind of boundary. A moment of panic as Emma looked up and their eyes locked. A delicious moment. A terrifying moment as she registered his look and something inexplicable passed between them. It was as if they had made love and were too coy to admit that such an outrageous thing could have happened.

"You know what's going on in her mind."

"I know what she says to me."

"What does she say to you?"

The disturbing wave of energy dissipated, but it left its mark.

"Is there someone else, Emma?"

It was an impossible question and she groaned under the weight of it. Having already answered his question by default, she said, "It's dead in the water as far as I can make out."

"How long has it been going on?"

"Not long."

"Does she want us to go on?"

"I couldn't say."

"Is she ready to talk?"

"I don't think so. She needs more time." A forced laugh. "She feels guilty, but not sorry."

"She said that?"

"I'm quoting."

"Interestingly put."

Their snacks arrived.

"I'd move slowly if I were you."

"Why should I bother, Emma?"

"You don't want to?"

He stopped eating to contemplate that.

"She's hurting for you as well as for herself."

A woman's summation of another woman's plight. A sliver of conscience? A way back? No way back?

"Give her a few days and come over unannounced."

Walking the length of the arcade at ground level with Emma not long afterwards, he said that he was going to spend a few more days in Sydney and would, if it were at all possible, like to meet with her again. She said that that was unlikely. Michael's new book on the state of the Labor party had reached proof stage and she would be caught up with editing. He looked at her to see if she were lying, but she seemed not to be. Her expression was open, uncomplicated and apologetic. They parted at the entrance to the arcade with another little hug, and he watched her walk away.

PART TWO

13
Recapitulation

The relationship between Laura and some unidentified man seemed to be over, but that did not comfort him. It seemed so unlike Laura. So unlike? He obviously had no idea what Laura was like; she had shown herself to be inscrutable. Guilty but not sorry? That required thought and he was not up to it. He repeated the words in his head and caught a glimpse of something, but it came to nothing. Dark brown eyes full of humour and intelligence, the lips sculpted, the hands slim and expressive. He groaned and faced the fact that Emma had got to him, that he had let the cat out of the proverbial bag and jeopardised their friendship. Two emotions struggling for precedence: his disappointment and astonishment over Laura's infidelity, and his inability to explain the how and why of his feelings for Emma. Guilty but not sorry. The something he had glimpsed back in focus and the realisation that he had always had a soft spot for his best friend's wife.

But was he any the less close to Laura? The answer was no. When he thought of her, all the affection and tenderness and love he had for her immediately bubbled to the surface; and that in spite of what had happened.

He was bloody annoyed with her, but he could not blame her — blame did not enter into it. He had neglected her and that was the price one paid. He had been too wrapped up in himself to notice how they were drifting apart, and when he had noticed, a hardness had already crept into her. And it would have been the same with any woman, Emma included. He was obsessed with his work and only felt real when engaged in it — fiction was his touchstone with reality, the so-called 'unreal' was his real.

He had never understood those who said they avoided fiction because it wasn't true; they had completely missed the point. Fiction was real and true for the very reason of its form — it was, at its best, a delicate and delicious exploration of the reality each of us lived. Every decent portrayal of the human condition was a lived fact, it was objective and factual in a way that factually recorded things could never be. To wake up to this was to be enthralled by fiction; it was to realise that life was a fiction in the very best sense of that word. Knowing this, he had let Laura down. He had let her harden through neglect and allowed their private fiction to take a nasty turn. He regretted that but realised at the same time that that was what living a fiction was all about — it was about risk. Hence his dislike of fiction in which risk was consciously manipulated, the kind of fiction where the characters were forced to do and say things because the writer had decided that that should be the case. One could feel the distortions as one read, feel and see and sense men and women being put through a utilitarian hoop for the sake of financial gain. This was what Laura had yet to learn — let loose a sensed mentality and you had to stay with it. We had no right to dictate what that sensed mentality should say or do; we had to watch and listen and not impose our will on that will. Free will belonged to the characters in a novel just as much as it did to us — our characters had the right to turn left when we thought they should turn right. When that was understood she would discover that she was possessed of all sorts of people with the capacity to speak and reason.

This was why she had had the affair — she had broken out of her mould. She had taken a risk and listened to some other voice. In spite of the jealousy he felt, he congratulated her on having achieved that. It was difficult when someone you cared for let someone else come close, too close. Three was a crowd, and it would ever be so. Which left him with the dilemma of what he felt for Emma, for when their eyes had met, he too had been guilty of infidelity, yet somehow innocent of any crime. Guilty, but not sorry. Guilty as he betrayed Laura with a look, but not sorry, not even now.

He had walked fast, and with purpose, towards Parramatta. It had been abominably hot. He had heard himself breathe, felt the scuff of his clothes on his body and his heels as they eased out of his shoes. Everything had been on the move, his tongue, his arms, his fingers, his eyelids. He had had a pain in his right knee and a tightness in his chest, and there had been a high-pitched whine in his head and a churning, empty feeling in his stomach: visceral intelligence. It had taken him a long time to realise that he was two people, not one, and that one of those people was driven by emotion instead of feeling. Emotion was reactive; feeling was evaluative. This discovery reflected the insight arrived at by Palfreyman's wise researcher — we were each engaged in an attempt to overcome the limitations of our natures, a process thwarted by banal notions of self-mastery. And that, basically, was Laura's problem — she treated her characters in the same manner as she treated herself.

Laura's problem was, however, as much his as it was hers — it was difficult to be real in the midst of our personal fiction. Thinking was all. Don't disturb me, we said, I'm thinking. Don't ask me to feel, I'm thinking. Yet the light of our existence was on — we were conscious and knew it. Or did we? Was the light on when caught up in thought? Was it really on when involved in problem solving? Or were we an empty shell in such moments, a being within whom something vital had dimmed? And, just as importantly, were the characters we created similarly empty, or impaired, similarly soulless when we soullessly pushed them around the way we ourselves were reactively pushed around? Did they in some sense die under our automated touch? That was the question that bothered Hennessey, the question he lived with, and explored, daily.

He did not believe in a ready-made soul; he believed the soul had to be built. He believed the soul to be our private creation, our responsibility, our task. He believed that he now possessed a rudimentary soul, a wee thing making and unmaking itself moment by moment as he stumbled about in his private world. And the growth of this wee thing depended on whether he would allow the 'other' in himself to surface, allow the 'other' to show its face. We were not one; we were two. It was a fluke of our complex geometry that we were so, and he had to find out what that meant. In connection with this he had had an important dream. In this dream, standing before the bathroom mirror, his reflected image had changed into that of a young man in his prime. He had not recognised himself at first, but as he looked, the joyous figure before him had become familiar — not some past self-projected, but in some inexplicable sense a potential self-intercepted. He was more than he seemed; but only to the extent that he built for himself a soul.

What had Harrenstein made of him when he turned up soaked with perspiration, he wondered. He should have taken a bus, but he did not know which one to take. Laura would have had no problem with that; she would have found out by doing what he disliked doing, she would have asked for help. Was this a male thing, or was it just his inadequacy showing? Was he perhaps programmed not to ask for help?

Very businesslike, Herr Harrenstein, whose name meant 'he who waits'. A smartly dressed man acting smart, talking smart, thinking smart. They had gone through the preliminaries and got to the question of his nationality, and from there on in everything had changed. Harrenstein had been quizzical, interested, open yet on guard. Even his movements had changed — they had slowed down and become deliberate. It was as if the mind behind them had been evaluating every syllable, and this deliberateness had transferred itself to his body parts. But the little Austrian had got into the part too well and allowed snippets of reality to pepper his returns. What did it matter if he mentioned Munich? What did it matter if he said his father had been a medical doctor? What did it matter if he mentioned his father's brother's death on the Russian front? It was all meaningless information to the man before him. And then, later, a moment's hesitation as he realised that he had perhaps gone too far in his description of Dean's behaviour, that he had offered a little too much by way of a character analysis for the man he was supposed to despise. Harrenstein's expression had become unhinged in that moment; it was as if he had fallen between mental stools. Dean the liar. Harrenstein the liar. Liars all. Two liars talking about a liar as they attempted to determine the truth.

Laura and he had been telling each other lies for some time; from the very beginning, perhaps. But always for the best of reasons. He had never tried to deceive her with words, just avoided too direct a calling of the truth. She had done likewise. Sins of omission. Dean's lies had been different, as were Harrenstein's. Their lies sprang from the intention to deceive. Unlike Laura, Harrenstein lacked conscience; he lied just as confidently as Dean, and probably as often. So, what was going on in his life, and to what extent was it connected with his father? The father had been highly intelligent and deadly — intelligence in a moral vacuum — but could the same be said for the son? Australia was not Germany *circa* 1945. And what of Harrenstein's son, and the talented daughter? Aussies through and through, Harrenstein had admitted ruefully.

Palfreyman's displeasure at being in a cheapish Indian restaurant had amused Hennessey; the tanned face had remained immobile with displeasure. But on seeing the notes on Giffard's confession, he had rallied and begun to discuss the nature of the phenomenon confronting them. The question uppermost in his mind had been: how deep does the rot go? Had the virus of haughty certainty taken root? Was it as organised as Giffard seemed to think? Was it about to develop a new, deceptive political profile, a religious profile, perhaps? These questions had led to them discussing whether Europe's two most important schools of thought — philosophy and literary criticism — had been contaminated at source. Could attitudes be passed on cryptically? In accepting relativism and deconstructionism, had we unwittingly imbibed nihilism in disguise, taken on a vision alien to everything we believed ourselves to hold dear? It wasn't just a matter of past political madness skulking somewhere in the Australian bush, it was a matter of that madness being given a spurious credibility and allowed to flourish all over again.

As they left the restaurant, he had begun to wonder what it was that drove a man like David Palfreyman. What made him tick? Why this particular line of work? Why a policeman of this sort? As they stepped into the light and heat of a late Sydney afternoon, he had sprung that question on Palfreyman and received a totally unexpected reply — his mother was a German national. An artist and a teacher by profession, she had, like Harrenstein, found her way to Australia when the war was over. Gently chiding Palfreyman for not having told him sooner, he had asked tentative questions, and Palfreyman had replied in German. In that moment, standing facing one another on a busy street, a whole new dimension had been added to their disjointed relationship.

14
A Veil of Silence

"You told him!"

"I admitted to the fact without saying anything. He took me by surprise — it was unavoidable." Emma's expression was an apology in itself. "He sprang it on me, Laura."

"How did he take it?"

"Calmly."

"That's my John."

They were in the lounge talking over coffee, Emma seated, Laura standing at the French windows, mug in hand.

"I told him it was over between you and... Is it?"

"I think so."

"You *think* so?"

"It's... over." Laura made a face of that. "It would never have worked; I think I've known that all along."

"And you and John?"

"That's probably over, too. Now?"

Ignoring the faintly accusative tone, Emma said that it did not have to be over between them, that John accepted his share of the blame.

"He said so?"

"In as many words."

There was a silence; Laura spoke first: "Look, I'm sorry to have dragged you into all of this."

"Don't be silly; it's what friends are for."

"I've been a fool; I realise that now."

"These things happen."

A silence as they evaluated each other's clichés.

"You managed to shrug it off." The 'real' reinstated. "I can't imagine John having an affair. He's probably immune to that kind of thing. I don't think he's had many relationships."

"That surprises me."

"What does?"

"That he hasn't had his fair share?"

Another woman evaluating her partner in that way made Laura hesitate. Turning back towards the French windows, she stared out into the afternoon heat. "He's too bright for his own good." A glance at her friend. "He thinks the world of you and Michael."

"Likewise."

"And I go and spoil it all." Back to looking at Emma. "What am I going to do now that he knows?"

"If I'd lied, he'd have known"

Laura's sigh was a quick expulsion of air. "I'll get out of your hair tomorrow."

"You'll do no such thing! John's going to be in Sydney for a few more days. You have to stay on."

"What for?"

"What for?" Emma's patience gave out. "Why do you think? To meet up. Talk!"

"He's not up here because of *me*." Laura's expression was simultaneously defensive and dismissive. "He's up here playing bloody detective."

"I don't think he's *playing* at anything, Laura. He wants to sort things out. Said so."

"Really? Are you sure about that? All I can see is someone getting on with things as usual. I don't know what to make of that. It makes me feel that what's happened to us is secondary. I get the impression he'll fit me in when it's convenient."

"He can't just sit on his hands waiting for you to respond."

"I know that, but…"

"You can't expect to have his undivided attention."

"I damn well do!" Laura's eyes blazed as she turned back into the room and faced Emma. "I want him to drop everything and think about what's happened to us. *Really* think about what's happened."

"He's doing just that."

"Yes, at the same time as he's planning his next bloody novel!"

Emma's patience was under strain. "What you don't realise," she said in a controlled whisper, "is that this Dean thing has escalated into something quite serious."

"Really? Which hotel is he in?"

"Why? What's that got to do with anything?"

"The Hilton?"

"He's in the Lancaster; it's a dump."

"Exactly," said Laura triumphantly. "But he's not there for reasons of thrift, Emma. It's *romance* that's driving him."

"He hates the place!"

"Which means it's perfect for his purposes."

Emma hesitated in her reply. "Do you really think you're reading him correctly?"

"Oh yes," said Laura. "I know my John."

***

Hennessey was at that moment sitting in the Giffards' kitchen listening to Mary rationalise the threat Dean posed to both of them. Norman, his arms folded, sat scowling. Yes, Dean would be annoyed at Norman for clouting him, Mary said, but as he had been drunk and Dean had got the better of him, he would probably let that one go. But not for snitching to the police; if he found out about that he'd come after them for sure. And then a statement that made Hennessey freeze: they were ready for him if he did; they still had a revolver Dean had given to Norman.

"Revolver?" said Hennessey. "Christ almighty, if you use that on Dean it'll be premeditated murder."

"It would be self-defence," said Giffard.

"It would be murder even if you had a license, which I'm sure you don't have." He sat staring at them.

"What you have to do is put yourself under police protection; it's the only way. They'll find you a safe house."

"He'd find us."

"He's not invincible, Mary."

"He's got the luck of the devil," she replied. "He doesn't think like you or me. He's bonkers. He never does what's expected."

"He's about to come a cropper, I can assure you of that."

"So, you hope," said Giffard.

Mary came back in with a caution. "Don't go telling the police about the revolver."

"I have to; I have no option."

"You don't have to be *that* honest."

"It's got nothing to do with honesty. If you use it and the police find out that I knew you, had it, I'll be for the high jump along with you." He came back in quickly. "If there was ever a reason for both of you to work with the police, this is it. Selling drugs up the Cross isn't the answer, Norman."

"How the fuck do you know about that?"

"You've got a police record that says just that."

The Giffards stared at Hennessey.

"Look, if you cooperate, they'll put you somewhere safe. But only if you agree to testify against Dean and his new cronies. That's the deal." Sensing strong resistance, he added quickly, "Think about it, Norman. Every newspaper in country will be after your story."

"That's not all that'll be after us," said Giffard.

"Dean'll be in custody by that time."

"The police can't be trusted."

"The people I know will protect you."

"They're not police?"

"They're a police unit independent of the regular force."

"Doesn't matter what they are, they won't give people like us a fair go, not ever," said Mary. Then, haughtily, "Their promises aren't worth shit."

"You'll be treated properly, fairly, *I* promise you that. But I want you to meet up with a journalist friend of mine first."

"What for?"

"He'll help you sell your story when the time comes."

"Can't you do that?"

"He knows the right people."

"And the police? What'll they be doing?" asked Mary.

"They'll make their own arrangement with you." He looked from one to the other. "Handing in that firearm will be a good start. Or you can give it to me, and I'll hand it in for you. That might in fact be the best way to go."

"I'd rather do that myself," said Giffard.

"Then make sure it isn't loaded."

"We don't have any ammunition," Giffard lied.

***

Frank Darby was expounding on the White Brotherhood, a group in the USA with a particularly nasty line in thinking. He was sitting wrong way round on a bentwood chair, a cigarette burning like an incendiary between the fingers of his right hand, his leather jacket open, the expanse of his red-shirted, vested stomach fully visible. He was a man in his late fifties who had run to seed. Anglo Saxons, he was saying, were the chosen people of the Bible according to the Brotherhood; non-whites were mud people and no better than animals. The Brotherhood had a pseudo-religious ideology that identified Jews with Satan and predicted a final, apocalyptic battle between whites and non-whites. It also advocated the establishment of a white racist state. Members were expected to commit extremist acts by way of initiation. The group was opposed to the banking system, interracial marriage and homosexuality. American intelligence sources considered it the most dangerous hate group to have arisen since the war years, and it was now operating in Australia.

Delivering his breakdown with pauses calculated for effect, Frank sucked on his cigarette and exhaled into the room with eye-watering precision. He was a law unto himself, an intellectual urchin in stained trousers who, if asked, would pontificate on almost any subject with scary exactitude.

Jack Murchinson sat hunched behind his desk, his jaw resting on the butt of his right palm, his gaze fixed on Frank's pock-marked face. But the director's eyes were not altogether still; they wandered occasionally in the direction of David Palfreyman, who was sitting on his right. Palfreyman was not aware of Murchinson's glances, he was giving Frank his full attention; the man's balding pate and lank black hair reminded him of a portrait of Francis Bacon.

"Which brings us to Giffard's morsels," said Frank, giving Palfreyman an appreciative nod. "As you're well aware, contact has been made between one of our hard-line groups and the Brotherhood's representatives now in the country, but we can't yet determine what's going on. There is no movement at the station; no word is being passed around. Which of course raises the question of who is running the show and how they have acquired control over so many individual elements. That's the assumption. How else explain the silence? Giffard's titbits do not throw light on that; they merely accentuate the fact that something is going on behind the scenes."

"We've got neither the manpower nor the funds," said Murchinson, breaking in, "and our cousins are getting edgy.

David Palfreyman swivelled round and asked if they had been asked to pass on their findings. Murchinson said that he had so far managed to avoid that commitment. Anyway, what did they know? Not much, really. All they had were rumours, some serious, some decidedly Mickey Mouse. The Giffard stuff sounded *Boy's Own Annual* in places. What did they think they were involved in?

"I find ASIO's interest of interest," said Palfreyman. "They may be thinking along similar lines to Frank."

"I doubt that very much. Frank?"

"I haven't picked up on anything."

"Resources," said Murchinson, returning to his hobby horse.

"It's a matter of using meagre resources more efficiently," said Frank. He turned and dunked out his cigarette in the moist earth of a nearby plant pot. As he swung back, he was already fumbling for the packet of cigarettes in his shirt pocket. "As we've identified which of our groups is considered numero uno by the Americans, we can now concentrate surveillance on that group's activities.

"The rest is bonkers stuff," said Palfreyman, referring to the numerous web sites under scrutiny. "Even if this White Brotherhood connection is for real, I hardly think Australia is itching to become a racist state."

"Depends how you read it all," said Frank, sending a plume of cigarette smoke in Palfreyman's direction. "There's intelligence at work here. Don't dismiss what's going on too quickly."

"And there's a bucketful of resentment out there," said Murchinson, referring to closed factories and the collapse of manufacturing. He was sprawled back in his leather chair now, his dark eyes moving from face to face.

"It's still a big ask," said Palfreyman. "Independents would have to independently corner around twenty per cent of the vote to make a dent in the status quo, and that's unlikely given how idiosyncratic each of them is."

"I think something a little more complicated is going on," said Frank. "It isn't just a matter of a few independents upsetting the status quo. I think it's a matter of a few independents getting in, then coming together later to form a political block. Perhaps even a new party. If the upcoming election proves to be close, such a group could end up as power brokers in a very real sense."

"That's asking a lot of such people," said Palfreyman.

"Bound by prejudice, but not stupid," said Frank. "And in alliance with some clever buggers by the feel of it. The silence being experienced at ground level attests to that. Someone has taken the reins and is pulling on them hard."

"I've had flak from customs," said Murchinson. "They didn't like having their arm twisted over who should be allowed in. Wanted to know why we were interested in letting in the very people they were about to refuse entry to."

Frank was dismissive. It was the only way they could potentially track who was talking to whom.

"How long is their stay," asked Palfreyman.

"A couple of weeks."

"And our cousins?"

"Watchful."

The telephone rang on Murchinson's desk, and he answered it. "Hennessey's on the other line and wants to talk to you," he said.

***

Palfreyman's greeting to Hennessey was in the form of one word. "Success?"

"They've agreed to meet with you on Monday evening."

"What's wrong with Sunday?"

"I've suggested they talk to a journo friend of mine first. He'll evaluate the possibility of a package on the basis of Giffard's info. It's my guess they'll be more amenable after that."

"You can't do that, John!"

"You said they could sell their story."

"Yes, but I didn't mean for them to start talking to a journalist this early. What were you thinking? These dolts blabbing half-baked nonsense to a journalist could unravel everything if it got out."

"First of all, the Giffards aren't dolts, David. They aren't dumb, they're *numb* from having to deal with the system. And the journalist in question is a close friend of mine with a lot of experience in this area. He'll help get the Giffards on side."

"You'll have to cancel."

"They won't talk to you if they can't talk to him first. That's their safeguard against being used and then dumped."

"You've got to make them see sense, John."

"I did. That's why things are set up the way they are."

Palfreyman's annoyance was almost palpable, but he kept his tone even. "They can sell their story officially *after* they've testified."

"There's nothing to stop them coming to an arrangement prior to that. They don't actually have a story yet, just bits and pieces."

"Murchinson will have a fit!"

"Murchinson will just have to put up with it."

Palfreyman paused to regain his composure. "You must have realised this would complicate things for me."

"I wasn't thinking about *you* — I was thinking about *them*. I feel responsible for having talked them into this."

"We'll have to talk to this *friend* of yours."

"*You* can talk to him this evening in the lounge bar of the Belvedere. I'm meeting him there for a preliminary chat at six-thirty."

"And the Giffards?"

"Same place same time tomorrow evening."

"They'll stand out like sore thumbs, John."

"It'll make them feel they're being taken seriously; that'll work to your advantage."

Palfreyman digested that. "Murchinson will have a fit."

"Blame it all on me."

"I intend to," said Palfreyman

***

It being early, and all but empty, the lounge bar of the Belvedere had a hushed atmosphere like that of a church. Palfreyman arrived shortly after six-thirty, and they got down to business. Nothing of what Norman Giffard passed on could be used without official clearance, he said. And that was not a request. Any attempt to circumvent that directive would result in serious consequences.

"You're whetting my appetite," Michael said.

"You'll have to sign this first." Palfreyman produced a document. "It's the Crimes Act." His pained expression became a smile. "It's to your advantage. You'll be all the more able to convince when telling how carefully we've handled this situation."

"The moment I sign that I'm stuffed," said Michael.

"Not at all. All it means is that you can't publish until after we're finished with the Giffards and given you clearance." He glanced at Hennessey, returned his gaze to Michael. "I've got nothing against the Giffards making a quick buck — eventually. It's the timing that matters." Palfreyman balanced himself on the edge of a half-truth. "We're not completely without heart."

"What about protection?" asked Hennessey.

"I'll arrange surveillance when Norman collaborates and agrees to testify."

"A safe house? They're really scared."

"Giffard being scared surprises me."

"Not for himself, for Mary."

"That's to our advantage." Palfreyman turned his attention back to Michael. "If you would be so kind," he said, glancing at the papers he wanted him to sign.

"Doesn't look terribly official," said Michael.

"It's what civil servants have to sign." A little laugh from Palfreyman. "Try breaking it and see where you end up."

"And if I don't sign?"

Palfreyman addressed his reply to Hennessey. "I suggest you advise your friend on the facts of life, John."

A smile and a shake of the head from Michael as he put pen to paper.

"The Giffards will have to do likewise."

"I'd approach that *very* carefully if I were you," said Hennessey.

"Only full cooperation will lead to riches," said Palfreyman, tongue in cheek. Back into his briefcase went the document. Then, in a completely different tone, he said, "I've got time for a quick drink."

"Then I'll be on my way," said Michael.

"John has my number." When they were alone, he added without embarrassment: "I'm taking my seventy-year-old mother dancing tonight. She prefers it to exercising in a gym."

"You never cease to surprise me," said Hennessey."

15
The Language of Rebirth

"They may be in trouble," Hennessey said, when the Giffards didn't show.

"They may have scarpered," said Palfreyman.

"I don't think so. Mary would have held him to it."

"He hasn't exactly delivered gold nuggets."

"I suspect he knows more than he's letting on."

"Even when blind drunk?"

"Being blind drunk doesn't make one utterly stupid."

"It does if you're stupid in the first place."

"Which I don't think he is."

"Look, a few scraps of disjointed information are all he's given us so far: locations that are weeks, if not months, old. He doesn't really know what's going on because he doesn't really understand half of what he's seen or heard."

"That's to admit that he's carrying important information without realising it."

"Yes, but—"

"Hence the need to sign them up?"

"We didn't want a garbled account getting into the press."

"Or too accurate an account?"

"They're innocents abroad, John."

"I wouldn't bet on that; I think you're underestimating the Giffards."

"So, you keep saying."

"Then why aren't you listening?"

Palfreyman looked as if he had been struck.

"This situation is about more than my stolen book, David. It now involves people's lives, and I can't treat that lightly."

"I understand what you're saying, John."

"I don't think you do. Even a mentally benighted Giffard does not deserve to be treated as worthless. And what about Mary? I remember you saying that it was 'touching' that they had married. What did you mean by that?"

"Just that it was unusual."

"Why unusual? What's so unusual about two people wanting to commit themselves to one another? Or is that the wrong question? Should the question not really be why are two *stupid* people pretending to be decent?"

"You're being overly sensitive, John."

"Do you know what intelligence is, David? Let me tell you first what it is not. It is *not* having a head stuffed with information. Intelligence is not about knowing anything in the concrete sense of knowing; it is the capacity to know that you *don't* know something, the capacity to face the black hole of one's own ignorance and do something about it."

"You think Giffard understands that?"

"I think they both do."

"Why?"

"Because it's in their eyes, David."

Palfreyman's frown was studied and stationary; he was staring into black hole, and he was not enjoying the experience.

A wave of a hand from Hennessey; he ought not to have said any of that, he said.

"I'm glad you did."

"Then find out what's going on with the Giffards."

A sharp nod from Palfreyman. He would have a car call for Hennessey in the morning.

"Where am I going?"

"To chat with Frank. It's time."

Hennessey waited until Palfreyman was well away, then headed for a telephone booth he'd spotted in the hallway. He would speak to Michael. Alas, he got Laura instead.

"John?"

"Is... Michael there?"

"Yes, I'll get him for you."

"No, no, wait! We have to talk!"

"Not on the phone."

"Of course, not on the phone! Let's meet somewhere in town and have dinner. Here in the Belvedere Hotel would be good."

"You're at the Belvedere. What are you doing there?"

"I had a meeting with Palfreyman."

"Are you sure you can fit me in, John?"

"Don't be silly, Laura! We have to talk!"

"Yes, about *me*. I don't know if I want to talk about me, John."

"*Us,* Laura."

A silence.

"Say seven o'clock?"

"No, I don't think so," she said, and hung up.

He rang straight back, and Michael answered. "She doesn't want to speak to you, John."

"That's ridiculous."

"She says it isn't ridiculous."

"That's even more ridiculous!"

Michael laughed in spite of himself.

"Ask her if the Belvedere thing is on or not."

"She's nodding, John."

"Good. Seven o'clock in the upstairs bar. Okay?"

"Yup, that's fine." After a pause: "Something happened?"

"The Giffards didn't show. Palfreyman's finding out why."

***

News of the Gifffards' plight reached Hennessey around ten that evening; it was not good news. The front door of their hovel had been shouldered in, and there was evidence of a struggle. A length of timber had been found lying in the hallway. An alert had been put out. When Hennessey arrived to meet Frank the following morning, nothing had changed. Palfreyman ushered him into Murchinson's office saying that Frank hadn't arrived in yet, and that Murchinson wanted to talk with him first.

"So where is he?" asked Hennessey.

"On his way. Traffic."

"And nothing on the Giffards."

"I'm afraid not.

"Harrenstein?"

"Going about his business as usual." Then a rather odd question. "You've discussed what's going on with your wife as well as Michael?"

"Peripherally. She's not terribly interested in my doings. We're temporarily separated, in fact."

"Oh, I'm sorry to hear that."

"We've arranged to meet on neutral ground this evening and sort things out. Well, hopefully. The Belvedere."

"Ah, *very* good, John. The kidneys are *sensational*. Ply her with kidneys."

"I rather think it's *my* kidney's she's after."

Palfreyman thought that very funny.

"Tell me about Murchinson?"

Jack Murchinson had been Special Branch before becoming OSI, Palfreyman said. He had been in injured in the line of duty and was not a happy chappie.

"This meeting is over my having made an arrangement with the Giffards?"

"Jack didn't say, but that's probable.

"I'm to be ticked off?"

"Your turn?" said Palfreyman.

Murchinson, when he turned up, was a man in his late fifties, lean and strong with chiselled eyebrows and dark, intelligent eyes — Hennessey could detect no sign of an injury. Internal, perhaps. There were a few things he, Hennessey, had to get straight before they went any further, Murchinson said. He had to recognise his limits and avoid trouble. Yes, he had signed a waiver, but they'd prefer he avoided getting his skull cracked open, or worse. A terse smile from Murchinson, followed by a sentence that confirmed some kind of tension between himself and Palfreyman. If he felt, he was being pushed to perform…

Hennessey's denials were emphatic. David had acted professionally at all times. Murchinson nodded, waited; it was as if he expected Hennessey to change his mind and blurt out some terrible misdemeanour.

"David's very bright," Hennessey added, conscious of having used Palfreyman's first name twice in Murchinson's presence.

"Oh, he's bright enough, there's no doubting that. First class mind." Said in such a way as to suggest

Palfreyman harboured some hidden flaw. Then a piece of information that caused Hennessey to freeze. The man they thought had betrayed Giffard to Dean — Dave Hollows — had been found dead that very morning. He had been shot twice in the chest at close range. His death roughly matched the time of the supposed abduction.

"Supposed?" said Hennessey.

"The Giffards may not have been abducted. They may have overcome their attackers and run for it. There was a fight, and Dave Hollows may have been shot during that fight. He wasn't found at the scene, but that doesn't rule out the possibility of his having been there. It's a likely scenario."

"A man like Giffard tends to rely on his physical strength," said Hennessey, fearful that the Giffards had been stringing him along about not having any ammunition.

"David says you've developed a liking for him."

"I don't dislike him."

"I get the impression David's not so keen."

"David is perhaps more perceptive."

"Perhaps," said Murchinson. He extended a hand. "We're obliged for the time you're putting into this."

"It's to my benefit, I think," said Hennessey.

Palfreyman's office was empty when he returned. A young woman approached and said that she had been instructed to take him to Mr Derby's 'room'. The emphasis placed on the word room alerted Hennessey to an underlying current of meaning. When he stepped into Frank's 'room', that meaning became clear. All trace of daylight had been banished. Squares of thick brown paper had been taped to the panes of a casement window, what light there was delivered by table lamps placed either side of a large oak desk. This, he learned later, was because Frank's eyes were sensitive to strong light. But what amazed Hennessey most was the general clutter of the place. There were piles of books, old newspapers, magazines and video tapes wherever one looked, and on the desk, amidst a debris of dismantled fountain pens and other assorted bric-a-brac, sat an immaculate Adler portable typewriter with a sheet of paper sticking out of it. Most noticeable of all, however, was a pyramid of cigarette butts in a black marble ashtray, and a pall of cigarette smoke racing towards a gently whirring extraction fan.

"Frank Derby," said Frank Derby.

They shook hands and Frank ushered Hennessey to a half-buried armchair which he cleared by sweeping its contents onto the floor.

"You're the writer?"

"For my sins."

As was his habit, Frank seated himself on a chair wrong way round — it allowed him to support his smoking hand and hide his paunch at the same time.

"Where do you want to start?"

"Wherever you think appropriate," said Hennessey.

Rescuing the remains of a burning cigarette from the ashtray, Frank drew on it, exhaled dramatically and launched into a monologue that Hennessey punctuated with an occasional question.

"It's been a very good year for bonkers types, John," he said, as if they were old buddies. "Almost as good as the late eighties. Lots of great stuff during those years. In '87 we had the West German neo-Nazi movement trying to make a big deal out of Hess's suicide. In '88 the Kurt Waldheim fiasco, and in '89 the shock of ultra far right parties in the West German elections, making a breakthrough in Frankfurt where they took six-point-six per cent of the vote." Frank was speaking, not to Hennessey, but to thin air, his tone that of a lecturer confronted by an auditorium of disinterested students. A glance that held for a moment or two. "A former officer in Hitler's SS took a ten per cent slice in Hesse. I was in Germany in '89 for the Fuhrer's one hundredth birthday. A one-meter-high block of granite from the concentration camp at Mauthausen in central Austria was unveiled in his hometown on April twentieth. Why was I there?" Another glance. "I was researching aspects of the neo-Nazi movement and needed something atmospheric for the opening chapter of the book I was planning. I got what I was after."

"Published?"

"Oxford University Press. I've got a copy somewhere..." Frank looked around disinterestedly, then returned to his subject. "As I stood in that West German border town and listened to the mayor speak of the necessity to acknowledge historical facts, I found myself asking the question that many people have asked themselves. Why did a nation as intelligent as the Germans give in to someone like Adolf Hitler? What was going on in the German psyche during the first three decades of this century that made them vulnerable to that kind of nonsense? And, just as important, why were the neo-Nazis again gaining credence in Europe?"

"You answered those questions?"

"Yes, I think so, but not quite in the manner I expected. I expected the answer to have something to do with the famed orderliness of the German mind, but that was not the right tack. The Germans hadn't given in to Hitler because they were in love with order, they had given in because they were fooled into thinking he was offering them some great truth — the chance to transcend themselves. That's what was at the bottom of the whole sad affair. Now that isn't the kind of answer one expects, and it isn't the kind of answer most people want to hear, but it's a perfectly feasible reading of history when one realises what was going on in the European psyche at the turn of the previous century. And I say European rather than German because the ideas and prejudices we associate with the Third Reich were in fact distributed evenly throughout Europe — they were not exclusively German. Knowledge was in a state of flux. Amazingly silly ideas were being considered alongside ideas of real brilliance. Darwin was up and running, as were Freud, Jung, Haeckel and many others, but some of these thinkers were influential way beyond their worth."

"I know nothing of Haeckel," said Hennessey.

"Haeckel was professor of zoology at the University of Jena — he dominated German evolutionary theory in the second half of the nineteenth century. Bright fellow. Just about everything written about Darwin in German was written by Haeckel, and that explains some of the distortions that arose in the German mind around the question of evolutionary biology — particularly the social implications. It was Haeckel, not Darwin, who formulated the theory that human beings had descended from simian ancestors, and it was Haeckel who insisted that evolutionary biology was a historical science, that it wasn't possible to think about human evolution without including disciplines such as embryology, palaeontology and phylogeny. Now keep in mind when this was happening. It wasn't the nineteen-thirties, it was the eighteen-seventies. Haeckel even published a book on human evolution before Darwin."

"Phylogeny?"

"The development of the human race mirrored or replicated in the stages of individual human development. Shades of Jung. Haeckel believed that the entire history of the species could be detected in the development and structure of an adult human being, and on that basis proposed the creation of a new religion." Frank chuckled to himself. "That's the kind of madcap thing people did at the turn of the last century. Haeckel argued that God revealed himself in all natural phenomena, and as such could be interpreted as the vital force or energy that drove the evolutionary process. And this wasn't disguised atheistic materialism; it was a blend of religion and science that just happened to coincide with a rejection of the Christian myth in Central Europe during the 1890s."

"Völkisch nationalism and a return to a golden age."

"Exactly. Folk nationalism mixed with madcap *fin de siècle* ideas of hereditary degeneration and quasi-scientific, quasi-mystical theories of racial purity. With an emphasis on nature worship — particularly the sun. German folk-nationalism amalgamated with Haeckel's new religion, which he called 'Monism', and by 1906 groups known as the Monistic Alliance were all over Central Europe. Experimenting with secular rites of passage under Haeckel's guidance, these groups came up with three basic demands: that a member reject organised religion, undergo an initiation to dissolve the boundary between body and spirit, and participate in local societies promoting Alliance ideas. But it all went terribly wrong. Haeckel was eventually forced to distance himself from the ideological excesses of these groups — which is really something given his own excesses — and in 1911 the chemist Wilhelm Ostwald became president of the Alliance in Haeckel's place. Ostwald won the Nobel Prize for Chemistry in 1909, and it was he who went on to initiate social Darwinian reforms in eugenics, euthanasia and economics."

"I think I get your drift."

"I'm sure you do, but bear with me, there's more. Haeckel was, briefly, a member of the Thule Society, a secret organisation with many prominent nationalists in its ranks. There was also the Society of German Believers, the Nordic Faith Fellowship, the All-Aryan Federation, the German Church of God and the Tannenberg Foundation. Each of these societies attempted to institute a new German paganism. But there was actually nothing new about it; the promotion of neopagan ideas had been going on steadily since the 1890s. It included things like nature-worship, hiking, nudism, vegetarianism, dancing round bonfires, magical ceremonies invoking the old Norse gods, horse sacrifice and an idealisation of the ancient Teutonic warrior — particularly Siegfried. But what has to be understood here is that the central tenet of German neopaganism was personal. Through its practices and philosophy, it promised the psychological and spiritual rebirth of the individual. That was its core promise, and that was the promise Hitler and his henchmen used to seduce the German nation. Even Ludendorff was taken in for a while; he heard in Hitler's rhetoric the language of rebirth and responded like millions of others."

"Ludendorff?"

"He was head of the Tannenberg Society; his wife was the famous völkisch writer Mathilde von Kemnitz."

"I studied the political scene in Germany prior to the outbreak of war — I was there '59 to '61 — but I didn't come across any of this stuff."

"It's of little interest except to historians like myself."

"What turned you on?"

Frank laughed in response to Hennessey's question. Two tabs of LSD was all it had taken, Frank said. His world view had undergone instant change.

Hennessey's astonishment was plain.

"That was it for me, John. I discovered there was more than one way to skin a cat."

"Where are you heading with this?"

"I'll explain in a minute — let me first complete the scenario for you. The Germans were up to their ears in völkisch notions at the end of the nineteenth century. By the turn of the century völkisch groups had formed throughout Germany, Austria-Hungary and Switzerland. Mixing theosophy and occultism with evolutionary theory the members of these groups, fraternities, lodges and societies became intoxicated with their own brew and ended up giving in to Haeckel's doctrine of biological inferiority. When that twist in public perception was established, the scene was set for the rise of Hitler in '33 and for what followed."

"David showed me the piece on Goebbels; it suggested we had perhaps thrown the baby out with the bathwater."

"Intuitions of splendour bastardised." Frank killed off another cigarette by pushing it into the pile of dead butts. "When I came across that piece, I did a double take; the writer had woken up to something important. I'd been fiddling around with the question of 'transcendence' for a couple of decades and couldn't decide whether it was a legitimate aim or not. My hippy youth and two tabs of LSD said it was my education said otherwise. Christianity preached transcendence as a fundamental truth, but only on its own fantastical terms. Then there was Nietzsche's superior man, his 'Overman', and Hitler's perfect Aryan that Nietzsche's sister so cleverly exploited. And on top of it all Jung's psychology based, as anyone who has studied the matter knows, on ideas not altogether dissimilar to those held by Haeckel. So, what did we do? We dumped the lot and started again. It was a matter of cleaning the stable of anything that even peripherally reminded us of Germany's dream of spiritual renewal."

"I've never been able to make up my mind about Jung."

"Nor I. But there are aspects of his thinking that can't be ignored. What bothered me was the way in which our intellectuals came to interpret reality; they saw it as a set of cold, brutal facts with no meaning other than the meaning we gave to them. Didn't matter that there were universal laws around which we could create hugely complex mathematical schemes. Just about everyone believed that reality was meaningless in itself.

The extraordinary complexity of animate and inanimate things could be written off as no more than chance endlessly multiplied by chance."

"You believe in something other than chance?"

"I don't believe in a manipulating God, if that's what you mean. I'm not a theist."

"What then?"

Frank hesitated. "Let me put it this way. Haeckel's argument was that human beings were an expression of the universe's complexity, and that that complexity was meaningful in its own right. To say that the universe only had meaning when we gave it meaning was to fail to recognise that we ourselves were direct proof of the universe's capacity to produce meaning."

"Cute."

"And irrefutable even if you reject the idea of a megalomaniac creator out there somewhere."

"And the point you wish to make?"

"More a question than a point, John. We're in the process of systematically dismantling our reason to live. That's my take on things. We've lost contact with what it feels like to be a human being. Everything is external. The moment is taken up with thinking about externals. Which is to say that the inner has been invaded by the outer to such an extent that we find it difficult to differentiate between the two. We've come to believe that thinking about things outer is our inner life in action, but we're wrong in that assumption. The outer has all but completely usurped the inner and we're paying the price for not having noticed. It's as simple as that, and that in itself tells us that a possible transcendence has been swapped for a growing utilitarian vision."

Hennessey stared at Frank. "They're paying you to think about stuff like this?"

"They're paying me to *think*, John; thinking is a risky business."

"David's on side? Murchinson?"

"They're battling, like everyone else, with a society in decline and are trying to get a handle on why it's happening.'

"You've been set a precise analytical task?"

"An analysis of Australia's social and cultural climate in relation to the far right. That takes in resident war criminals of all sorts and the influence of visiting crackpots. Most of our old Nazis are inactive; their ideology, alas, is not; it's now hydra headed."

"Harrenstein?"

"Affiliations not yet proven."

Hennessey watched Frank draw on his cigarette and blow a stream of smoke towards the fan. "I find it hard to believe you're being allowed to consider stuff like this."

"It's snowballed. Started a couple of years back." Frank tapped ash into the ashtray, stared into the pile of twisted butts as if scrying it for some terrible truth. "Government advisers woke up to the fact that Australian society was creaking. A general breakdown in young people's attitudes. A growing disregard for the most basic of social demands and a hike in the adolescent suicide rate. Something was going on and it could not be ignored. That *something* is now taking on shape and substance in relation to the refugee question and militant Islam."

"Sounds like social engineering in the making."

"Not at all. That old Soviet notion doesn't belong in this context."

"I suspect the Liberal party wouldn't agree."

"John, if the Liberals get in this time they're going to have to face up to some very difficult questions, and the rule of law won't be sufficient in itself to answer those questions. We're going to have to *think* our way out of this one."

"What's the difference between believing in God and believing that the universe is in some sense meaningful in its own right?"

"The difference is stark. A universe capable of expressing an underlying coherence does not have to be conscious; God, on the other hand, has to be defined as conscious to allow for the moves he is believed to have made throughout world history. The problem with this God is that it is a God with aims and objectives, likes and dislikes, loves and hates — a projection in anyone's terms — whereas all that's needed is a more adventurous conception of complexity. Darwin's basic theory of evolution and natural selection is the governing paradigm, and on this basis the tendency in all of our major disciplines is to explain life, human intelligence and self-consciousness in physical terms. It's either religion's big fella beyond the sky playing puppet-master, or a physicalist interpretation of reality defined as beyond dispute: a new fundamentalism, in other words." Frank fell silent for a moment; then he said, "There's a huge problem here, John, we don't actually know what physical matter is apart from saying that it's physical. That, to my way of thinking, constitutes a tautology; it does not properly address the phenomenon of conscious awareness or how it arose. Consciousness may have been an *in potentia* property of matter right from the moment of the Big Bang, and if that's so, then we bloody well ought to be talking about it."

"That's an astonishing hypothesis," said Hennessey.

"Yet easy as pie if we upgrade the language we use to talk about such things. If life came out of dead matter, John, then dead matter isn't as dead as we have come to believe — it may be of an entirely different order and require a much subtler theory of complexity to explain its nature."

Hennessey drew breath and audibly exhaled. "And I thought we were going to talk about Gavin Dean's shadowy friends."

"We are, John." Frank's smile was enigmatic. "It's my bet they're all in there somewhere."

16
Betrayer and Betrayed

Frank's diatribe on völkisch idealism and Hitlerite metaphysics had helped clarify something for Hennessey: the OSI was comprised of individuals of considerable flexibility and imagination. That was a healthy sign; it was what was expected of intelligence organisations but too seldom realised in practice. His own stint with army intelligence had revealed a sad lack of imagination alongside great technical expertise. Break a stubborn code his colleagues had been able to do, but they had had the habit of cocking things up when it came to thinking their way into the mental processes of their intelligence counterparts. He had not had their puzzle-breaking kind of mind, but he had possessed the novelist's ability to empathetically enter another's mental space, and this curious sensitivity had given him the edge in many an encounter. The encounter he was about to embark on, however, was with Laura, and that, as he was well aware, would be on a whole other level.

She of the new hair-do appeared in the Belvedere at five to seven. She had on a new blue dress, and from what he could remember of her old handbag, one of those as well. He signalled and she caught sight of him.

Sliding onto an adjacent bar stool, she said, "Bit posh for you, isn't it?" Her hair was darker than usual and very well cut. He smiled and asked what she wanted to drink.

"Brandy."

"You've lost weight."

"Have I?"

The innocence of her look completely threw him. Catching the bar tender's attention, he ordered her drink. When he looked back, she was leaning on the bar's polished surface, her face all but hidden by her hands, her attention internalised. She made a little movement with her head, but no words came out; that was when he realised, she was on the verge of tears.

"Laura," he said, but he didn't touch her.

Not looking at him, she said, "You must think me an absolute bitch."

"I don't. Really, I don't."

"Don't be saintly!" Her gaze met his. "If you had taken a lover, I'd have kicked you out on your ear."

"You kicked yourself out."

Giving him a tight smile, she took a deep breath and forced the conversation in a different direction by asking if Giffard and his wife had been found. Michael had filled her in.

"Not a breath," he said, hoping his words were not prophetic. "They could be anywhere. The powers that be think they may have beaten off their attackers and scarpered."

"Or be dead?" She gave him one of her looks. "Why you, John?"

"It turned into a saga. I like sagas."

"Yes, but why you?"

"What about our saga?"

She lifted her drink but did not partake. "I don't know if we still have one."

Her tone was flat and listless, and he did not know what to say back, so he changed tack the way she had done and told her about the Giffard household. She listened gravely, her eyes on his face all the while.

"Dean bashed Giffard's wife while he was in prison."

There was a flash of the old Laura: "Bloody animal!" she said. Then, "He must know by now that you're involved."

"That's for sure."

"That doesn't worry you?"

"I won't be sticking my neck out."

"They could be dead," she said again.

"I wish you'd stop saying that."

She looked away. When she looked back her eyes were glistening again. "I almost didn't come."

"You would have missed out on the kidneys," he replied. "Another?"

She nodded and he signalled to the barman. When he looked back, she was lighting a cigarette. With one of her don't-say-a-word looks, she said that it was temporary. When her brandy came, she poured what remained of the other into the fresh glass and took her courage in both hands: she didn't think it was going to work out for them.

"You're all out of love?"

"I'm not in love with someone else, if that's what you mean."

"That's something."

"I'm in limbo, John."

"I know the feeling."

Her next sentence sounded as potentially final as the others, but he knew she was hiding behind words. "I betrayed your trust."

"There's often not a lot of difference between betrayer and betrayed."

She objected to that. Her adultery had been a statement and she was not going to surrender it. A generous sip of brandy as she weighed what to say next. "I want to break out of my life. Does that make sense?"

"To me it does."

"Your advice would be?"

"Keep going the way you're going."

"Even if it means the end of us?"

"Even then."

She drew deeply on her cigarette and exhaled with the satisfaction only an ex-smoker can muster. "You wake up one morning and sense that everything's about to change, that your life is about to come out of a holding pattern."

"Some people never wake up, Laura. Or if they do, only for a moment or two. Before they know it, they're fast asleep again, comatose or dead to what they've glimpsed."

"That's not a comforting thought." She pondered that and flicked the ash from her cigarette. "I've been putting it off. Endlessly. All my life, I think."

"It's another bubble," he said, alluding to what she had said about marriage prior to his leaving for London. "Double-bubble-trouble?"

Another smile as a waiter approached: their table was ready.

When they were seated, Laura again asked why the people he was dealing were being so cavalier about his welfare. He decided to tell her about his interrogatory past, about Palfreyman tracking him down and the purpose of the OSI as an organisation. It was just one of those things, he said. A fluke. All the factors had come together, and he had been so mad at Dean he had decided to follow through.

She stared at him for a long moment, then she said, "You've never talked about that side of your life."

"I didn't think it important. I still don't."

"But it must have been fascinating."

"Not something I look back on with any pride."

"You didn't enjoy the subterfuge?"

"In a twisted kind of way; that's what I didn't like about it."

"And now it's war criminals?"

"The OSI's task is the identification and prosecution of war criminals who got into the country post 1945. That applies to quite a few nationalities; not just Germans. It also applies to far right groups and their sympathisers with similar ideas and agendas."

"And you've kept all of this to yourself?"

"You upped and left just as things came together. I would have told you otherwise."

"Michael's involved?"

"The Giffards wouldn't open up without a sweetener; Michael has agreed to a write up for one of the national newspapers. Perhaps even a book when we get to the full picture. In my case it was either help out or be left guessing. My nose got the better of me." He dug out his wallet and handed her the latest rigmarole on Dean's supposed Irish background. "He's still at it, Laura."

She read the piece and handed it back without comment. The drinks waiter appeared. She would have another brandy, she said, throwing him a glance. He declined, consulted the wine list and chose the same bottle of red that Palfreyman had chosen when they talked Wagner and Nietzsche. It was a forty-six-dollar bottle, but he was beyond caring.

"I'm seriously thinking of jacking in my job."

"Bravo."

'But it scares me."

"I sometimes write a sentence twenty times before I get what I'm after," he said, jumping the gun, and realising it.

"That's not what I'm referring to."

"Sorry, I thought you were referring to the writing process."

"In a way I am, I suppose."

"It's all relative," he said, trying to smile away a *faux pas*. "Perhaps you want to succeed too much."

"Why shouldn't I want to succeed?"

"What shall it profit a man…"

"Your point?"

"Souls aren't dished out like Smarties."

"Souls are outside my province, John?"

"The *real*, Laura."

She studied his face. "What do you consider to be real?"

"*Everything*," he said back.

"Yes, but—"

"The real is a bomb ready to explode every second. That's why we keep on defusing it."

Laura laughed outright. "Only a bloody Irishman would choose a metaphor like that!" Her stare was suddenly disconcerting. "What's gone wrong between us?"

"We've let habit strangle us, Laura."

"Is that all? Why didn't you say something?"

"I was as caught up in it as you were." Palfreyman's exquisite wine arrived; he sampled the sample. "The blind leadeth the blind," he said, more to himself than to Laura.

***

A mate's taxi was being used to shift the Giffards. It had a driver's protection screen of thick Perspex behind the driver's seat, and a locking system that gave the driver control over his passengers. Dean was in the back with Giffard, Mary was up front. Their hands had been secured in front of them with plastic ties, and they had been blindfolded. Dean had a revolver levelled at the big man's stomach — he kept prodding at Giffard with it.

"Where are you taking us?" asked Giffard.

"Depends," said Dean.

There was a cut above Giffard's left eye, and his left knee continued to beat out a steady pulse from being whacked with a length of timber.

"I've told you everything I know about Hennessey. He's just a fucking writer. I told him to get lost, but he kept coming back."

"He turned up at Rosie's asking questions. He could only have got that from you."

"He already knew about that."

"You mouthed off."

"Why would I?"

"So, tell me what you told him."

"I told him you ran drugs. Stuff like that. I gave him a sob story about Mary. You'd have thought he'd won the fucking lottery when I said you holed up most of the time in Brisbane, which you don't."

"Keep going."

"He wanted to know everything about you. I told him you were a right bastard but that you were fair to your mates."

"That was nice of you, Norman. What else?"

"He asked about Heather. Wanted to know if she lived in Sydney. I told him I thought she was in Melbourne. I didn't think that would do any harm."

"He gave you money?"

"He gave Mary fifty bucks."

"What did you get?"

"Promises."

Dean's smile reduced his eyes to slits. "I've always liked you, Norman," he said, prodding at Giffard's stomach with the revolver to prove it. "You've got a bit more up top than most. Not a lot, but enough." He nodded in the direction of Mary. "So why do you hang around with that black bitch?" Laughing at his own words, he lowered the revolver. "It could all be different if you'd only wise up."

"How do you mean?"

"Dump her, son. That's what you do with trash, isn't it? You fucking *dump* it."

Giffard's mind was racing."

"I'd call it quits if you dumped her." Before Giffard could reply, Dean added, "Believe me, it's the best fucking offer you'll get today."

Giffard could smell violence.

"Call itself interest, Norman. I want a good man back and you want that bitch to keep her face. Right?" A beaming smile. "Dave said you wanted to come back."

"You'd let her go?"

"She'd be my insurance, wouldn't she?" A laugh. "It would be trust, all round"

"You're on if you let her go right this minute."

"It would be for keeps, ol' son."

Norman Giffard hesitated, then nodded. Leaning forward, Dean rapped on the Perspex and signalled for the car to be stopped. Going round to the passenger door, he hauled Mary out onto the dimly lit street. "Tell her to fuck off, Norman!" he shouted. When Giffard hesitated, he rammed Mary's face against the glass and repeated his demand. Giffard said the words, but still not to Dean's satisfaction. "Tell her to fuck off to her big black face!" he shouted, whereupon Giffard mustered his hate for Dean and shouted the man's choice of words at Mary. Both of their blindfolds had shifted, Mary's due to Dean's manhandling, Giffard's due to his hauling at it with his bound hands: Mary found herself looking into her husband's bloodied face at close quarters.

"Cut her loose, Gavin!"

Caring little if he nicked Mary's wrists, Dean produced a blade and set about cutting Mary free; she took off immediately, Giffard having propelled her with a jerk of his head.

Dean's delight was genuine but gone in an instant. Getting back into the cab he cut Giffard loose and shouted to the driver to get them the hell out of there. Then, "That's better, isn't it, ol' son?" To Giffard's astonishment, he added: "Fancy a beer?"

The turnaround was bizarre, and it continued. It was as if nothing had happened between them, as if Mary had never existed, as if time had stopped and started again.

"Where are we going?" asked Giffard.

"Uptown." Producing a wad of notes, Dean peeled off two fifties and handed them to Giffard. "There'll be more when you've earned it." Pleased with himself, he sat back into the corner of the cab and stared out into the brightening streets. It did not matter to him that he had set up an impossible situation; all that mattered was that betrayal had been punished, the books balanced, order restored. If Norman defaulted, the bitch would pay. End of story. To have brought the mighty Norman to his knees before a crowd had been sweet, but to have him sitting here now mute and dejected was sweeter still. With all of this in his look, in his tone, Dean turned to Giffard and asked what he had made of Hennessey.

"We've already been through that."

"No, we haven't. I want to know how he came across."

Giffard thought carefully before replying. "Smart *and* stupid," he said. "Thinks he knows what's going on when he doesn't."

"And the smart bit?"

"Forgets nothing; bit like you."

"How did he get on to you?"

"Some Bondi cop mentioned my name when speaking about you. He knows how to work the system."

"And you said you'd help out."

"I told him to get lost, but he came back. It was Mary who saw the chance to make a quick buck."

"You've got a contact number?"

"He gave me a different number from the one he gave Mary."

"Got it on you?"

"Yeah."

"Good boy," said Dean.

***

"He stood me a beautiful dinner."

"He's staying on in Sydney?"

"As far as I could make out."

"You?"

"It's back to Hobart for me, to face the music."

They were sitting either end of the sofa, Laura nursing a cup of tea, Emma a hot chocolate. Michael was in bed, reading; he had been packed off the moment Laura returned.

"You talked about Mark?"

"Not by name."

"His reaction?"

"As he was with you, very civilised about it all. I didn't feel put down."

"But you don't think it's going to work."

Laura did not reply immediately; she sipped at her tea, then carefully returned her cup to its saucer. "We were more honest with one another than I would have thought possible a few days ago, but he spoiled it, Emma. The male thing surfaced." Her head went back in defiance. "He's so *bloody* superior!"

"He respects you more than you know."

"I sometimes think he's got more respect for you than he has for me."

Emma did not reply.

"The wise woman of Lindfield?"

"Huh," Emma said.

Closing her eyes, Laura opened them again wide. "In the end everything was left hanging." An empty laugh, and a glance. "He told me souls weren't dished out like Smarties."

"At least you got a meal out of it."

"And he didn't hold back, I'll give him that." Her expression underwent a subtle change. "You probably think I didn't try hard enough. *Don't* try hard enough."

"I have no way to judge that," Emma said.

"Judgeless Emma," said Laura, articulating a judgement. Then, with a little explosion of feeling, she said, "God! How I wish I was more like you at times!"

"John doesn't just see people doing things, Laura; he sees them being something, expressing something. He's looking all the while for the hidden dimension. His books are full of people trying desperately to understand one another. The danger is that you read things into people that aren't there, that you make demands on them that are impossible to fulfill. But I haven't seen him do that, not ever. He told me once that life did not have to be parochial and boring, that life was meaningful in and of itself over and above the meanings we imbued it with."

"That's his Catholicism speaking; I've been there."

"I don't think it's that at all."

"They can't shake it off, Emma, not ever. Once a Catholic?"

"That's not how I read him."

"You don't *know* him. Not really. You know the charming visitor; I know the man obsessed."

"That doesn't sound at all like the John we know."

"As I said, a visitor."

Hennessey's attempts to make sense of things had now completely worn off for Laura. Her feeling was that they should have got straight down to practicalities and not wasted their time on what it meant to have, or not have, a soul. What was the good of having a soul if the universe was just a big black hole full of debris crashing around aimlessly? For that was what it was, and everyone knew that that was what it was. Except John, it seemed; he seemed to think something else was going on but could not say what.

Swinging her legs off the couch, Laura glanced at Emma dejectedly and headed for the kitchen with her cup and saucer. Her movements conveyed despondency, her sigh, resignation. She was on the slippery slope of change, and there was no way back.

17
The Buried Nerve

Hennessey was surprised to find Mary Giffard asleep in the foyer of the Lancaster when he got back. Glancing at the young man in reception, he received a shrug, and a grimace. Wearing the same thin dress, he had first seen her in, Mary was curled up in a corner of the big red sofa that dominated the entrance hall. She had been there for over an hour, the clerk said, and had been very agitated on arrival. She had asked for him by name. To allay suspicions, Hennessey asked if he could use the telephone, but Mary woke with a start in the same instant.

"You've got to get out of here," she said, springing to her feet. "Dean must know where you are by now."

"Where's Norman?"

"He's with Dean." She grabbed at his sleeve. "You've got to get out of here!"

"How did you get away?"

She gabbled out the story of their abduction.

"He let you go. Why?"

"He's bonkers. The deal is that he'll let Norman work for him again if he dumps me. I heard everything."

"Where are your shoes?" asked Hennessey

"I wasn't wearing any when we got lifted."

He led her back to the sofa and asked quietly about the revolver.

"Dean's got it."

"Did someone get shot?"

She shook her head; nothing like that. Dean and another man had bashed their way in and set about Norman, Dean with his fists, the other with a length of wood. The clerk, who was all ears, suggested that he ring for the police. Hennessey vetoed that idea. Mary continued with her saga, and he learned how she and Norman had been bundled into a taxi and held in a dilapidated shack overnight. They had been blindfolded during the journey, but her guess was the back of Redfern somewhere. They had gone round in circles. She was sure about that.

"Is Norman badly injured?"

"He could hardly walk, and he's got a big slash across his forehead."

"Then just like that he lets you go?"

"If Norman plays up, I cop it. If I play up, he cops it." She proffered something resembling a smile. "It's my bet we'll both cop it whatever we do."

Palfreyman said little when Hennessey got through; he grunted a few times, asked if Mary needed medical attention, then hung up. When he arrived, he found a steely-eyed Mary sitting next to Hennessey. Hennessey was being quizzed by the hotel manager. Palfreyman presented his credentials and the quizzing stopped. He turned to Mary. He was here to help Norman in any way he could, he said, but he had to know everything that had happened down to the smallest detail.

Mary told her story graphically, glancing at Hennessey from time to time. They hadn't been given anything to eat, had had no water, and had barely slept. The same thing had happened that morning; nothing to eat or drink all day. Then in the evening Dean had turned up with his mate and bound their wrists with plastic ties.

"Did he say what he intended to do with you?"

"Nah. But he told us a joke. He was in a good mood; really cheerful. Norman pleaded with him to let me go, but he just laughed. I thought he was going to kill us right there and then, but he had something else in mind." She added as an afterthought, "He had the gun he'd given to Norman and was playing with it."

"What gun?" said Palfreyman.

Hennessey intervened. "Dean gave it to Norman some time ago; they didn't have any ammunition."

"You knew about this?"

"They were about to hand it in."

"Oh, that's nice," said Palfreyman. He turned back to Mary. "You're sure it was the same item?"

"There's a spot of red paint on the handle. I saw it. He was playing cowboys."

"How do you mean?"

"Twirling it." She demonstrated the action. "Kept pointing it at us, kept twirling it and laughing."

"John said you were freed while in a taxi?"

"We were driving along, and he stops and lets me go. Just like that. Well, not quite. He roughed me up a bit and made Norman tell me to fuck off. So, I ran for my life."

"Why do you think he did that?"

"Because he's a fucking psychopath!"

Mary's psychological profile of Dean surprised Palfreyman. He registered her use of the word 'psychopath' with a glance at Hennessey.

"What makes you think the shack was in Redfern," asked Hennessey.

"That's where we were when he let me go. I know the area. We'd been going round in circles for ages. I could tell."

"*That* is exactly the kind of information we're after, Mary," said Palfreyman. Then to Hennessey he said, "She can't go back to Marrickville in this state, John."

"It's *him* you should be worried about," said Mary, pointing at Hennessey. "Dean'll come after him here."

Mary's concern for Hennessey's welfare was not lost on Hennessey, nor on Palfreyman: it suggested genuine attachment. Palfreyman stood staring at them for some seconds, then with a little laugh he made up his mind and said that he was going to do something untoward. It was either a hotel the other side of Sydney for the both of them, or makeshift beds until something more appropriate could be worked out.

"A safe house?" said Hennessey.

"My mother's; there's plenty of room."
"She won't mind?"
"She's very flexible."
"Must be all that dancing," said Hennessey.

***

Gunther Harrenstein's tone was censorious; he did not like being interrupted; and in particular he did not like being interrupted by someone like Hal Tannerman. Allies in the fight against multiculturalism they and their American colleagues might be, but that was where the similarity ended. The White Brotherhood — a ridiculous name as far as he was concerned — and the Freedom Party of Australia were of the same ilk, but not of the same calibre, and this fact was becoming obvious as Harrenstein and three colleagues from the FPA's central committee laid out their theoretical stance.

In comparison with the Brotherhood's heavy-handed politico-religious approach, the line of thinking developed by the FPA was politically sophisticated. The Americans, the Brits, the French and whoever else might be interested, would have to grapple with that fact when they got down to basics. The days of full-frontal attack were over; it was now a matter of determining the ingrained likes and dislikes of the populous, and of allowing the energy of their marshalled distrust to work its own corrosive miracle through the ballot box. There would be no direct arraignment against race or culture, no obvious inflaming of the country's old-style patriots. Just a careful grading of issues and a low-key directing of attention towards what really mattered — a return to the old values. The way forward was through a subtle handling of the political process; to believe otherwise was to be out of step with reality and history.

"What has to be understood," said Harrenstein, eyeballing the larger and more aggressive of the two Americans, "is that as the nations of Europe move economically and politically closer, and the European Union cancels national divisions, provincial separatism is growing at a terrific pace. Border controls and trade barriers may be vanishing, and a single European currency may be on its way, but the people themselves are pulling apart and insisting ever more loudly on their regional differences. That will not diminish. The Maastricht II process is a blueprint for a quantum leap in the powers of federal Europe over the sovereign rights of individual states, and that fact has made a lot of people very nervous."

"What's that got to do with your great Australian experiment?" drawled Hal, his eyes fixed insolently on Harrenstein. "All of that EU stuff's a world away."

Tannerman's head was unusually small for the bulk of his body. It was as if God had been in a hurry and had picked up the wrong bit.

"It has everything to do with it." Harrenstein measured his words carefully. "It is intrinsic to the forces that will be unleashed when the attempt to impose the same social and economic policies across Europe fails, and it is intrinsic to the forces we are attempting to mobilise here in Australia, forces that will prime the political situation and lead, eventually, to radical change on a wide front. Economic uniformity is one thing, cultural uniformity is quite another. By its very nature the creation of the EU makes the possibility of war in western Europe all but impossible, but at what cost? That is the question not being asked, and the answer is a united Germany strangled in perpetuity for fear that its radical spirit might resurface. It's the Germans who will be made to pay. So, what am I saying? I'm saying that the attempt to contain and control the German spirit is the principal factor at work in the resurgence of that spirit. I'm saying that the imperatives of unity are heightening the realities of difference throughout Europe. And I'm saying that the FPA's future success is, in real terms, linked to the inevitable and necessary collapse of the EU."

"Time scale?"

The question came from Elmer Garrett, Tannerman's companion. Aware of the smaller man's foxy intelligence, Harrenstein said politely, "Turn of the century, maybe later. Twenty years at most is the estimate. The rot should have well set in by then."

"And here in Australia?"

"We'll be well on our way to having a three-party system within eighteen months. The Democrats and the

Greens won't be any match for us when the groundswell starts "

"And the British?"

Harrenstein's smile broadened. "The Brits — the English, that is — are Eurosceptical and likely to be among the first to bail out." He laughed and added, "The Scots, the Irish and the Welsh will prove to be the true Europeans."

"I meant; will the British interfere?"

"Not in a republic they won't."

It was unlikely that either Elmer or Hal were familiar with Australian politics, but Elmer did seem to register comprehension, so Harrenstein talked on about the republic to come and how its unsettling effect would offer, during a critical period, a further window of opportunity. But although sent specifically to negotiate some kind of deal with the emerging FPA, the Brotherhood in its Hal Tannerman form did not warm to Harrenstein's gradualist approach, whereas Elmer Garrett, sharper by half than his much larger companion, could see the sense in building a populist base. The two men began to argue, and Harrenstein joined in, only too happy to divide and conquer.

"What you have to realise," said Harrenstein, directing his comments at Hal, "is that people in out-of-date uniforms or smothered in gowns and hoods look pretty silly nowadays. What used to frighten people makes them laugh now. Or angers them. You can't turn the clock back, and you shouldn't try. What you have to do is touch the buried nerve and keep on touching it until you get a response. That's the secret. There isn't a human being alive who doesn't harbour some level of dislike or fear for some other culture. No one is immune. Homo lovers do not love homos in their heart of hearts — they just put up with them. Same with Blacks. Multiculturalists can only take so much of multiculturalism, and everyone is afraid their neighbourhood will be swamped with undesirables. Values are skin deep. Scratch at them long enough, and they bleed."

Hal's response was to say that the groundswell for their agenda was presently so great in America that it was propelling Pat Buchanan towards the White House. So, they were in fact doing what the FPA planned to do, except they would have results within a few weeks, not in a few years.

Harrenstein was not impressed. First, he said, Buchanan was not part of the Brotherhood, and therefore not under their control, and second, he was unlikely to get more than thirty percent of the vote in each state, and that would not carry him into the Oval Office. The problem with someone like Buchanan was that he was far too honest. He had admitted that Christianity was superior to all other faiths, had rebuked the Justice Department for wasting time hunting down war criminals, and even described Martin Luther King as an evil demagogue. He had even suggested Holocaust survivors suffered from group fantasies. Courageous to a fault, one might say. But in the end useless because he would not be taken seriously by the broad sweep of the American electorate — an electorate bullied through leftist education to believe that such talk was indelicate and dangerous. No, another approach was necessary, and the FPA had developed and refined that approach with the assistance of some very cluey marketing people.

"We've got marketing people galore in the States," said Hal, turning to look at Elmer by way of a rebuke to Harrenstein.

"Then use them," said Harrenstein, beating at Hal with his eyes. "Use the system to overpower the system."

"He's got a point," said Elmer.

Hal eyed his colleague with distrust.

"We've lost grassroots support, Hal. You know we have."

"The country's gone soft."

"That's not what you were saying a moment ago. What happened to the groundswell that was going to put Buchanan in the White House?"

Elmer cut in before Hal could reply. "That's all single issue stuff. Buchanan doesn't have a worked out philosophy; his platform is a grab-bag of issues set in an isolationist foreign policy belonging to the thirties. He's Left, he's Right, he's New Deal, he's all over the place. Go for single issues and you're bound to pick up votes. So what? You're not really making a mark and you never will with that kind of policy base. There has to be a larger picture."

Harrenstein was impressed. Not only was Elmer bright, he was capable of handling blockheads like Hal. And he had accurately isolated the cause of Buchanan's impending failure — lack of vision. It was one thing to shout the odds at American immigration policy, champion creationist science and advocate a legal ban on abortion, it was quite another to present such issues in a coherent fashion. As the only workable context was wealth redistribution, and Buchanan had neglected this old-fashioned populist move, his claim to be a populist in the traditional sense was false. Yes, he had broadened his message by pointing to those involved in job losses, and to the economic pressures on families, but his attention to the voiceless and the downtrodden had no edge to it. The older populists had sought to redistribute wealth through huge government programs, whereas Buchanan had little or no interest in involving himself in such schemes. Consistent in his rhetoric he might be, but it was the rhetoric of a conservative demagogue with no real sense of direction.

"I couldn't agree more," said Harrenstein. "Getting a percentage of the electorate on side is all very well, but it's not enough. It's the broader political picture that's important. If we want our program of radical political change to be taken seriously, we in turn have to show that we take seriously the more mundane issues of the day. This has always been the problem with parties like ours, we've only ever paid attention to the big issues, and as a result have neglected the rank-and-file's more immediate concerns. Get that right, and everything will fall into place. Packaging is what we've neglected, and packaging is what we now have to concentrate on."

They talked on for an hour, Harrenstein progressively enlarging on the FPA's *modus operandi,* his colleagues — silent up until that point — supplying the facts and figures that Elmer and Hal would carry back with them to the States. What the Americans were not told was that the FPA had close ties with Australia's underworld, men and women with a deep and lasting grudge against the system and its institutions. Organised into groups, not a few of those individuals were being trained to function as the party's security wing, the brighter of them schooled in the organisation's philosophy. Expanding the FPA's policy base was the next priority. For that purpose, minor groups would be flattered and absorbed, their concerns made part of the larger FPA vision. The public's deep unease over immigration, refugees, the growing unrest in Europe and the threat of regional attack would all play their part, the expected change in government after the general election the spark that would ignite a more sympathetic approach to the FPA's concerns. Everything, Harrenstein assured his listeners, was on track.

***

"David, they disappeared around eight in the evening and reappeared just after eleven." Murchinson's face was half in shadow, only the small desk light being on in his study. It was the first time Palfreyman had been in Murchinson's home, and he was impressed by the man's vast collection of books. "How did they do that?"

"Insider knowledge obviously," said Palfreyman.

Murchinson chewed on his words before uttering them. "Police informers, David?"

"Seem likely," said Palfreyman, pleased that it was Murchinson who had come up with the notion.

"They're laughing at us, David. They went into dinner just before eight. By twenty past they had disappeared into thin air. They knew the hotel was being watched, but still managed to pull a Houdini."

"They obviously weren't being watched hard enough."

"So where did they go? Who were they with?" Murchinson's pause was brief. "This was supposed to help us get a handle on the ringleaders, but all it's done is reveal our ineptitude."

"Could be that Special Branch isn't treating this situation with the seriousness it deserves."

"They're under resourced and think we're exaggerating the seriousness of the situation. They had one man watching the front of the hotel."

"We could pull them in for questioning. One of them might let something slip."

"Not feasible. Have you checked the taxi firm they used to get back?"

"They were picked up in the middle of the city, so they must have alighted from one taxi and hailed another. As for their disappearing trick, that was easily done. They went out through the kitchen saying they were arranging a surprise party for someone."

"And Hennessey and the girl?"

"I've tucked them away safely, sir. But the Giffard woman wants to go home first thing tomorrow. I think she's right about that. She has to be seen around to keep Dean thinking he's in the clear."

"She's, okay?"

"Tough as they come, sir."

"Hennessey?"

"Riding it out."

"Loyalty to Hennessey by the wife probably means disloyalty to Dean by the husband," said Murchinson. "That's to our advantage." Then, with resignation, he added, "Just about everything that can go wrong has gone wrong, or is going wrong, David, and our inability to keep tabs on the Americans for even a few hours was the last straw."

"Shall I let the Giffard woman return home?"

"Yes, let her go back."

"Then I'll say... good night, sir."

"You mean 'good morning', surely?" said Murchinson.

***

It was two-thirty a.m. when Palfreyman returned to his mother's flat. She had asked that he be there too in spite of the crush. As he passed through the lounge where Hennessey lay sweltering under a single sheet, Hennessey said, "Problems?"

"Murchinson. He's not a happy chappie." A thumbnail explanation followed. Then, "It's another hotel for you in the morning; unless you want to go back to Hobart."

"I was just getting to like my brick wall."

"You'll stay on?"

"He knows where I live; I'm safer here. Mary?"

"Jack agrees she should go home. She wants to go home. Dean will expect her to go home."

"Murchinson asked me if Giffard was armed. I sidestepped his question by saying he was the kind of man who relied more on his physical strength."

"Not telling anyone was risky, John. Not loaded? Honestly!" He turned away, turned back. "Careful from here on in. Okay?"

"Of course."

When alone, Hennessey closed his eyes and listened to the sound of a police siren in the distance, and to the muffled hum of the city. Then, as if only moments had passed, it was morning, and he could hear Palfreyman and his mother conversing and smell freshly ground coffee. He surveyed his sleeping quarters in the diffuse morning light: bits and pieces of another country all around, another world, another time.

"How did you sleep, Mr Hennessey?"

Emmi looking down at him from behind the couch; her short, sandy-coloured hair had retained most of its colour, but it was her piercing blue eyes that held Hennessey's attention: they were of the most delicate shade of blue he had ever seen.

"I'm not used to the heat, and please call me John."

"But you did sleep, eventually?"

"I was *very* tired."

"Would you like some eggs? Scrambled eggs? I'm about to make some for David."

"Please," said Hennessey.

"There are fresh towels in the bathroom. The shower's not working, I'm afraid."

"No bother," he said, using an Australian expression.

He washed as best he could, dressed, and went through to the kitchen. Palfreyman was seated at an already laid table in an adjacent breakfast room reading the morning papers; he looked disgustingly fresh for someone who had gone to bed so late. A glance as Hennessey seated himself, followed by, "I've mentioned you to Emmi from time to time. She'd like to hear about your time in Germany."

"Mary's still asleep?"

"Hasn't stirred."

Hennessey helped himself to coffee and reinstating the day's dismal reality. "Who do you think shot Dave Hollows?"

"Dean's the most likely candidate."

"Yes, but why? Dobbing Giffard in must have got Hollows a few Brownie points."

"The abduction may have been Dean's way of setting up a replacement for Hollows. It almost amounts to a confession."

"He seems to like having Giffard around."

"I think affection improbable."

"Intelligence?"

"Muscle's my guess. We'll find out how intelligent he is if and when he testifies." Palfreyman's smile was condescending. "He's a thug, John, hadn't you noticed?"

"He's desperate, they both are." Hennessey's impatience was in his tone. "I think there's another Giffard trying to get out."

"Dean's a maniac and Giffard's a fool," said Palfreyman. "What you're sensing as intelligence is no more than street cunning. You get to know it after a while."

"I think there's more to him than that."

"And Dean? Is there more to him as well?"

Hennessey toyed with his coffee cup, then quickly and succinctly laid out how he read both men. Dean and

Giffard were chalk and cheese, he said. Dean's intelligence was brutal in its effect; it lacked human feeling. How else could he have bashed Heather or have treated Mary the way he had. Norman's kind of intelligence was different. He was oddly reflective, and reflection was the basis of intelligence. Dean was probably cleverer than Giffard, but Giffard was a damned sight better balanced.

"Norman?"

"That's his name."

"*Norman* sells drugs up the Cross, John."

"Mary wouldn't have gone for a dolt."

"I still think you're overestimating both of them."

Their breakfasts arrived. Without preamble, and to Hennessey's surprise, Emmi said, "Our maniacs had no regard for human feeling either. We thought they were gods at first, but they were not gods." She smiled a weary smile. "It was 1938 before my father admitted that something was wrong."

"Some never did," said Hennessey. "I came across not a few in the late fifties who were still enamoured."

Emmi made to turn away but changed her mind. "We went along with it like lambs to the slaughter, but not everyone. There *was* resistance. There *were* attempts to stop him."

Hennessey knew about those attempts; it had been part of his briefing as an interrogator. The most dangerous of the resistance groups had been broken up by the Gestapo within days or weeks, those who had done no more than accuse the Nazis of incompetence and corruption dealt with brutally. Others managed little acts of courage, like sharing news gleaned from BBC broadcasts with people they hoped were still their friends. Some had given assistance to undesirables. The atmosphere had been one of unbelievable restraint on a broad front: a loose word could produce dire consequences. The very air they breathed had seemed infected with the regime's poison.

"I was still carrying a lot of their nonsense in my head at twenty," Emmi admitted. "It was instilled into us at school. There was no escaping it." She was silent for a moment. "What people don't realise is how silly it all was to start with. It looked and sounded silly. They were not always the sure-footed technicians they later became. I can remember them milling around in newsreels like black clowns. They looked utterly ridiculous. But they got the hang of it. They turned theatrical ineptitude into the most sinister thing anyone had ever seen.

"My father's awakening terrified my mother. And me. I had been taught that Hitler was a genius, a kind of god, almost. Had he not rid Germany of the Versailles Treaty, faced up to the Allies, ended the Depression and made Germany prosperous again? Who could doubt him? He was obviously a genius. And for those who believed the Fuhrer's own rhetoric, he had also ended class division and created true community. We had no idea what was coming. Hitler's tirades against the Jews made some people feel uneasy, but almost everybody believed they were to blame for Germany's social and economic ills. It was a common perception. I believed it. And I did not just believe that Jews were money-grubbing parasites, I believed they were inferior to us Germans. I believed, God help me, that they were subhuman and that the Aryan race was superior to every other race."

"What a pity Stauffenberg failed," said Hennessey.

Emmi's smile became sardonic. "It's argued that the upper-class conservatives only wanted to get rid of Hitler because they thought he would drag Germany down to ruin. I don't agree with that; not wholly. I believe Stauffenberg's was a moral decision, not just a political one. There were a great number of planned attempts on the Fuhrer's life that didn't come to anything. If he had died because of that bomb Stauffenberg would have been a national hero."

"He would have been shot as a traitor," said Palfreyman. "The hero bit might have taken longer."

"He was a disciple of the poet Stefan Georg," she said by way of justification, "and Georg hated everything the Nazis stood for. Georg died in exile the same year as Hitler became chancellor."

"Frank says it's Georg we should read if we want to understand the peculiar spirituality of the Germans," said Palfreyman. "Problem is, many of the people who eventually joined the National Socialists were fans of Georg, so where does that leave us?"

"With a headache," said Hennessey.

18
Either Symbol or Parable

They pulled up outside a neat two-storey unit in the Nedlands district of Perth, having flown across from Melbourne late that afternoon. In Melbourne they had delivered some parcels picked up in Sydney the evening before. On this occasion the pickup had been 505 grammes of cocaine and 805 grammes of amphetamine in paste form, the street value of which was somewhere in the region of two million dollars. Dean, as usual, was meticulous about procedure, each step of the journey being planned and executed with the precision of a military exercise.

Tired out by their convoluted overnight drive to Melbourne, they had completed their business, snatched a few hours' sleep and headed for the airport with two briefcases of cash. Dean slept during the flight, Giffard did not. From the moment they left Sydney to the moment they left Melbourne, Giffard watched, listened and wondered when the facade of friendliness would crack, for in spite of every indication to the contrary, he knew it to be as false as the smile on Dean's face.

The house in Nedlands was tidily suburban, the man who answered the door a picture of respectability.

Small and dapper and dressed in a dark blue suit and shiny-toed black shoes, James Atherton looked like a bank manager. And in a sense, he was just that, for this hard-working individual with the round face, slicked-back hair and neatly clipped moustache was a financial wizard, a man of the city with an eye on the main chance. But more than that, he was also a political animal, a man who believed that Australia required radical change, and that he, James Atherton, had a part to play in bringing such change about. Admitting the two men to his beautifully furnished home, Atherton accepted the briefcases, placed them on an occasional table, and on being given the combinations, opened them to reveal tightly packed bundles of used one-hundred-dollar bills. Satisfied, he closed their lids and snapped their catches back into place.

"You followed procedure?"

"To the letter," said Dean.

"And now you'll want a taxi." Atherton turned away and attended to that, then to Giffard's surprise he offered them a drink.

"I could go a whisky," said Dean.

"And your friend?"

"Same," said Giffard.

Dean's behaviour and tone surprised Giffard; he was subdued and differential in Atherton's company. It was almost as if he expected to be punished and was surprised when punishment didn't come, as if punishment had been meted out on some other occasion and the memory of it lingered. Waving them towards a large white sofa, Atherton prepared the whiskies and talked with his back to them. Looking out through the French windows that fronted the house, Giffard appeared not to be listening, but that was not so.

"There's another shipment due," said Atherton. "Not as large as the one you've just handled, but not insubstantial." He approached with their drinks. "You'll get your instructions in the usual manner."

"And the big one?" asked Dean, referring to a drug shipment coming in from Thailand.

"Next month, if it works out."

"You expect trouble?"

"I think we're always in danger of the police getting lucky. Don't you?"

Reading Atherton's glance, Dean said, "Norman's solid."

"He's certainly big," said Atherton, turning his full attention on Giffard. "But does he have a brain?"

It was such an insulting thing to say Giffard did not know how to respond; it was like being back at school, he remembered. Finding his tongue, he said, "I'm not stupid, if that's what you mean."

"No, you're not, are you," said Atherton. "Your eyes are bright, and you have a good brow. But you've been fighting." The little man's gaze swivelled back to Dean. "With you, perhaps?" Before Dean could reply, he added, "Keeping the troops in order, eh?"

It was an astute deduction. Dean acknowledged it and Atherton returned to the business in hand. How were things shaping up in Sydney, he wanted to know.

"Pretty good," said Dean. Then with what was obviously a sense of injustice, he said, "I'm not exactly at the hub of things yet, am I?"

"A soldier's place is on the front line."

"Gunther keeps everything to himself."

"And that's how it should be," said Atherton. Then to Giffard he said, "Do you understand what's at stake?"

"I think so."

"You think so?"

"You aim to change things a bit — a lot?"

Atherton smile was a glancing blow. "We intend to change just about everything, and soon. And legitimately. Everything will be done legitimately."

"You're running drugs," said Giffard.

"An interim necessity, not a policy. But a good question nonetheless."

Emboldened, Giffard asked why it was a good question.

"Because it opens up the question of what I meant by *interim*. Interim means 'between' or 'intervening'. It was used to name certain edicts of the German emperor during the Reformation for the regulation of religious and ecclesiastical matters *yet to be determined*." A self-congratulatory smile followed. "The selling of drugs to an already drug-soaked society is therefore no big deal. It is a pragmatic decision based on the necessity to raise capital as quickly as possible. In the society we envisage, there will be no hard drugs of any kind. *That* has already been determined."

"No one's managed to get rid of drugs so far."

"No one has had the *will* to do so. That's what separates *us* from *them*. Gavin understands what I'm saying. Don't you Gavin?"

A grunt from Dean.

"He says you're going to bring the whole bloody thing down about their ears. Is that right?"

This was more than Atherton had expected from the big man. Pleased as punch he launched into an impromptu lecture. "The main political parties have lost the plot, Norman, as have the religious community. That's what has to sink in. They're pandering to the weakest sector — homosexuals, prostitutes, artists, asylum seekers — and it's our job to reverse that trend."

"Big ask," said Giffard, getting into the swing of things.

"Big ask or not it has to be done. If it isn't, where will we end up?" As Giffard was not expected to reply, Atherton answered his own question. "Jews and left-wingers are running the show, Norman. They're everywhere. The media is full of them, as are the universities. It's wall-to-wall political correctness with hardly an historian gutsy enough to speak out against the left's interpretation of Australian history. It's bleeding hearts versus common sense, Norman, brains versus wishy-washy sentiment, action versus paralysis."

Atherton's head went up in recognition of his own brilliance, an insightful brilliance rooted in the past. "Few realise what the Allies were up to prior to the Second World War, or how Germany was driven by bloated Jewish financiers into declaring a war it had tried to avoid since the early thirties. Did you know that?"

Giffard shook his head obediently.

"Why do you think there's been such a resurgence of interest in radical political ideas throughout Europe? Eh? People are waking up, Norman. It's dawning on them that democracy isn't all it's made out to be, that democracies take on the values of their lowest strata if allowed to run their course — a point ably made by Nietzsche — and this one has undoubtedly run its course."

"You think Hitler was a good bloke?" asked Giffard.

Atherton hesitated; the question seemed to displease him. "Is anyone good?" he asked. "Am I good? Are you good? I don't know what you mean by good, Norman, and I don't think you do either. Goodness is relative. What's good to me is evil to someone else. So, when people say that Hitler wasn't good, they aren't really making much sense. Nietzsche understood the problem; he damned the democracies long before Hitler came to power. You don't know who Nietzsche was? He was the greatest of the German philosophers, a man of searing vision and honesty who called it as it really is. And like all geniuses he was shunned during his lifetime and driven mad. He refused to compromise his vision, Norman, the vision supplied to him by his instincts. We have to follow our instincts. Do you know what Nietzsche called history? He called it the invention and pride of the moderns because it lessened the integrity of the instincts."

Giffard's expression indicated perplexity.

"The instincts are what we are hard-wired to know and understand outside of thought and feeling. If we obeyed our instincts, most of our decisions would be other than they are."

The telephone rang and Atherton cut short his lesson in the new ethic, an ethic within which selfishness and egoism had been carefully redefined. According to the gospel of James A. Atherton, our problem was that we had swapped the horse for the cart and allowed feeling or whim to underpin our power of decision. That was our basic mistake. We had swapped intelligent self-interest for a manufactured altruism and ignored the facts. Self-interest had been defined as selfishness, and demoted; but it was actually altruism that was the problem. Altruism, based as it was on the uncertainties of feeling and emotion, led to decisions of questionable validity, whereas decisions made on the basis of intelligent self-interest relied automatically on hard facts. Western society was set on a course of self-destruction because of its philosophical alliance with altruism.

Giffard watched the small figure march across the room and lift the receiver. He was all hustle and bustle, his tone clipped and severe like his moustache. And then everything changed, not in substance, but in style, and Atherton was saying yes, yes, yes, and the smug abrasiveness of his tone had been exchanged for a respectful arrogance. It was a pecking order, and Atherton was in the process of being pecked.

Dean was sitting forward, legs apart, forearms on his knees, his attention on Atherton's back. Giffard, his huge frame filling one end of the sofa, did not know which was the more fascinating to watch, the talkative Atherton or the ultra-respectful Gavin Dean.

"I have to go out," said Atherton, when the call was over. "Drink up, gentlemen. "

Giffard, whose whisky had disappeared in two gulps, pushed himself up out of the sofa's luscious depths with difficulty and stood towering over the scene. Dean rose more slowly, more self-consciously; it was as if he were trying to make a statement. When he was on his feet, he drank down what remained of his whisky and handed Atherton his glass.

"You'll be contacted in the usual fashion," said Atherton, laying the glass aside. "Give my regards to Gunther." And then to both men's surprise he said, "We have a few minutes before your taxi arrives. Would you like to see my garden?"

Dean mumbled "Yeah," and glanced at Giffard.

Following Atherton, the length of his unit, they filed out into what was a very small garden indeed, but one beautifully appointed and drenched in afternoon sunlight. Terracotta paving and walls of similar colour were contrasted against turquoise timbers supporting a balcony, and directly ahead, affixed to the gable of a brick garage, an impressive lion's head of sandstone dribbled water into a matching basin with scalloped edges. A flowerbed filled with roses and assorted plants dominated the centre of what was a small courtyard, and on the right a large wooden gate with heavy hinges and ornate door handle completed the garden's visual impact.

"It's an Italian design," said Atherton, surveying his little kingdom with delight, "but I could not resist a touch of Grecian audacity." He was referring to his use of turquoise for the timbers. "What do you think?"

"Mary would like it," said Giffard.

"Your wife?" said Atherton.

"His ex-wife," said Dean.

"Marriage is important," said Atherton, staring at a rose. "I've been married for twenty-five years and would recommend the estate to anyone."

Giffard stood thinking of Mary and their dilapidated house in Marrickville, of the overgrown garden with its diseased nectarine tree. Dean, dourly glancing around and unable to fathom anyone's interest in gardens, listened for the taxi's arrival.

"Do you know what's happened to us, Norman?" said Atherton, surveying his little kingdom, "we've fallen foul of an inverted morality, a morality that holds evil to be good, and good to be evil. We've swapped reason for emotion and allowed altruism to overpower instinct. No one has the right to demand the sacrifice of intelligence or ability for the sake of the stupid or the incompetent." Turning, Atherton fixed his gaze on Dean. "Justice is dealing with men as they objectively are, with what they objectively deserve. It has nothing do with faith. Altruism, as we have come to understand it, is faith by another name. Faith is the fantasy that hopes against hope that what cannot be avoided will be avoided, that what cannot be attained will be attained. Do you understand what I'm saying, Gavin?"

Atherton's change of focus took Dean by surprise.

"Yeah, of course," said Dean.

"Then you are on your way to a new beginning, and you will never regret it."

The man's face had come alive as he spoke, the tone of his voice changed from that of schoolteacher to that of poet.

"You're good with words," said an emboldened Giffard.

"Which means you've been listening," said Atherton, his estimation of Giffard's intelligence up another notch. Then, "Ah, your taxi."

And that was how they parted, with Dean secretly miffed at the attention Atherton had given to Giffard, and Giffard, alert to Atherton's seriousness, trying to work out the pros and cons of what he had just heard.

"Grand Hotel," said Dean.

They raced down Ocean Drive, a choppy sea and swaying palm fronds indicating that the expected late afternoon breeze had come in more strongly than usual. To their left, beyond the remains of a defunct racetrack, the city's Dallas-like outline of glass spikes and tinted concrete soared into a cloudless sky. A few minutes later they mounted the steep ramp to the Grand's entrance and found themselves embroiled in a traffic jam. The row of taxis hugging the right-hand wall had made the entrance lane too narrow and it was now blocked by a small white bus. As they waited, a hotel employee ran out to say that the holdup would be of short duration.

"Bunch of cripples," said Dean, who was able to see something of what was happening up front.

"I'm almost a fucking cripple," said Giffard.

The bus pulled away and they slid into place.

"We could have got out back there," said Giffard.

"And miss out on the flunkey opening the door? Not on your life, mate."

"Why are we here?" asked Giffard.

"To have some *fun*, ol' son."

Dean's whole demeanour changed from that moment: he seemed suddenly taller, his expression removed from the mundane, his stride confident. Giffard, on the other hand, felt ill at ease and decidedly out of place in his checked shirt and blue windcheater. He hobbled in behind Dean, the pain in his right knee ascending to his brain in sharp bursts. But there was no doubting that this was a break in routine, and a welcome break at that. The Grand *was* very grand. The ground floor with its central bar on a carpeted podium, where drinks or afternoon tea could be ordered, was imposing enough, but when one looked up it was like looking into the heights of a cathedral, the circular balconies ascending tier upon tier appearing greenish and unworldly.

"You've stayed here before?"

"Many a time. They know me." Then, "A cold one, Norman?"

"Yeah, why not?" said Giffard.

Headed straight for the bar, Dean selected a corner table with a clear view of the entrance. "This'll do," he said, looking around. When they were seated, he produced a roll of notes and tossed it at Giffard. "Behave yourself and this is how it'll be from now on."

Taken aback by what seemed to be a genuine note of affection, Giffard pushed the wad into his windcheater pocket without comment. And on it went, this affection, in little things. They drank beer for half an hour, but talked little, then sallied over to the desk where Dean picked up their key cards, Dean holding on to both. Giffard was a little under the weather by then, but not drunk. When they got to their rooms on the third floor, a cheery Dean informed Giffard that female company had been arranged.

"I'm not into that kind of stuff."

"I can get you a black bitch if that's what you want."

"Don't push your fucking luck!" said Giffard.

Dean's look of innocence was patently false, his smile cruel. Going to the minibar he pulled open the door and surveyed its contents. "Another beer? Something stronger?"

"Whisky," said Giffard.

"That's my boy!"

As Dean attended to the drinks, Giffard looked around what was almost an apartment. "What's this going to cost?"

"An arm and a fucking leg, mate." He handed Giffard his whisky. "Doesn't take long to get used to it. You'll see."

And again, they settled in to drink, and an hour later they had done serious damage to the contents of the minibar.

"I need a piss," said Giffard, struggling to get up. He fell back, but on his second attempt succeeded.

"You hungry?" asked Dean.

"Famished," said Giffard

"Steak and chips?"

"Do me."

Dean headed for the telephone.

"They'll bring it up?"

"They'll do any fucking thing you want if you've got the cash, mate."

"I've gotta have a piss!" said Giffard, lumbering away.

When he returned, a fresh can of beer and a whisky were waiting for him. He flopped back into his chair and reached for the beer.

"You okay, mate?" said Dean.

"Never felt better," said Giffard.

"Nor me, mate," said Dean. Then out of the blue he said, "What did you make of the little guy?"

"A shit," said Giffard. Then, smiling to take the edge off what he was about to say, he said, "Had you licking his arse."

"You betcha," said Dean, taking the swipe. "He's got the contacts, Norman. You can't do anything without contacts."

When their food arrived, they had not talked for about ten minutes. Uncovering his plate, Giffard eyed his meal.

"Not bad, eh?" said Dean.

The girls arrived at six-thirty. They came into the room looking and smelling like newly cut flowers, their dresses bright, their hair long, smooth and glistening, their tans deep and natural. Giffard stared at them, speechless. He was now very drunk. Their names were Cheryl and Anne, and they weren't much older than twenty. Giving Anne the nod to attend to Giffard, Dean put an arm round Cheryl's waist and asked if she and her friend would like a drink.

"Champagne," she said.

Anne was already sitting on the arm of Giffard's chair; she had swung her legs across his body and was leaning into him provocatively. "I don't think your friend's up to it," she said.

"He'll be okay."

"You guys up from Sydney?" asked Cheryl.

"Brisbane," said Dean.

As they discussed preferences, Anne continued to work on Giffard without success. "He can't keep his eyes open," she said.

Dean got up and came over to where Giffard was sprawled out. "Come on, you stupid bastard!" he said, shaking him. But Giffard was beyond response. The deluge of alcohol had carried him off into a world of roaring sounds and up-rushing sensations.

They stood staring down at Giffard's slumped figure, Dean annoyed at not having managed to sexually compromise his now comatose companion. Then, taking both girls into the larger of the two bedrooms, he set about satisfying his own peculiar appetite.

***

Hennessey's new hotel was markedly superior to the Lancaster. There was a bar and a small restaurant downstairs, and the rooms had both a telephone and a television set: a set with good reception, that is. Most important of all was the fact that his room looked out onto George Street — that helped remove the feeling of isolation he had experienced at the Lancaster. So it was with relief that he unpacked his few belongings and laid Emmi's copy of *The Erl-King* next to his bed.

Palfreyman had dumped him outside the Bartlett around ten saying that he would return for him at six — Emmi had issued a dinner invitation for seven. As he unpacked, Mary Giffard headed across town in a taxi for the uncertainties of Marrickville in a pair of borrowed tennis shoes. She had slept straight through until lunchtime. Stretching out on the bed, Hennessey lifted Tournier's controversial novel and opened it at random. It opened at a blank page with a quote by Paul Claudel opposite.

All that passes is raised to the dignity of expression; all that happens is raised to the dignity of meaning. Everything is either symbol or parable.

When Palfreyman returned, Hennessey answered the door with Tournier's novel in his hand.

"You haven't budged?"

"I had lunch downstairs, and a bit of a walk."

"We've got Mary covered, but Giffard's a worry. Anything could happen there." Palfreyman went to the window and looked out. "We lost track of a couple of people last night. Jack was livid."

Hennessey slipped the book into his jacket. "That why you were so late?"

A nod from Palfreyman, and a bit of a laugh. "We're moral knights with hardly a horse between us, John." They moved out into the corridor. "There's an echelon of government that would close us down if they could. Have done in the past. If it wasn't for Jack's days as a high-flier in Special Branch, we'd be hamstrung most of the time. Getting sufficient money to keep the department running is a full-time job."

"I would have thought what you were doing rather important."

"We're an embarrassment. We're a reminder of things that can't be imagined by the younger politicians. Our political masters think we're paranoid; others are less kind." They entered an elevator. "We're seen as too imaginative in our interpretation of events — ASIO sees us as bothersome meddlers."

"What made you take on the job?"

"I was approached in much the same way as you were approached. It felt right."

They came out of the elevator and made their way to the front entrance where Palfreyman's car was cheekily parked.

"How did things go at the Belvedere?"

"She doesn't see us getting through this."

"Said so?"

"In as many words." They got into the car. "She sees me as a problem she doesn't know how to solve."

Palfreyman engaged gear. "We all have one of those. What's yours?"

"I've never been any good at making money. Real money, that is. Laura can't get to grips with that."

"My father was very good at making money." Palfreyman's face betrayed nothing of what he was about to say. He changed gear again, glanced in his rear-view mirror. "He was driving the car in which my wife and unborn child were killed. He had been drinking." A glance. "He was brilliant but flawed."

"Your wife was pregnant?"

"A whole other kind of life was taken from me in an instant."

"Your father died too?"

"Mercifully, yes."

A silence.

"Laura didn't want children."

"You?"

"I was an only child. I think that predisposed me to not caring one way or the other."

"It was also my mother's loss," Palfreyman said graciously. "She never speaks of the accident, or of my father."

After a longish pause, Hennessey said, remembering, "I studied Georg's poetry at university."

"Too esoteric for me," said Palfreyman.

"Frank's pretty esoteric."

"Frank is Frank."

They turned off Edgecliff Road into the forecourt of Bellevue Mansions. Hennessey had not seen the outside of the place in daylight. Everything was shaded nooks, flowerbeds and neatly corbelled red brick. A grand half-circle of steps led up to an equally grand entrance that in turn gave way to a wide wooden staircase and a dado of sparkling green and white tiles. The doors on each landing were panelled and heavy with architraves, their brass handles and letterboxes burnished, their dark wood polished. All in all, an impressive four-storey building with cream and green windows looking out into the branches of towering eucalypts. Palfreyman applied his key, and they moved up the passageway to the kitchen where Emmi was busy cooking.

"I hope this isn't too hot for you," she said, looking round. "I've made a Hungarian goulash with sauerkraut."

Going over to where she stood, Hennessey looked into the pot where pork bits and sauerkraut bubbled and heaved in a rich, chilli-enhanced sauce.

"And I've made you Austrian dumplings." She pointed at the oven where the dumplings could be seen cooking in a deep tray. "Have you had them before?"

"Never," said Hennessey.

"And pea soup!"

"I've got a single malt I think you'll like," said Palfreyman. He beckoned and Hennessey followed him into the lounge where he poured two large scotches. Drink in hand, Hennessey watched Palfreyman open a bottle of shiraz and place it on the ledge of a bookcase next to a pre-set table. "Are all the paintings by the same artist?" he asked.

"There my mother's work."

"She's very good."

"She trained under Harbel as a youngster."

There was a large, dark canvas above the empty fireplace. It was of a furnished room from somewhere in Emmi's past. In it a cigarette burned in an ashtray on a table, a pair of spectacles lying half-folded on an open book. It was an atmospheric work, dark and brooding and full of skill, the enlarged words seen through the lens of the spectacles in perfect perspective. The other pictures were mostly landscapes, one of a large, walled Bavarian-type house with wrought-iron gates and a central courtyard seen from an odd angle. Hennessey's eyes strayed from the paintings to a writing desk of mellowed yellow timber that straddled a corner of the room; he had not paid it much attention previously. It was surmounted by two standing columns of tiny drawers, each with a tiny black knob, each knob with red and blue wildflowers painted either side. It was an exquisitely made piece.

"A relic from the past," said Palfreyman.

"We're all relics from the past," said Hennessey.

When his soup arrived, it was Palfreyman who delivered it. Hennessey was sitting at the table by himself.

"She has a bit of tremor; hot liquids are difficult."

The pea soup was lumpy and delicious, the brown bread Emmi brought in newly baked and dense. She sat down and beamed at him. "I can't eat your fluffy white stuff," she said, "and it's useless for making dumplings."

"I still buy black bread occasionally."

"David says you speak excellent German."

"University," said Hennessey.

"You were stationed in Bielefeld?"

"Yes. You're familiar?"

"I know that it is sometimes called 'Little Paris'. I know that it is on the outskirts of the Teutoburg Forest. I know it had — and probably still has — a famous children's choir. And I know that it is equally famous for its linen."

"You know a lot."

"This tablecloth is from Bielefeld."

"What she's not telling you," said Palfreyman, "is that she lived there for some time."

"I had a very handsome lover in Bielefeld."

Hennessey was reminded of a dark-eyed girl of twenty in a polka-dot dress and floppy-brimmed hat, and of Sparrenburg Castle with its round tower and terraces where they had met to talk and eat ice cream.

"When were you there?"

"The summer of forty-three; I was seventeen years of age."

Thinking of the Sparrenburg terrace with its crowds of promenading visitors, Hennessey said, "I have fond memories of the place."

"Did you go to the theatre much?"

"Quite a bit. The Anglo-German Club organised theatrical parties to the Old Market Place theatre. I saw my first modern ballet in Bielefeld — *Glück, Traum und Tot.*"

"Have you been back?"

"Not to Bielefeld. I've been in Vienna a few times. Twice in Berlin."

"You had a German lover?"

Hennessey smiled at Emmi's directness. "I met a very beautiful girl called Ursula. We had a bit of a fling during the Rosenmontag wine festival. I was tempted to stay on when I completed my stint."

"Why didn't you?"

"I'm not really sure. I just didn't."

"I went to Essen and got myself a studio after Bielefeld"

Hennessey made a movement with his hands to indicate the pictures that hung around the room. "You're very talented. The big oil is superb."

"I had a… friend who smoked."

Having imbibed a large single malt and three glasses of shiraz, Hennessey became talkative. He was in his element but refrained from speaking German because his hosts stuck doggedly to English. The conversation ranged from art to literature to music, then to Australian politics, then back again to the arts, then quite suddenly veered off in the direction of first-century history, which was apparently one of Emmi's passions. Then, finally, inevitably, to Germany's experience of its own psyche run amok.

"It's an irony that from Nietzsche onwards it's the German glorification of the golden age of antiquity that caused all the problems," Emmi said, her delicate blue eyes searching Hennessey's face. "We Germans were so deeply taken with ancient Greek society and philosophy, with Greek art, Greek courage and the Greek contempt for weakness that we unwittingly laid the foundation for fascism." She sat back into her chair, glass in hand "As I admitted earlier, I succumbed to it. My father and my mother succumbed to it. Some of the best minds in Germany succumbed to it. We felt ourselves to be part of something majestic, something wonderfully... prescient? I can remember waving a Nazi flag and feeling liberated. Can you imagine such a thing?"

Hennessey admitted that he could not.

"Hitler's achievements during his first six years were so astonishing even his enemies began to show respect. Who could have guessed that he had such talents? No one. Certainly not before thirty-three. No one believed he was capable of accomplishing anything at that time. But his detractors were proved wrong. He surprised everyone by being hugely successful. There were six million people unemployed in Germany in thirty-three. Three years later there was full employment."

"What about the SA? Surely…"

"Surely?" Emmi laughed outright. "John, we'd already had the Nationalist Stahlhelm, the Social-Democratic Reichsbanner and the Communist Roter Frontkämpferbund. No one was surprised when Hitler launched the SA. It was just another group, another uniform. What you have to realise is that the SA, brutal as it was, was never half as brutal as we Germans expected it to be. We expected a bloodbath in thirty-three; it did not take place. We expected those threatened by Hitler — the prominent figures of the republic he had sworn to deal with — to disappear without trace. They didn't. They were locked up in camps and treated abominably, but most were eventually released. Even the official boycott of Jewish shops lasted only one day and was almost bloodless. What were we to think?" She leaned her elbows on the table and continued. "Between thirty-three and thirty-four the terror subsided. Between thirty-five and thirty-seven Hitler amazed everyone by turning the economic situation around and re-arming the country. It seemed miraculous. One minute there were soup kitchens and massive inflation, the next, normalcy. Well, almost."

Taking up the theme, Palfreyman said that Frank had described the terror of the early years as stage-managed. What Hitler had done was create fear through threats, wild threats, then fall short of completely fulfilling those threats, then introduce normalcy with sufficient terror in the background to keep everyone on their toes. Intimidation had been cleverly regulated to avoid driving the masses into opposition; it was never allowed to divert attention from Hitler's economic miracle. By this method those who had been against Hitler had come to think of the regime's earlier excesses as a transition period. By 1936 he had had such a hold on the country that the idea of rebelling against him had become unthinkable. He was God. Children in school were singing hymns to him. He was an armoured knight on a white charger. A saviour. A redeemer. The atmosphere throughout the country had been one of awe and fear: awe in the face of what appeared to be Hitler's almost magical powers; fear of the wrath everyone knew would be unleashed if as much as a finger was raised against him.

"But the dream did eventually fall apart," said Hennessey, switching his attention back to Emmi.

"Yes, but it was too late by then. He had the whole country stitched up and opportunists were everywhere." She shook her head as if trying to dislodge something. "There were terrible rumours, but the sun shone as usual, if you see what I mean? And I was a utopian, which complicated things further still. I belonged to a banned group. All groups other than those created by the Reich were banned early on. Symbols had been used to rouse the masses, and Hitler did not want us around to explain the significance of those symbols. Hence the

Nazi flag with its red background, sun and swastika. The red background symbolised purity of blood and set the scene for a huge misunderstanding." She was momentarily agitated. "What people don't realise is that völkisch symbols were everywhere at the turn of the century. They were on posters, armbands, banners and the covers of magazines throughout the whole of central Europe. It was believed that these symbols heralded a utopian age, and we Germans believed we would initiate it." She looked away for a moment, then back. "Well, we did, didn't we? Only problem is, it was back to front and upside down."

"You still think these symbols have efficacy?"

"We sold our birthright; we may never get it back."

"Our birthright being?"

"The ability to touch the centre of the Earth with our foot," she replied mysteriously.

There was an empty page here and I attempted to move it up!

19
An Unspeakable Presence

Hennessey was horrified when news of Michael and Emma's Lindfield home being fire-bombed reached him. No one had been hurt; the home-made Molotov cocktail had hit an astragal in the French doors and failed to penetrate the room to any real depth. But there had been a moment when everything could have got out of control, when the flames engulfing the window could easily have spread into the room itself, or into the ceiling. Quick action with an extinguisher had stopped that from happening. But it had been touch and go.

They were altogether now in that same room, plus a Special Branch detective who listened, but said little. In the garden, Special Operations Group police were deep in conversation with David Palfreyman.

"No one could have anticipated such a move," Palfreyman said later, aware that he had not picked up on Dean having access to Michael's telephone number through Giffard. "We thought he might strike at the Lancaster."

"John has *really* annoyed him," said Laura.

"I gave Giffard your number on our very first meeting," said Hennessey. His expression carried an apology. "Giffard told me then that I didn't know what I was getting myself into."

"Get your daughter out of Sydney for a few days," said Palfreyman. "A relative? Where is she now?"

"With a neighbour," said Emma.

Michael said in a low, almost anguished voice, "This isn't shaping up too well, is it?"

"He's overplayed his hand," said Palfreyman. "His superiors won't like this bit of flamboyance. It could be a costly mistake presuming it was Dean who did it.

"It could be a simple warning," said Hennessey, taking in the room's blackened devastation. "He, or some other, may have been ordered to do it."

"That would raise the stakes considerably," said Palfreyman.

"What about the training sites?" said Hennessey.

"Boy's Own Adventures stuff was our first thought," said Palfreyman.

Flames had badly damaged the wall either side of the French doors, the blackened ceiling above those doors hacked away for fear of smouldering timbers. The brigade's size eleven boots and a torrent of water had completed the sadness.

Michael had been in his office, Emma upstairs helping their daughter Alix with her homework when Dean struck. Laura had taken the brunt of the attack. She had been in the lounge and experienced it firsthand. Her screams had brought everyone running. And done in broad daylight with the kind of bravado Dean delighted in. He had stood for some seconds admiring his handiwork before melting away.

With the questioning over and the police gone, Hennessey and Michael went into the garage in search of a tarpaulin, leaving Palfreyman to face an interrogative Laura. Emma stood listening. When they returned, Laura was quietly but firmly suggesting that he had not had the right to involve Hennessey in the way he had. Palfreyman was sympathetic, but just as firm in his response: John's help had been invaluable, and voluntary, he said. Laura would not leave it at that; she had another go at Palfreyman, but he smilingly disengaged himself. Try as she might, she got no further with him. Going over to what was left of the French doors, Palfreyman asked if Hennessey were ready to go, but he wasn't. He was needed to help with the tarp, he said, and he wanted to speak to Laura before leaving.

"She's just gone upstairs, John," Emma said, her look a warning. "I'd leave it for now."

"I'll be in the car when you're ready," said Palfreyman. "I've got a few calls to make."

***

Hennessey headed for Glebe early next morning, his port of call Gunther Harrenstein's busy little office; he was in a bad mood, and he intended to use it. He was greeted in the now expected offhand fashion, but when he accused Harrenstein to his face of playing a double game, everything changed.

"Don't be ridiculous!"

"Convince me."

"Of what?"

"That you're *kosher*."

Harrenstein's rapid blinking told Hennessey that he had unsettled the little man: proof of this was immediate. If Hennessey had heard about his recent meeting with Dean at Rosie's Steak Bar that could be explained. Dean had appeared at his home without warning and all but forced him into a cab. Next thing he knew he was being stood a beautiful meal at the Cross.

"You witnessed the fight?"

More blinking. Yes, he had witnessed the fight.

"The two of you had a cosy little evening from what I've heard."

"Hardly cosy," said Harrenstein. "Dean was in one of his incomprehensible moods, and I had no choice but to go along with it." Harrenstein's tone then turned conspiratorial. "He wanted to know all about you, what you were up to, what you had said. I told him everything, like I said I would."

"Why didn't you notify the police?"

"I was told there would be repercussions if I did."

"So why are you telling me now?"

"Because there's no point in not telling you; you already know we were there together."

"Did Dean tell you his attacker was Norman Giffard?"

"I asked him if he knew his attacker and he said he didn't."

"Do you know what I think? I think you and Dean are working together. I think you've been working with him from the very start."

"That's a preposterous suggestion!" Harrenstein reached for the telephone. "You leave me no option but to ring my lawyer."

Hennessey's hand went down on top of Harrenstein's. "Listen to me for a moment. The home of a close friend of mine was firebombed by Dean last night. If I find out, you had anything to do with that…"

Genuinely alarmed, Harrenstein asked if he was sure, it was Dean's handiwork.

"It's got his arrogance stamped all over it."

"Was anyone hurt?"

It was the right question; Hennessey withdrew his hand. Someone close to him had barely missed being drenched in lighted petrol, he said, and there had been a young child upstairs.

"I don't know what to say," said Harrenstein, and he seemed genuinely shaken by the news.

"There's more," said Hennessey. "Dean abducted Norman Giffard and his Aboriginal wife from their home a few nights ago. He then let the wife go and took Giffard back into his employ. The wife is now Dean's insurance policy against the husband turning on him."

"I'd never seen Giffard before that night." said Harrenstein. "Good God, you can't possibly think I had anything to do with that!"

"You deny *all* involvement with Dean?"

"Absolutely!"

With a final twist, Hennessey said, "As much as a whisper from that man and you let me know. Right?"

A nod from Harrenstein.

Producing his diary, Hennessey read out the number of his new hotel and watched as Harrenstein wrote it down. "*Me* first if anything interesting comes up," he said. Then, with a hard look and a bit of Belfast twang, he added, "If he turns up on my doorstep, I'll know who to blame."

***

Dean's aim had been good, but not good enough. The bottle had hit the right-hand French door on an astragal and shattered the thin glass, its contents only partially penetrating into the room. Using the garden's natural cover, he had slipped back out onto the road and walked casually back to where the car was parked. Minutes later he and Giffard had been safely out of leafy, blossomy Lindfield and headed for central Sydney, Dean's delight at fever pitch, the surface severity of the blaze sufficient to convince him that substantial damage had been inflicted.

They were now eating breakfast in a workers' cafe in Redfern, having returned the previous evening to where the Giffards had been held captive. He had a few such spots, each with a purpose of its own: either pleasure, or terror. Situated on a corner, number 62 Nyland Avenue was surrounded by straggly eucalypts and a fence of weather-beaten planks. Having celebrated the fireball by opening a bottle of whisky, both men were now nursing hangovers as they munched toast and pushed bacon, eggs and a mountain of beans into their mouths. Giffard ate in silence. Dean, his eyes hidden behind sunglasses, talked mostly without looking up, his flat cap hiding the fact that his sandy hair was thinning on top. Alluding to the big shipment of drugs coming in from Thailand, he said that if they got this first batch through there would be no stopping them. Customs had been taken care of. How, asked Giffard. Dean placed an index finger on the side of his nose and tapped at it to signify that some things could not be talked about; then he shocked Giffard by revealing that Dave Hollows was dead.

The beans Giffard had loaded onto his fork began to slide off.

"He thought dobbing you in had made him invulnerable. It didn't. It just made the big boys more watchful." Dean's knife and fork were poised above his plate as if waiting for the signal to attack. "I told the silly bastard to watch his step, but he didn't listen."

"They had him shot for skimming?"

"There's skimming, then there's skimming, mate." Dean's knife and fork descended back into his plate. "He expected to disappear for good afterwards, well he did."

"You shot him?"

"Didn't have the pleasure." Dean's smile was enigmatic. "You got off real light, Norman." A look that told Giffard absolutely nothing. "You got lucky, ol' mate."

"You call three years in Pentridge lucky?"

"Better than six feet under, mate. That's why I dobbed you into the police; you'd have been a goner otherwise.

"You're having me on," said Giffard.

"Without *me* you'd have ended up on a slab."

"Why did you do that?"

"Because I *like* you, you stupid bastard!" Dean leaned forward to reinforce his statement, but also to make an extra point. "I'm not the non-entity some of these fuckers think I am," he said. "I've got plans for the future that they don't have."

"You think they're all shit?"

"It's all just guff," said Dean. "Guff and more fucking guff. But the gloves are about to come off, mate, and that's just how I like it."

"Starting where?" asked Giffard

"Starting with that *fucking* Irishman as far as I'm concerned," Dean replied.

20
Morality is for the Plebs

Harrenstein immediately reported Hennessey's visit to his superiors. Dean had gone berserk, he said, giving what details he had. Hennessey was on the warpath and there was no telling what Dean would do next. What had been an act of stupidity on Dean's part — the stealing and publishing of Hennessey's book — had now turned into a personal vendetta. The man was a menace, and Hennessey was not going to let go until he had him behind bars. The voice on the line gave terse assurances; the matter would be attended to. Harrenstein rang off, relieved to have passed the buck, relieved to think that he might never have to deal with Gavin Dean again.

On the other side of town Hennessey was in his hotel room scoffing sandwiches and reading a long, obtusely written article by an archbishop on the ordination of women.

No more than a kilometre away, on an inter-agency intelligence course, Palfreyman was listening to a lecture on web hate sites, the audience a mixture of men and women from all walks of police life. The speaker was a woman Palfreyman had known years earlier, and as he listened to Linda Carter introduce her subject, he realised with a jolt that he was attracted to her. That shocked him. The idea of being attracted to someone other than his dead wife did not seem right.

"A hate site is a site where an organisation or an individual advocates violence against, or unreasonable hostility towards, persons or organisations identified by race, religion, national origin, sexual orientation, gender or disability."

Linda was red-haired and tall with a good figure and a PhD in information systems.

"There are around ten hate sites here in Australia, between two hundred and five hundred worldwide. The number changes constantly. The Web is perfect for such groups in that it offers access to large numbers of people at low cost, and a sense of community, anonymity and the means to circumvent national laws and boundaries. What's of interest here is that racists value the Web for exactly the same reason as civil libertarians: the fact that it is democratic in nature."

Her eyes met Palfreyman's.

"Due to almost constant legal opposition when engaged in meetings, protests or marches, many hate groups have adopted the Web as a strategy to influence public opinion: terrorist groups are already showing interest in it as a recruitment tool. In Australia, the major growth area in hate email is in the area of anti-Jewish intimidation. The Executive Council of Australian Jewry filed a complaint this year against email abuse and threats coming from a known source in Adelaide.

That complaint is presently being investigated. The problem that arises here is that in Australia speech inciting racial hatred is outlawed under the Racial Discrimination Act, whereas in the States it is protected by the First Amendment."

As she developed her subject, dealt with control strategies and moved on to suggest workable solutions to the problems presented by the vast, dispersed and borderless Web, her eyes came to rest on Palfreyman's face a number of times. When her lecture came to a close, he had to hang around for a further twenty minutes before he could get anywhere near her.

"David!"

He kissed her on the cheek, and she immediately asked how married life was treating him.

"Not too well, I'm afraid." Still inexpert at explaining how his wife and unborn child had come to die, he changed the subject. "Got time for a coffee? Lunch?"

She agreed to coffee, but he had to wait while she spoke with two others. When they left the building, he congratulated her on an excellent lecture. Avoiding the topic of his marriage, she rambled on about herself until they were safely closeted, then asked what he had meant by his remark.

He explained quickly and fell silent.

"She was pregnant?"

"Five months."

"How awful."

"I'm working here now. With Jack. Jack Murchinson. Do you remember Jack?"

"We've met a couple of times."

"And looking after my mother," he added, knowing that that was not quite true. The waitress came and went, and he said, "You've become a high-flier."

"I decided to specialise."

"Have you married?"

"I'm married to my job."

"Where's home?"

"Sydney."

He registered surprise.

"I've been here about a year." She corrected herself. "Nine months. I got fed up with Canberra." She corrected herself a second time. "A three-year-old relationship collapsed — I asked for a transfer."

She had been about to say 'died' but stopped herself. Palfreyman, too, had mentally inserted the same word into her sentence. That, he mused later, was the difference between himself and just about everyone he knew. They were able to move on when a relationship 'died'; he was left with the memory of a woman he still loved and would always love.

Their coffee arrived and the little silence that had arisen between them continued, but not awkwardly.

"I see you're still OSI."

He looked up.

"Your name was on the list of those interested in coming to my lecture." She smiled. "You've changed hardly at all."

"Nor you."

"I'm fatter." She pinched at her waist. "You look like you've spent time in the sun, and in the gym."

"I swim, when I can."

There was another silence; Linda broke it with an observation. "I've heard they're trying to close you down."

"Where did you hear that?"

"Around."

"Wouldn't be the first time."

"Too costly. No future," she said, repeating the reasoning she had picked up on.

"We must be getting close."

"To what?"

He hesitated, then, because it was Linda, he spilled a few basic facts. Successive Australian governments, he said, lowering his voice, had been shielding war criminals from prosecution for over fifty-five years because of services rendered. Evidence to this effect was now surfacing, and it was only a matter of time before that information moved into the public domain.

"That's a serious allegation."

"It's gospel. We were closed down in ninety-two for stumbling too close to that truth, and we're back in the same position now. Investigate anyone you like, but don't expect any help from government if you home in on an individual shielded by protocol." He sipped at his coffee and continued. "The OSI was set up in eighty-seven. Five years later it was closed down. I joined the unit when it reopened in ninety-four. During that five year period we investigated eight hundred and forty-one cases at a cost of fifteen million dollars. Three trials failed to secure a conviction because of lack of evidence. The unit was described by an ex-Labor finance minister as a crazy exercise, and the Liberal opposition constantly attacked the cost of the unit's existence and the obvious futility of its efforts. And they weren't wrong. We were getting nowhere because we didn't have access to the evidence we needed."

"You believe that evidence was in the government's own files?"

"Not in every case, but in quite a few, yes." He laughed to himself. "Their loyalty would be touching if it weren't so misplaced."

"We're not really talking loyalty, though, are we?"

"No, we're not. We're talking government present shielding government past."

"Understandable."

"But not acceptable. Benign neglect on the prosecution front to avoid embarrassment is not an argument I can go along with. A former director of the OSI summed it up best. He said that past governments not only lacked the political will to effectively prosecute war criminals, but also the moral fibre to even try. That's quite an indictment. Morality, it seems, is for the plebs. Politicians, whatever their hue, have the right to ride roughshod over society's moral structures whenever they feel like it. That can't be right. It makes a nonsense out of my life, and I can't afford to let that happen even if it appears to be unavoidable." He shrugged, doubled back and tried to qualify his misgivings. "The common good is important. I know that we all know that; but we can't allow the idea of the common good to rule every situation. That's downright dangerous. There are occasions when pleb morality has to come first; ignore that fact and you run the risk of a public backlash at the ballot box."

He was fighting himself as he spoke, fighting his own lies, his own opportunism, his own capacity to turn a blind eye. She watched his face as he traced his misgivings and his fears. Released from the usual professional constraints because of her high clearances, he let his frustrations surface and immediately regretted it. "So speaks the hypocrite," he said in summation.

"We're all hypocrites, David."

They sat looking at one another and realised that a mutual chemistry was at work.

"I take it back," she said, keeping her eyes on his. "You have changed. Quite a bit." He made no comment, and she came back in with a question. "Your mother was… German?"

"Still is."

Linda laughed. It was one of those quick Palfreyman responses that she remembered liking.

"She's got an Australian passport, but she'll never be anything other than German." He glanced towards the entrance and watched an elderly couple enter the coffee shop. "I can think in German, but I'm Australian through and through. She can think in English, but she's German through and through. Is there any real difference between us? Yes. Memory. Memory maketh the man, and the woman."

"Sounds complicated."

"You don't know the half of it. Listening to her talk is like listening to a stranger at times. I sometimes think I don't know her at all."

"Does anyone ever know their parents?"

He smiled at that, nodded. "Do you know what she said to me last night? She said that too much clarity plays havoc with the soul. I asked her what she meant, and she said that ambiguity was by far the better state. Why? Because it reduced arrogance and encouraged trust. Faith, if you like." He pushed his empty coffee cup aside. "She said that faith had nothing whatsoever to do with belief, only with trust. She said the church had reduced faith to a grocery list of impossible-to-believe-in nonsenses."

"Trust in what? God?"

"Our deepest instincts."

"Which is to say what?"

"That we've become disconnected from our world and are paying the price."

"My mother died last year," Linda said, remembering the moment. "My father trundles on; he's in his eighties."

"Didn't you have a brother?"

"I still have."

They laughed and she said that her brother had gone into medicine. Then, doubling back, she surprised him with a difficult question: had Germany the right to criticise Israel's treatment of the Palestinians?

"I would have thought it had every right. Within limits."

"Isn't that the catch?" She leaned forward and spoke softly. "Back in eighty-eight, Jitzhak Ben-Ari — he was Israel's ambassador to Bonn at the time — said that any German could criticise Israel so long as they had no personal responsibility for the Holocaust. And even then, they had to be moderate and tactful." She moved back a little. "Which, of course, was a problem for West German politicians and media commentators. Where did you draw the line? A hundred Palestinians were killed by Israel's security forces in eighty-eight and no one knew how to handle it. Diehard racists and the German far left had a field day. Everyone else was at a loss."

"Nothing's changed."

"Exactly. It's a policy that has to be in place but it's working against itself. It might in fact be why Germany's neo-Nazis have recently been so successful in by-elections. The German government is afraid to be thought of as forgetting its past, and that frustrates ordinary law-abiding Germans who want to register protest at Israel's actions. That ends up playing into the hands of the extremists."

"And the extremists then use that frustration to fuel anti-Semitic feeling on an ever-expanding scale."

A sharp nod from Linda. "Add the far left's denunciation of Israel for what it terms Zionist expansionism and you've got an intractable problem on your hands."

"So, what's the answer?"

She counted off the points she had to make on the fingers of her left hand. One: not allowing criticism to turn into anti-Semitism. Two: not allowing the past to blunt the capacity of Germany's younger generation to speak out against brutality wherever it turned up. In other words, three: being German should not be a reason for keeping quiet, it should be the fundamental reason for speaking out — witness one of Richard Wagner's sons. She drank down what remained of her coffee and replaced the cup carefully on its saucer. Those who propagated a new anti-Semitism disguised as moral outrage should be dealt with severely. But if Israel broke the rules of civilised behaviour, then she should expect censorship like anyone else, particularly from Germany.

"That's a quite daring angle."

"I'm still developing the ins and outs of it."

"And then what, run for cover?"

"Yes, I suppose." She gave a little hiccupping laugh. "I'm expected to break new ground. It's my job." He was about to reply, but she cut back in. "If we falter because we fear the difficulties, then we fail the values we profess to honour."

"Who said that?"

"You did, almost." She smiled at him, then surprised him with a verbatim quote. "You said you couldn't afford to agree with something that made a nonsense out of your life... even if in some obscure sense that something was true by definition. I knew I'd heard something like it before."

"Your quote is better."

"Perhaps."

"Another coffee?"

"I can't." She glanced at her watch. "I've got five minutes at most."

"Am I going to see you again?"

She stared at him.

"There's a lot I'd like to catch up on." He sensed hesitancy. "If you'd rather not..."

"Don't get me wrong. I'd like to."

She rummaged in her handbag, produced a dog-eared card and scribbled her address and telephone number on the back. He glanced at it before slipping it into his pocket.

"I really do have to go. A silly appointment." Getting to her feet she dove back into her handbag for change, but he said there was no need. He'd ring her towards the end of the week.

"Thursday's best," she said, coming round to brush his cheek with a return kiss. Then with an uncertain look she said, "Bye," and headed for the door.

***

"You're mad to have come here in broad daylight! I'm under surveillance."

"I came in over the wall." Taking Harrenstein by the arm, Dean, smiling all the while, pushed him towards his office, his fingers gripping into the man's flesh through his shirt. The door closed behind them.

"What've you been saying about me?" He let go of Harrenstein's arm. "I've been called in."

"Hennessey was here."

"And?"

"I had to report on what he told me."

Dean stared hard at Harrenstein. "Upset, was he?"

"Ropeable." Harrenstein chose to sit on the edge of his desk and talk from there. "You've really got him going this time."

"That'll teach the fucker. So?"

"So, they want an explanation."

"What did you tell them?"

"What Hennessey told me. The fire? The abductions?" Harrenstein smiled as if amused by Dean's antics. "Heavy stuff, Gavin."

"What's it to them — they cut up rough with Dave."

"On your recommendation."

"How the fuck do you know that?"

"I know because I was told. I was around long before you appeared on the scene."

"So, what do they want?"

"They want you to forget about Hennessey and get on with the job you're paid to do." Harrenstein corrected himself. "At least that's my guess. You're engaged in a personal vendetta, and they don't like that."

"I do my job."

"That's not the point."

"Who the fuck are you to tell me what the point is?"

Ignoring Dean's outburst, Harrenstein said, "Hennessey knows we had dinner together at Rosie's. I had to do some fast talking to get out of that one."

"Fucking Giffard," said Dean, turning away.

"Where is he now?"

"Two streets away, at least that's where he's supposed to be."

"He's working for you again?" Harrenstein did not know what to make of that. "I think you had better go. I'll ring Hennessey and tell him you've been here. I promised I would."

Dean turned back to face Harrenstein. "Wait a minute. Norman's never met you. And even if he'd been watching us, he wouldn't have known who you were."

"He may have described me."

"He was too pissed to describe anything to anyone."

"So?"

"So where did Hennessey get the info?"

"From the police, I suppose."

"One of the squad was there, but he wouldn't have said anything," said Dean. "And the CIB don't know what the fuck is going on." He pondered his own statement. "Hennessey give you a number? Is it for the Lancaster?"

"It's better that you don't know where he is."

"*Give,*" said Dean.

"This is not a good idea, Gavin. Last thing he said was that if you turned up, he'd know I'd given you the number."

"I'll show him this, this'll explain everything." Dean opened his jacket to reveal the ribbed butt of a revolver. "I'm sure he'll understand your dilemma."

"You're losing control, Gavin."

"I'll be the judge of that. Give me two hours."

"This is exactly why they've called you in." Harrenstein was losing patience. "You're acting irresponsibly."

In reply, Dean pulled the revolver out of his belt and pointed it at Harrenstein.

"Don't be absurd!"

"Give it here."

Harrenstein obeyed. Pushing the revolver back into his belt, Dean snatched at the piece of paper and looked at it, and as he did so Harrenstein dipped a hand back into the drawer and produced an automatic. Levelling it at an astonished Dean, he reached forward and took the piece of paper from him. If he did not leave immediately, Harrenstein said, he would kill him and say that he had had no choice.

"You don't have it in you," said Dean.

"Try me," said Harrenstein.

Dean paused. Then he said, "I need to know who Hennessey's working with. Something's going on that doesn't make sense."

"You're right about that, but you're not the person to do it. You'd fuck up and we can't let you do that; there's too much at stake." Harrenstein lowered the automatic slightly and pointed it at Dean's genitals. "Let me give you a piece of advice, Gavin. If you ever speak disrespectfully to me again, I'll have you horsewhipped, then I'll shoot you. Do you understand what I'm saying?"

Dean was staring at Harrenstein with a kind of admiration.

"Don't underestimate me."

"I still don't think you have it in you."

"Neither did Dave Hollows."

There was no bravado in Harrenstein's claim; it was delivered as a flat statement of fact.

"*You* shot Dave?"

"Unlike you, I obey orders," said Harrenstein.

As he descended the staircase and made his way through to the back of the building, the shock of learning about Dave Hollows' death melted into surreal unimportance for Dean. Fixated on the question of how Hennessey had known that Harrenstein had been present at Rosie's Steak Bar, he pumped Giffard on his return and was rewarded with blank incomprehension. Satisfied, he signalled that they should move on.

"Where are we headed?" asked Giffard.

"Tell you in a minute," said Dean. Taking out his mobile, he made a call, talked to someone briefly, then directed Giffard to George Street. His ability with numbers had paid off yet again.

When they arrived across from the Bartlett, and parked, Dean made no move to get out.

What are we waiting for?"

"Christmas," said Dean. Pulling his cap forward, he slumped in his seat and closed his eyes, or at least appeared to. "Time for a snooze, ol'son." he said.

***

Hennessey emerged at two-thirty and began to walk in the direction of Circular Quay. Dean was immediately jubilant.

"What happens now?" asked Giffard.

"Turn her round. Get ahead of him and park."

"Then what?"

"We scoop 'im up."

And that was what Dean did, and he did it expertly. Catching Hennessey off guard, he bundled the Irishman into the back of the car, and they took off fast.

"Slow down!" shouted Dean.

"You're stark raving mad!" said Hennessey, glancing at the piece of blue-black metal in Dean's hand.

"Shut up, you *cunt!*"

Catching sight of Giffard's face in the central mirror, Hennessey said, "I thought you had more sense!"

"Leave 'im alone!"

All the way to the shack Hennessey and Dean bickered, the Irishman's sarcasm causing Dean to mouth threats. When they arrived, a fuming Dean got out of the car backwards, the revolver levelled at Hennessey's middle.

"I'm not stupid," said Hennessey.

The shack was stinking hot inside and none too fresh; Dean told Giffard to open a window. Sitting Hennessey down at a small deal table in what had once been the lounge, Dean followed suit and came straight to the point. He wanted to know what kind of arrangement Hennessey had with the police.

"I don't have any kind of arrangement. You had my book vanity printed in UK and shipped into Australia. The police want to talk to you about that."

"*Fuck* you and your book!" said Dean. "What I want to know is how you knew I was at Rosie's Steak

Bar with Gunther. Who told you that? I know you didn't get it from Norman."

"I guessed it was you when I heard about the fight," said Hennessey.

"Who told you about the fight?"

"*His* wife," said Hennessey, thumbing backwards. "I put two and two together and got Harrenstein as the most likely person you had been arguing with."

"That came from you, Norman? You had been watching us?"

"I didn't know who the guy was," said Giffard.

"Jesus!" said Dean.

"Put it down to prejudice on my part," said Hennessey. "But when I tried it out on Harrenstein, I got an immediate confession."

"What kind of confession?"

"He said you had forced him to go there, that you had a screw loose. Hence the argument."

Dean thought that very funny. Pushing the revolver back into his belt, he got up and made his way through to the kitchen. When he returned, he was carrying a bottle of single malt and two glasses. During the time he was out of sight Hennessey glanced twice at Giffard but got no response. Two equal measures of whisky were poured.

"What's the occasion?" asked Hennessey.

"Life," said Dean.

Hennessey did not know what to make of that, but drinking whisky was preferable to having a revolver levelled at one's gut, so he went along with the charade. His principal worry was that a few whiskies might make him less sharp in his responses. This worry took on substance when Dean topped up their glasses long before they were empty and Hennessey realised, he was intent on his inebriation.

"You think I'm a loser and that you're a winner," Dean was saying, his gaze fixed on Hennessey from across the table. "You think that you're right and that I'm wrong, that you understand things and that I don't. But it's the other way round, mate. It's you who doesn't understand. It's you who's blind. I can see what's going on out there because I'm a part of it. All you can see is the story that's been made up for you. You don't write stories, mate, you live a fucking story! You're trying to wake up to what I already know and have always known: out there is a total fuck-up. Truth is, mate, people like you are a bigger fuck-up than I'll ever be. I'm raw meat, and I admit it, but I'd rather be raw meat than over-cooked meat."

"I know what you're saying. But—"

"No, you don't, you only *think* you do."

"I'm from the back end of Belfast for Christ's sake!"

Dean threw back his head and laughed. "You'll be telling me next your old man was IRA!"

Hennessey's smile was tight. "My mother was Catholic, my father Protestant. He worked for the railways and had no interest in religion or politics.

Started out as a pole man. Do you know what that is? It's the guy that separates the wagons in the shunting yard and writes up the fucking tickets. That's *my* background!"

"So what?"

"So, I didn't have a privileged start in life the way you seem to think I had. My father's father was a stonemason."

Glancing at Giffard, Dean said, "He'll have me in tears in a minute." Then to Hennessey he said, "You'll have to do better than that. Start with what that big cunt over there told you about me?"

"He told me next to nothing."

"You gave him money for next to nothing?"

"I gave his wife fifty bucks in the hope of learning something later. They were broke. I reasoned it was a good investment."

"So, what did he tell you?"

"He told me that you ran drugs, that you wanted to change society in some way, and that you wanted to get your own back on the nobs. Stuff like that." Hennessey was free-wheeling and conscious of the dangers. To distract Dean, he downed the remains of his whisky and slapping the glass down on the table. "You want to drink?" he said, pushing his glass towards Dean. "Then let's do it!"

Dean obliged; he filled Hennessey's glass to the brim. Then in a blank voice, he said, "You won't beat me at this." With that said he filled his own glass. So, what else had Norman told him, he wanted to know. Nothing else? He had given the Giffards good money for that dribble of shite.

Hennessey found the situation disturbing; he could sense Dean was winding up to something.

"Do you know what I think?" said Dean. "I think you're having me on, ol' son. I think you and the police are sweet."

"They think you used my book to bring drugs into the country and that Harrenstein was involved in some way. That's what all of this is about as you damn well know!"

Giffard was now half-perched on the windowsill behind Hennessey; he was listening intently.

Dean got to his feet. The revolver was out of his belt. Coming round to where Hennessey sat, he stuck the muzzle into his cheek. "You're lying your fucking head off, and I want to know why," he said hoarsely.

Hennessey could feel Dean's breath on the side of his face. "I'm an innocent wandering around in the thicket," he said, remembering Palfreyman's summation of his early efforts.

"Yeah, but whose *thicket*?" said Dean.

"The Bondi squad fucked up and the Hobart lot gave me a look at your file. Then came Harrenstein and your peculiar arrangement with him over the book. Didn't take rocket science to work out that something might be going on between you two."

"Let me sort something out for you," said Dean. "The squads don't warm to the likes of you; they don't like writers nosing around in their business. So, what's driving you?"

"You," said Hennessey.

Lowering the revolver, Dean leaned on the table, his face close to Hennessey's face. "You just don't get it, do you? You think I'm an idiot and that you'll talk your way out of this. But you won't, can't. I know what's going on in these stations better than some of the people who work there. That's how it is. I scratch someone's back, and they scratch mine. I look away when one of the lads is helping himself, and he does the same for me. It's a game, mate. The whole fucking thing's a game and you're in it up to your fucking ears. So, who are you with? Special Branch?"

The interrogator was being interrogated.

"May I?" Hennessey indicated that he would like another whisky.

"Be my guest," said Dean. He straightened but remained close to Hennessey's shoulder.

Bringing the glass to his lips, Hennessey took a sip. Not to be outdone, Dean reached for his own glass and followed suit. They kept this up until both glasses were empty. Dean immediately filled them again and asked who Hennessey was working for, or with. ASIO, perhaps?

"A minute ago, it was Special Branch. Make up your mind."

Dean's reaction was to cuff Hennessey quite hard about the head. Then, accurately reading the tension in Hennessey's limbs, he said, "Don't even think about it."

"All of this started with the Hobart drug squad," complained Hennessey. "You were on their radar over the book, Bondi fucked up over the book, and the rest is history."

"I don't buy that."

"That's your problem, *mate*, not mine!"

Another cuff about the head almost knocked Hennessey off his chair. "You know more than you're letting on," said Dean. Then, to heighten the tension, he returned to his seat and placed the revolver on the table just out of Hennessey's reach. "You haven't asked me about the other night. Why not? Nice little blaze."

"What you did beggars the imagination. There was a child upstairs."

"What *we* did," said Dean, compromising Giffard, "was a warning to you to keep your nose out of my fucking business!"

"This is ridiculous!" said Hennessey. "You're creating something out of nothing."

Turning on his polite voice, Dean repeated Hennessey's statement word for word.

"I don't know what it is you want from me," said Hennessey.

"I want to know who I'm dealing with."

"We've been all through that."

"We're only starting, ol' son."

"Then you'll need another bottle."

That was as far as Hennessey got. Lifting the revolver, Dean let off a shot that narrowly missed Hennessey; it ploughed into the woodwork to the left of Giffard's head.

"Christ!" said Giffard.

"Where, when and with whom?" said Dean, ignoring the big man's alarm.

Deeply shocked, and aware that he was on a knife's edge, Hennessey said that he had been approached by someone from a police unit dealing with crime syndicates. He had turned up in Hobart and given him the third degree over the book. "And with my having been in contact with you and your girlfriend," Hennessey added, "they thought at first you and I were working together."

"Huh," said Dean. Then, "You have a name for this guy?"

"Detective Sergeant Brownley. You started the ball rolling, and I ended up as keeper."

"Who do you report to?"

"I don't *report* to anyone. I meet with Brownley at intervals. Cafés. An occasional lunch. They don't like me snooping around but they can't stop me looking after my own affairs. I was trying to gather information for a civil case against you."

"Sounds like fucking ASIO to me."

"They'd be flattered." Hennessey forced a laugh. "Brownley's team, if you could call it a team, is small and under-resourced. He's a complainer. Hasn't got this, hasn't got that. Understaffed. Not being taken seriously. He goes on a bit."

"How many of them are there?"

"Three. Perhaps four. They operate out of Canberra."

Dean was frowning.

"The Hobart police weren't interested in the fact that my book and been stolen," said Hennessey, going over old ground to deflect Dean from his thoughts, "only in what it may have been used for. They told me I would have to track you down and put you through the courts myself."

"And you've come up with what?"

"Nothing, so far. They knew you were involved in drugs long before I turned up, but they seemed to think you were now involved with a crime syndicate and wanted to find out what that meant in real terms. I was convinced Harrenstein was lying, but I couldn't prove anything. I got bits and pieces from *him*," Hennessey again thumbed at Giffard, "but none of it helped me get any closer to you. I would have been on my way back to Hobart yesterday but for what you did at Lindfield."

"Empty your pockets."

"What?"

"Empty your *fucking* pockets!"

Hennessey obeyed knowing what Dean was after.

Lifting Hennessey's diary, Dean pored over it for some time, then with a look of satisfaction asked who

David Palfreyman was. Feeling the hole, he was digging for himself deepen, Hennessey said he was one of Brownley's associates.

"This his number?" said Dean. Not waiting for a reply, he produced his mobile and punched in Palfreyman's department number. When he got through, he was told by switchboard that Detective Inspector Palfreyman was out of the office at that moment. Did he wish to leave a message? Dean said no and hung up.

"Office of Special Investigation?"

"As I said, a special unit looking into crime syndicates."

"It's a Sydney number," said Dean, eyeing Hennessey. "You said the mob you were dealing with were in Canberra."

"It was a contact number if I couldn't get Brownley; I haven't had occasion to use it."

"Detective Inspector Palfreyman?"

Hennessey shrugged his innocence.

"You know what? I'm going to have to pass you on, ol' son. What a pity."

"On?" said Hennessey.

"To-whom-it-may-concern?" said Dean. Then to Giffard he said, "Time to move out, mate, nothing that this fucker says adds up."

21
Double Act

Shepherding Hennessey out of the house at gunpoint, Dean made him lie face down on the floor of the cab's rear cabin, and on entering placed both feet on the Irishman's back. It was an uncomfortable ride, and a humiliating one. About three-quarters of an hour later they entered the grounds of a large Georgian mansion in a secluded corner of Surry Hills and followed the driveway round to the front door. The door to this most English of houses opened and a tall, wiry man in a grey suit appeared.

"We've got a problem," said Dean.

The man in the grey suit said nothing. He just stood to one side and watched as Dean and party filed by.

"Anyone else here?" asked Dean.

"Not as yet."

Prodding Hennessey through to what had once been a large kitchen, Dean pushed him in and pulled the door shut behind him. "I've brought him in for questioning," he said, turning the big rim lock key.

"On whose authority?"

"My own; I had no option."

The man in the grey suit stared at Dean; his expression was that of someone trying to fathom the unfathomable.

"There's more to this fucker than meets the eye."

Left to his own devices, Hennessey checked out the room's windows, but they were screwed shut and heavily barred, their panes of ripple glass reinforced with wire. He looked around. Whitewashed walls and an empty cupboard with its doors lying open. The blocked-off remains of two pipes where taps had once been. In a doorless cubicle a seatless toilet and a roll of toilet paper. A bare wooden floor. A light socket complete with bulb in the ceiling; but no light switch and no visible ventilation. No furniture of any kind. The muffled sound of footsteps and voices from above made him look up and stand listening. And then someone shouting followed by more muffled talking and a door slamming. Then the sound of feet coming down the staircase, and the front door opening and closing. Surveying his prison, Hennessey concluded that the only vulnerable point in the whole room was the door's large rim lock, an ancient affair with paint-encrusted roundhead screws. But Dean had made him empty everything out of his pockets, so tackling that was out of the question.

By the time James Atherton arrived, Hennessey was tired out, his attempts to sleep with his jacket as a pillow a complete failure. He had managed to rest a little, but as darkness approached and it looked as if they were going to leave him to rot overnight, even this ability deserted him. And the whisky he had consumed had not helped; his head was pounding, and his mouth and throat were intolerably dry, his disbelief at what was happening to him tempered only by the thought of what might be next on Dean's agenda. And every so often the question of why Giffard had not made his move would recur, and with it the memory that he too had not been able to grasp the moment.

***

"He's secure?" asked Atherton.

The man in the grey suit nodded.

"Gerald?"

"A parliamentary get together."

"Dean?"

"On an errand. I've informed Gerald of Dean's brazenness."

"He's pushy, but he's effective," said Atherton, whose opinion of Dean was greater than that of Harrenstein's. "And on this occasion not without reason, it seems. Gunther's in the picture?"

"Gunther alerted us to what Dean might be up to." The man in the grey suit smiled. "It would have been awkward for Gunther if you hadn't been available."

***

Hennessey came back to himself with a start, cursed, stretched painfully and squinted at his watch: ten fifty-five and dark outside. He had been twisting and turning for hours but had eventually succumbed to sleep. Getting up, he stood listening, but the house was deadly silent. At least he wasn't thirsty any longer; it had dawned on him that the toilet's cistern was full of water, and he had availed himself of that. He returned to the cistern now, removed the plastic lid and scooped out a few handfuls, wet his face and neck and stood in contemplation. No signal from Giffard at any point; not even when he had turned and looked directly at him. So, had the big man changed sides? Had he gone over? It was a possibility. Fear of what could happen to Mary if he tried something could have left him so indecisive as to be utterly useless. And he'd had a go at Dean once before, and failed, and the bullet slamming into the woodwork so close could have further unnerved him.

Standing in the darkness, water dripping from his chin, Hennessey suddenly lost patience and did something quite out of character — he demanded, at the top of his voice, to be let out. As the sound faded, he repeated his demand with even greater force, deciding to keep up the harangue until something happened. As his outbursts rang throughout the house, he began to take pleasure in the act, and when, after a few minutes, a sharp voice from beyond the door instructed him to shut up, he took to thumping the door with the flat of his foot and shouting at the same time.

Atherton came out on to the landing and stared down the lit staircase as his grey-suited companion threw a switch and illuminated Hennessey's prison. The shock of the light coming on silenced the Irishman for a moment. Then the door opened and the man everyone knew as Arthur walked into the room. Expecting a shouting match, Hennessey stood his ground, but Arthur had not come to argue. He produced a small leather cosh and struck Hennessey hard across the side of the neck. Hennessey collapsed. Only one blow, but expertly delivered. As the door closed behind Arthur, Hennessey struggled to rise, but when the light blinked out again, he sank back onto the floor.

Moments later, Gerald Korn, businessman and self-proclaimed rationalist, returned from the city. His mane of yellow-white hair was tousled from the fire-threatening breeze that was now sweeping Sydney's chalk-and-cheese suburbs. When he entered and saw Arthur coming away from where Hennessey was being held, and saw Atherton staring down from above, he knew something was wrong. Arthur said nonchalantly that Hennessey had been playing up and that he'd dealt with him. Unconcerned by the news, Korn made his way upstairs, acknowledging Atherton's presence with a wave.

"I wish you had been with me this evening," he said, when he reached the landing, "you would have enjoyed yourself enormously."

In his mid-fifties, Gerald Korn was a striking man to look at, big with a neatly trimmed beard. The head was well shaped with a good brow, deep set eyes and a slightly hooked nose; the lips were sensuous.

"Anyone of interest?" asked Atherton.

"A frontbencher with an interesting slant on things; we'll be meeting again soon." Korn turned away, but immediately turned back. "What are we going to do about Hennessey? Is he dangerous, do you think?"

"Gunther thinks Hennessey and Dean equally dangerous. He sees Dean as a liability and Hennessey as too clever by half."

"What do you think of Dean?"

"He's a good operative. Could be said that he thinks well on his feet."

"The fire? Was that him thinking on his feet? The book? What else don't we know about him?" Before Atherton could reply, Korn said, "I trust Gunther's judgement on this."

Atherton sucked at his cheek, waited for a pronouncement. He did not have long to wait.

"Tell Gunther to deal with Dean. I'll make up my mind about Hennessey after we've talked to him." With that said, Korn turned away abruptly and Atherton, used to the man's abrupt manner, headed for the telephone.

***

It was late evening when David Palfreyman realised something was wrong. He had rung Hennessey to say that forensics had found a thumbprint on a shard of bottle glass at Michael's, only to be told that Mr Hennessey had not returned to the hotel since going out mid-afternoon. A call to Michael's and a second call around six to the hotel had met with the same result. Then a call from the manager of the Bartlett had come through to say that a rather terse message had been left for Mr Hennessey by a Mr Harrenstein. The manager had been apologetic; he had only just learned of the call. A visit to Harrenstein's home followed. Listening to the man's tale of woe, Palfreyman questioned him unaware that a train of events was already under way that would bring the whole sorry business to a swift and deadly conclusion.

"What time did you ring Mr Hennessey?"

"Quarter to three."

"When did Dean leave here?"

"Just before I rang."

"Why didn't you leave a more explicit message?"

"He wasn't there; what was I supposed to do?" Harrenstein took in a breath. "Hennessey's parting words were that he'd know who to blame if Dean found out where he was. I phoned the moment Dean left."

"What kind of firearm was it?"

"A revolver."

"He threatened you with it?"

"Pointed it straight at me."

"Did he say why he wanted to know Hennessey's whereabouts?"

"It's a personal thing. Hennessey's persistence over the book has annoyed him."

"So, what do you think he's up to?"

"Do you have to ask?"

"You think he might harm Mr Hennessey?"

"He got mad at me for holding back on where Hennessey was staying."

"Brave of you to stand up to him."

Harrenstein looked tired suddenly. It had been a very frightening experience, he said.

"You could have contacted the police."

"And told them what?" There was an edge of irritation in Harrenstein's voice. "They wouldn't have known what the hell I was talking about, and we'd have gone round in circles."

"We think he's abducted Hennessey."

Silence.

Palfreyman scrutinised Harrenstein for a moment. "If there's anything you think I should know, now's the time."

"If I knew *anything* I'd tell you," said Harrenstein, and like Gavin Dean he sounded as if he really meant it.

***

Gingerly feeling around the large swelling that had come up on the side of his neck, Hennessey sat marvelling at the speed and efficiency of the attack. In and out in a trice and not a word said. Which meant he was in the hands of men with very strong aims, men not unlike Dean in their ferocity, but different perhaps in their pathology.

Dean and Giffard arrived back around one in the morning; Hennessey heard them come in, Dean's voice high-pitched and excited. Giffard was his only hope, and Giffard, it seemed, was now hopelessly entangled with Dean.

Sometime later the light came on, but no one appeared. Hennessey was reminded of the bullying tactics of someone at school, of the day he had been battered to the ground inside one of the bike sheds and had lain face down on the concrete shielding his head from blows. The playground silent and the slow realisation that there was no one there, that he was alone. He had felt intolerably foolish in that moment. And now here he was facing bullies armed with guns and truncheons, grown-up bullies with grown-up objectives; having learned to box at university was not going to be enough.

The door opened and Arthur came in followed by Dean. Giffard was standing at the foot of the staircase. Ushering Hennessey out, they took him upstairs to what Arthur referred to as the 'conference' room, but it was actually a very large and comfortable lounge arranged with armchairs like in a gentleman's club. Hennessey glanced at Giffard as he passed but elicited no response.

"Ah, Mr Hennessey!" said Gerald Korn.

"I don't think I've had the pleasure," Hennessey said.

"Find Mr Hennessey a seat, Arthur. Yes, that one will do."

Korn was seated in a large, winged armchair, Atherton in another. Giffard had been left downstairs.

When Hennessey was seated, Arthur sat down near to him, within reach. Dean remained standing.

"What happens now?" said Hennessey.

"Indeed," said Korn. Then, in the tone of a question, he said, "You appear to be some kind of spy."

"Hardly," said Hennessey.

"But certainly, an informer of some kind; you've been caught passing information to a government agency. I'd like to know more about that."

"I've been answering questions posed by the police."

"The police, you say. Really?"

"A unit of the police set up to investigate syndicated crime. I stumbled into association because of my stolen book. Do you know about my stolen book?"

"Yes, yes, we know all about that," said Korn impatiently. "What we really want to know is the exact nature of the questions you've been asked. The OSI isn't police in the ordinary sense of police, Mr Hennessey. What does the acronym stand for?"

"Office of Special Investigation," said Hennessey, feigning puzzlement. "As I said, a unit set up to investigate crime syndicates."

"So, what did you talk about when you met up? And why *you*, Mr Hennessey?"

The bullies were getting into stride; it was Atherton's turn.

"Your being singled out by the OSI suggests expertise of some kind. What could you possibly help them with?"

"Dean. We discussed Dean mostly. Why he had stolen my book. What the book might have been used for. His having belonged to a prison reform group was of interest to them." Hennessey's laugh was dismissive. "They thought that a hoot."

"But in relation to *what*?" said Korn. "What was the context of your discussions apart from Gavin's exploits?"

"They were interested in his politics, what he believed in, what he felt strongly about. I couldn't help them with any of that."

"And?"

"That was it. They didn't explain why. I asked, but they wouldn't say."

"Who put you on to Giffard?"

"He was mentioned in passing by the Hobart drug squad. They told me all about Dean as well. Showed me his police file. Have you seen his police file?"

Dean's expression suggested that he did not like being talked about in this removed manner.

"Gavin understands things that someone like you will never understand," said Atherton. "For instance, he understands that justice is more important than sacrifice. Why? Because that is what a democratic society demands of its citizens, constant sacrifice. The ruling principle of all Western-type democracies is that virtue be turned into a liability."

"I didn't understand a word of that," said Hennessey, "and I very much doubt he did either."

Atherton's next statement astounded Hennessey: social activism should not be ridiculed. Dean had worked hard to reform the prison system from the inside, and that should not be mocked. He had even written a play to that effect.

"Really?" said Hennessey. "Do you happen to have a copy?"

"We deal with men as they objectively are, Mr Hennessey, not as we have been trained to perceive them. What democracy does is change the vice of dependence into a moral asset and endlessly sacrifice men of virtue, intelligence and ability on behalf of the stupid and the incompetent. Which is to say that we have swapped justice for altruism and allowed weakness to take the place of strength. Altruism teaches that wealth does not have to be earned, that love does not require standards, that a promiscuous love for all other human beings should be the common denominator in social interactions. I do not believe that to be true, and deep down neither do you."

The whole tenor of the interaction had lurched suddenly in a didactically obtuse direction. Conscious of Dean's attentive stare, Hennessey said that that was an interesting slant on altruism, but that he thought it garbage.

"This *garbage* is about to have its day because the alternatives have failed and are now seen to have failed by the majority of thinking people," said Atherton. "You must surely have noticed the swing in public opinion."

"I'm not really sure what it is I've noticed; there's a lot of game-playing going on out there. Truth being told, I'm not all that interested in politics."

"An Irishman not interested in politics? How can that possibly be?"

"I left Ireland when I was fifteen."

"And went on to take an honours degree in classics at the University of London."

"You've been checking up."

"But there's more, isn't there?"

"You tell me."

"Much more, *Captain* Hennessey."

Hennessey stared at Korn, wondering how the hell he had got access to his military record.

"Military intelligence?"

"I interviewed people. That's all."

"Don't you mean interrogated?"

"If you know so much then you must also know all I was doing was vetting German civilians for jobs."

"You were a *trained* intelligence officer."

"If you say so."

"And you're now working for the OSI in exactly that capacity."

"*With*, not *for*. Getting to know more about your friend here was to my advantage. I wanted to put him through the courts over my book and took whatever opportunities presented themselves."

"I'm sorry, Mr Hennessey, but that's just *too* neat," said Korn. "The OSI isn't a police unit looking into syndicated crime in Australia; it's an active 'war crimes' unit working alongside Special Branch and ASIO."

"You're very well informed."

"I make it my business to be so."

"What exactly is your business?"

A wave of the hand brought Atherton back into the conversation. Australia was undergoing political change, he said. What had once been taken for granted in Australia was no longer being taken for granted. People were waking up to what had been going on. The day of the handout was over. The day of letting hordes of foreigners into one's country was over. And not just in Australia. European society had also awakened to the fact that it was headed for cultural and spiritual bankruptcy, that its moral fabric was threadbare and in danger of coming apart at the seams. Australia was now in lock step with Europe. The myth of multiculturalism was just about defunct: zero immigration of undesirables was on its way. When the political situation settled, immigrants already in the country would be required to integrate by taking on not only the language, but also the culture and customs of Australia. If they refused, or were incapable of doing so, deportation would be in order.

Hennessy did not reply, but his mind was racing.

"It's the tenor of things everywhere," said Atherton, who was Korn's political strategist. "Certain politicians may pretend that it is otherwise, but it is the feel of the country."

Korn came back in with a monologue of his own at that point. Pushing his large frame into a corner of his armchair, he prodded at his chin with two fingers and said that the metaphysic hidden behind democracy was that all men were equally unworthy in the sight of God. To compensate for this lack of worth, democracy had made all men equal in the hope that altruism would save them from that worthlessness. But that was not what had happened. What had happened was that the idea of equality had taken over and reduced human beings further still. Worthy they may now appear to have become, but it was an imaginary worth. To break out of that imaginary worth we had first to break with the metaphysic that underpinned it, then break with the idea that altruism had in any sense saved us from it.

"All I know," said Hennessey, "is that that man over there almost killed me, and that this man beat me to the floor with a truncheon. Explain that if you will?"

"My apologies for that. Arthur is in charge of security, and you were being very, very difficult, hence your being brought here by Gavin in the first place. You are on some kind of mission, Mr Hennessey, and we want to know the ins and outs of that mission."

"Everything I've done is because of *him*." said Hennessey, pointing at Dean. "It's *him* I've been tracking, not *you*. And you haven't answered my question."

"Security, Mr Hennessey. That's all."

"Brutality," said Hennessey.

"Unflinching resolve in the face of someone intent on causing trouble for all the wrong reasons," said Korn. "We are *not* war criminals, Mr Hennessey. "We are a group of concerned individuals attempting to put Australia back on the rail of decency and common sense."

"With the likes of Dean in tow?"

"A concerned citizen, Mr Hennessey; Gavin has shown that to be case even when in prison."

"He's an opportunistic thug who firebombed the house of a friend of mine and endangered the life of a child *and* my partner."

"Yes, that was unfortunate. I'll be speaking to Gavin about that."

"You didn't order it?"

"Don't be absurd."

"Did you know he enjoys bashing women? His last partner suffered brain damage and is in a wheelchair."

"I'll look into that," said Korn, attempting to sound reasonable.

"Did you know he also runs drugs big time?"

Korn was about to reply, but Atherton cut him short. "I think we're straying from the point somewhat," he said, glowering at Hennessey. "We're here to question *you*, not be questioned *by* you."

"Once an intelligence officer *always* an intelligence officer," said Korn, almost as a compliment.

"Wishy-washy liberalism has had its day," said Atherton. "Altruism without a strong element of self-interest is self-sacrifice, Mr Hennessey. Self-sacrifice on behalf of the incompetent and the stupid is injustice at its worst. That's what this country has to wake up to."

"That's a screwy argument," said Hennessey.

"You think so? You believe self-interest isn't man's basic goal?"

"That pushes the idea of species survival way too far. We're not biological robots; we have consciousness. We can think."

"Supported by *instinct*, Mr Hennessey. Instinct tells us that an endless pandering to the stupid and the incompetent is to *be* stupid and incompetent."

"No, no, no," said Hennessey. "Instinct is as much a learning process as it is hardwired. No one's absolutely sure about that one."

"Instinct is *obviously* hardwired," said Atherton.

"Some aspects of instinct *may* be hardwired; others probably aren't. We can learn by more than one route. You're mistaking the body's functional systems for *psyche*," said Hennessey. "Psyche *isn't* unconscious in that subterranean sense; psyche is the upper echelon of everything that we are in terms of higher order thinking. Instinct in the sense you mean is no more than involuntary prompting. We're no longer animals in that basic sense. We've brought our survival instincts under control through the rule of law, the rule of law you are in the process of dismantling with your false ideas about altruism. Your philosophy is a kind of mixed-up infantile nonsense based on limited categories of understanding. Yes, the instincts can overpower rational thought, but only when rational thought atrophies due to self-interest being allowed to run the show. *That* is your political platform, it's your fundamental problem, and it's all been seen before."

Hennessey's return serve so surprised Atherton and Korn, that they fell silent for a moment. Rallying, Korn said that left-wing taboos did not automatically constitute rational thought. Common sense and raw experience told us that things were not as they ought to be. We *sensed* that this was the case but were seldom allowed to articulate what we sensed because of those taboos. But the resentment of ordinary folk against mainstream political idea had now intensified to pressure-cooker proportions and could no longer be denied. And it was the same all over Europe, and in America. America was well on its way to adopting a more sensible political philosophy, and the European Union had been forced by sheer weight of public opinion to rethink its distorted and distorting direction. If the EU continued to ignore this groundswell of public opinion in its member countries, then it would collapse. And if that happened all the left-wing arguments in existence wouldn't stem the flood of truth and tears that followed.

"He was arguing for something a little more basic."

"James was arguing on behalf of a biological truth, Mr Hennessey. We care *because* we want to be cared for. Recognise that fact and everything falls into place. Fail to recognise the strong element of self-interest in altruism and you fail to recognise the inherent pragmatism of nature."

"We are animals with consciousness."

"But no one knows what consciousness *is*, Mr Hennessey."

"It's what separates us from the animal kingdom in spite of our being animals. It's what allows us to *know* that we know and *feel* what we feel *beyond* blind process. You're saying we have no say in the matter, that we don't have it in us to consciously move from self-interest to an altruism that transcends self-interest. Well, that's not how I experience my life, or the life of others."

"Come, come," said Korn. "Look around you. It is our false notion of altruism that's causing all the problems in the West. If we sit back and allow hordes of people with belief patterns contrary to our own to swamp our culture, undermine the best of our laws and usurp employment, then there's something wrong with us. Is that what you want to see happen here in Australia?"

"You're once again mixing categories of thought," said Hennessey. "As understood in the West, altruism isn't suppressed biological interest; it's human consciousness struggling with the necessity to go beyond limited ideas. It's too damned easy to say that altruism is a biological given and turn one's back on the needy. Yes, we're animals, but we're animals who have struggled to make sense of the world and managed to create a *humane* society."

"And if Asians suddenly turn up on our beaches in tens of thousands? What then? I'll tell you what, Mr Hennessey. It will be machineguns on every sand dune."

"You can't sense the jump in your logic when you say something like that?"

"What I've just said is perfectly logical," said Korn.

"Logical, but not sensible. Logic requires a well thought out, reflected upon premise for it to make proper sense. You're trying to stabilise an ever-wobbly society by introducing a moral vacuum within which the most outrageous acts will be permissible in the name of your screwed up logic. You've chosen scientific materialism as your base structure and you're using it as an excuse to do whatever the hell you like!"

"You reject scientific materialism?"

"I reject the ransacking of good minds to justify whatever takes your fancy."

"Europe is waking up of its own volition," said Atherton, itching to re-join the fray. "One spark and the whole edifice will come alight." He smiled obscenely to himself. "Your ideas are dependant almost entirely on feeling and that disallows your conclusions."

"Better to rely on feelings than on emotional claptrap. Emotion and feeling are not interchangeable propositions, *James*. Emotion constitutes a spectrum. At one end you have a devil, at the other, an angel. Appreciating something through feeling does not cloud the mind, it *enriches* the mind. Feeling is *evaluative*; it allows us to intuit subtlety and become aware of complexity. It's what allows us to transcend the limitations of logic and become truly creative. In the reactive sense, emotion is the opposite of that. How do I know? I know because I'm continually giving in to my emotions and having to appreciate that fact *through* my feelings. When we say we're only human, *that's* what we mean. When we say that someone has transcended the human, *that's* what we mean. What we're talking about here is *grace* through feeling, the human capacity to *care* deeply without reward, and that, gentlemen, is altruism."

"Grace?" said Korn.

"Insight," said Hennessey.

"New Age twaddle," said Atherton.

"An easily observed fact of our existence," said Hennessey.

"Vaguely religious," said Korn.

"Shite," said Dean.

Gerald Korn sighed; it was the sigh of a man who has to put up with lesser beings.

"You're trying to convince me that you are all reasonable men, but you're not. Who in their right mind would sanction the firebombing of a suburban house?"

"We sanctioned no such thing," said Korn.

"He's *your* man, damn it!"

Korn had had enough. Raising a hand, he turned it into a pointing finger. "It is *you* who are here to be questioned by *us*," he said irritably, falling back on Atherton's reasoning. "The OSI's function is the tracking down of war criminals, and that tells me that you are a naive fool caught up in something way beyond your understanding. You're a meddler, Mr Hennessey. What you refuse to accept is that the world *as* experience is not a pretty place and that it isn't going to get any better. Dire measures will have to be taken against those who threaten our culture and way of life. That does not allow anyone to equate us with war criminals, we are not of that ilk; we are pragmatists and proud of it. We are, in everything we say, articulating a weary truth, and it is here in Australia that that truth will be worked out for the whole world to see. We can't keep on being kind to those who threaten our existence; there has to be an end to that. There has to be a raw understanding of the situation and a taking on of responsibility. We are ready to do that. We're mentally prepared to carry the guilt and get on with the job. And we're not alone. There are patriots all over Australia — all over the world for that matter! — who will rise to the occasion, men and women unencumbered by your rationalised weaknesses. The socialists and everything that crawls or flies left of the socialists have had their day, Mr Hennessey. It's *our* turn now, and we will not shirk from our duty."

"Carry the guilt and get on with the job?" said Hennessey. "What in God's name are you saying?"

"We're saying that an overdue set of truths are about to be unleashed on a broad scale after the general election."

"Your so-called independents?"

"You see, you do understand."

"What are you going to do with me? Have me shot?"

"We are *not* barbarians, Mr Hennessey. We've taken the time to present our manifesto and argue its merits; there was no requirement for us to do so. We thought you might be interested, but alas, you're not." Korn was momentarily reflective. "What you have to understand, Mr Hennessey, is that we've only touched the surface of a great truth being worked out with greater precision elsewhere. There is a great work and a wonder afoot."

"Are you referring to what's going on in philosophy and literary criticism?"

"Truths raised from our depths cannot be refuted, Mr Hennessey. The inherent darkness of our natures has to be faced, not sidestepped. This… *mysticism* of yours is no replacement for the cold hard fact of our biology and the findings of brain science.'

"Academia is entranced by the seemingly irrefutable logic of its own discoveries."

"That's novel."

"It soon will be."

"What you've just described as an entranced academia, Mr Hennessey, is academia finally awake to the biological and neuronal facts of human existence. Ethics and morality and religion and politics will soon be in the hands of those who have rejected your rubbery nineteenth-century notions."

"And you'll do the rest, I suppose."

"It's a biological given that some human beings are superior, some weaker, some, well, fundamentally unfit. It's always been so, and it will ever remain so."

"So, what are you going to do with me?"

"He's seen the front of the house," said Arthur.

"I was brought here face down. I saw absolutely nothing. This house could be anywhere."

"Leave him to me," said Dean.

"Are you afraid, Mr Hennessey? You look afraid."

"I'd be a fool not to be."

"Fear is the beginning of wisdom, they say."

"No, fear of God is the beginning of wisdom, they say."

"Ah, the good Catholic boy surfaces at last."

"You mean the good Catholic boy's education surfaces. I learned a long time ago to trust my *own* depths."

"Then we have something in common."

"I'm not referring to my biology."

Korn glanced at Atherton, then wearily, he said, "Mr Hennessey, it's time for you to leave."

"Where am I going?"

"Back to your hotel, of course. Gavin?"

Dean's expression was one of sheer bewilderment; he looked as if he were about to argue with Korn.

"*Do* it," said Korn, throwing Dean a look. Then, for devilment, he said, "Which of your novels would you suggest I read first, Mr. Hennessey?"

"How about my next one," said Hennessey.

***

Once again, he found himself lying face down in the hot, sticky darkness of the taxi's rear. Nearby, Dean and Giffard were arguing about something. Their disagreement was muffled and accompanied by gravel-crunching steps, but Hennessey could make out the occasional word. Then he heard Giffard say, "Place'll be like a bloody oven!" To which Dean replied that it would be for only one more night. They moved off soon after, Giffard driving, Dean with his feet resting impertinently on Hennessey's right hip. Knowing Dean's propensity for sudden violence, Hennessey kept his mouth shut. But as the journey progressed, and the lights and noises of the city gave way to silence and a moon-illuminated darkness, he realised sickeningly that they were not heading, as he had forlornly hoped, for George Street, but more probably for the old shack in Redfern.

"Home sweet bloody home," said Dean, when they reached their destination.

When they emerged, Hennessey's worst fears were confirmed.

"A nightcap?" said Dean.

"You were told to take me back to my hotel."

"That's what you *think* I was told." Said with a terrible nonchalance, and a smile. "I was told to *do* it; I know what that means."

"He's going to kill me, Norman," Hennessey said, turning toward Giffard, but Dean wouldn't have any of that.

"Shut the fuck up!" he said, pulling Hennessey away.

When inside, Dean directed Hennessey back to the chair he had occupied earlier and produced what was left of the whisky. The room was stifling. With his back to the empty fireplace, Giffard watched a smiling Dean fill two glasses and push one towards Hennessey.

"One for the road, ol'son?"

"He's going to kill me, Norman."

"Drink up," said Dean. The revolver was in his right hand, side down on the table, and it was cocked.

"Did you know that Harrenstein's father was a war criminal?" said Hennessey. "He was a top-ranking Nazi physicist brought in from Germany by the Australian government in '45 to help them keep ahead of the Russians. No questions asked. Family as well. All expenses paid and a plum job in Melbourne when he arrived."

"Is that so?" said Dean. Then, "Do you like homosexuals, John?"

"Pardon?"

"Do-you-like-homo-sexuals, John?"

"Live and let live."

"Men fucking men?"

"Killing someone in cold blood is your alternative?"

"I think you're a homo-lover, John, that's what I think."

"You obviously think more about homosexuality than I do," said Hennessey.

Dean's expression hardened, but he did not follow through. "What I want to know," he said, his finger pointing across his body at where Giffard stood, "is what that big fucker over there really said about me."

"Bloody useless right from the start," said Hennessey, giving Giffard a disgusted glance. "Got pissed and fell all over me."

Dean glanced at Giffard. "That's my boy," he said. Then, cottoning on, he said, "You could have said he told you heaps and wound me up."

"Not my way of doing things."

"Do you know what I think? I think it's time you said your prayers, mate." Up came the revolver. "Goodnight, John."

That was when Giffard made his move. He came across the space as fast as his injured leg would allow, but it was not fast enough. The revolver barked and he went down hard, his face contorted with pain, his eyes full of a terrible surprise. But as he went down Hennessey upended the table and Dean found himself under it with Hennessey on top. He fired two shots, but they went into the skirting. Bucking madly, he tried to dislodge the table, but Hennessey kept his weight where he knew it mattered most and punched down at Dean's face with every ounce of strength he had. Dean did eventually manage to free his left arm and land a punch or two back, but Hennessey's downward driven blows proved too much for him. It was a mad free-for-all, and it seemed to go on for ever, and then quite suddenly it stopped, Dean giving a gasp and ceasing to fight back. Fearing a trick, Hennessey continued to hit him, his unrestricted punches quickly reducing Dean's face to a pulpy mass. Then, realising that no one could possibly take such punishment without flinching, he stopped hitting Dean and watched for any sign of movement. But there was none, for Dean the bully was not just unconscious, he was dead.

22
Bitch

Hennessey attended to Giffard as best he could, but he was unconscious and bleeding badly from the right shoulder and, strangely, from the head. Having padded the shoulder wound with a none too clean cloth that was to hand, he turned Giffard onto his right side and turned back to Dean in search of his mobile. Avoiding the man's blank, bloodied stare, he pushed the table aside and rummaged in Dean's pockets hoping to find the diary he had taken from him, but it wasn't there. Knowing only the number of the house — it was in larger black letters on the front door — he then left the shack in search of a street name. This took some minutes due to limited lighting, minutes he knew Giffard could ill afford. Then suddenly there it was, Nyland Avenue. Punching in triple zero he explained in a crazy shorthand that a man had been shot, gave the street name and was transferred first to the ambulance service then to the police. No, he did not know the district, but thought he might either be in Redfern or Marrickville. Yes, that information plus the street name had been given to the ambulance service. To the question why he did not know where he was, Hennessey said he would explain the reason for that later. After a pause, he was told to go back to the house and remain there; they would liaise with the ambulance service and track his location. What was the number of his phone. Hennessey said he had no idea; he was using a borrowed mobile. Another silence; then a double directive: he was to stay put *and* stay online.

The police and an ambulance arrived simultaneously. They found Hennessey sitting on the floor next to Giffard in a state of shock; he had by that time successfully quenched the flow of blood with an old towel. Undeterred by Hennessey's state, a Detective sergeant by the name of Powell questioned him rigorously about the man now confirmed to be dead. Powell was a small, red-haired individual with a testy nature, and his only concern was how the dead man had come to be dead. Hennessey said he would speak only when Inspector David Palfreyman was present.

"What has this… Palfreyman… got to do with what's happened here?" Powell wanted to know.

"Inspector Palfreyman will explain the context," said Hennessey.

"How can he do that? He isn't here. Was he here?"

"Not *this* situation; *how* this situation arose."

"What's Palfreyman's division?"

"OSI: Office of Special Investigation."

"Never heard of it."

"It's a unit with specialist concerns," said Hennessey, his attention usurped by what was going on with Giffard. He looked back at Powell. "They're a war crimes unit."

"War crimes?" said Powell.

"It's a complicated situation."

"Involving war criminals?"

"Not on this occasion."

"I am not following *any* of this," said Powell.

"And I'm not at liberty to explain without Palfreyman being present."

"Why is that?"

"Because under the circumstances silence has to remain golden."

"What's that supposed to mean?"

"It means what it means."

Powell laughed outright. "What are you, ASIO? Are you under cover?"

"Nothing like that. "

"Then *what*?" snapped Powell.

"I've just told you; I can't say why!"

Detective Powell stared down at a now seated Hennessey as if at a species of bug, he had not come across before. Then, glancing at Dean, he said, "So who's the dead man?"

"Gavin Dean."

"How did he end up dead and looking like that?"

Hennessey was momentarily lost for words.

"Well?"

"I killed him."

"You admit to killing him?"

"If I hadn't, he'd have killed me."

Powel glanced at a fellow officer who was listening in. "You did that to his face?"

A nod from Hennessey.

"I didn't hear that," said Powell.

"Yes!" said Hennessey. "He had just shot Giffard and I managed to get the better of him." Aware of the ambulance crew fighting to stabilise Giffard, Hennessey added, "*He* got shot attempting to come to my assistance. If he hadn't it's me that would be dead. He knew what Dean was about to do."

"Have you moved the body? It looks as if it's been moved."

"I had to get at his mobile, so I moved the table." Hennessey took a breath and closed his eyes, opened them again. "I also moved Giffard onto his injured side to stop blood draining into his chest cavity."

"Now you're a doctor?"

"A little something, I picked up in Belfast during the Troubles."

"You're Irish?"

A nod from Hennessey.

Having stabilised Giffard, the ambulance crew moved him out. He was still unconscious.

"You stink of booze, mate. How come?"

"He was forcing me to drink whisky." Hennessey immediately corrected himself. "At least he had been. This was his idea of a permanent goodnight nightcap."

"How long have you been here?"

"We'd just arrived back. They abducted me mid-afternoon; we returned about an hour ago."

"Abducted?" The detective's frown was now comic. "Then you share a bottle of whisky with him and his mate? Or have I got that wrong? He abducted you *and* the big guy?"

"Giffard was his driver."

"So, the two of them abduct you, then the big guy puts his life on the line for you? Is that what you're saying?"

"Yes, that's what I'm saying, but not quite. It's true that Giffard helped abduct me, but I have to presume against his will, given that he couldn't let Dean kill me in cold blood." Hennessey's energy had all but given out. "Ring the Hobart drug squad; they'll give you Palfreyman's number."

"What have they got to do with this?"

"Everything; nothing. Just do it!"

Powel digested Hennessey's tone and responded in kind. "Don't tell me what to do, mate!"

"Ring Palfreyman!"

"Not until you and I have had a little chat down the station, mate."

"I've got nothing more to say to you," said Hennessey.

Powell's hands were deep in his pockets, his head tilted slightly, his expression that of a man with a mission of his own. "You're saying that this Palfreyman fella can explain why one man is dead and another got shot? Eh? Well, I'm, sorry, I don't see how that's possible. It's *you* we found here. It's *you* who has admitted to killing the deceased so it's *you* who's going to have to explain how all of this happened."

Aware that a nightmare of words would follow if he even vaguely attempted to unscramble the situation, Hennessey looked away defiantly. Unimpressed, the detective produced a pair of handcuffs.

"I protest!" said Hennessey.

"Tell it to the desk sergeant," said the detective, and with that said he read Hennessey his rights and signalled that he should be taken out.

***

Redfern police station was a drab, brown-brick two-storey building with a flagpole out front. Hennessey was unaware of its charms; it was too dark, and he was too exhausted to notice. Incapable of being interviewed further, he was checked in, examined, and put in a cell. Thankful for any kind of bed, he sank into oblivion and dreamt that Laura had been killed in a car crash, and that he had been driving. Palfreyman arrived next morning early and was taken straight to the interview room where Hennessey and Powell sat in sullen silence. When proceedings got underway, Powell asked an already identified Palfreyman if he knew the defendant.

"Yes, I know him. This is John Hennessey. I request that you release Mr Hennessey into my custody immediately."

"Do you now," said Powell. "And what exactly is your relationship to Mr Hennessey, *sir*?"

"He's been assisting the OSI with research."

"I've never heard of the OSI, *sir*."

"We keep a low profile."

"War criminals?"

"That's our brief."

"But not on this occasion?"

Palfreyman stared at Detective Powell for a moment or two, then icily, he said, "My chief is with your chief right this minute, so I suggest you drop that tone."

"All I know," replied Powell, "is that one man is dead, another is fighting for his life and the only person capable of explaining how all of that happened is sitting right here next to me.

"Yes, but—"

"He's admitted to killing Dean with his bare hands, and to moving the bodies. For all we know he could have set up the whole scene. Wouldn't be the first time that's happened."

"Not in this case," said Palfreyman.

"You know that for certain?"

"I know Mr Hennessey." With a pained look, Palfreyman added, "Don't force me to pull rank on you."

"Pull away, sir, it won't get you anywhere. This killing took place on our patch, and that gives us, me, the last word on what goes on around here."

"The last word is about to drop on you from a great height," said Palfreyman. "I suggest, therefore, that you start transfer proceedings immediately."

With undisguised hostility, Powell said that Palfreyman couldn't just waltz into someone else's station and start throwing his weight around. Hennessey had confessed to killing Gavin Dean and that put him firmly in their grasp.

"I'm not trying to steal your case," said Palfreyman. "You'll get full credit for getting a confession out of Mr Hennessey; what you won't get is a conviction based on that confession."

"I wouldn't be too sure about that, sir."

"And I'm equally sure Mr Hennessey will be put into my custody at any moment."

Powell was about to reply, but didn't get the chance, for a fellow officer entered the room in that very moment and informed him in a low voice that Mr Hennessey was now in the keeping of Inspector Palfreyman. With a snort of disgust Powell gathered his papers together and headed for the door, but not without a parting shot: he would be putting in an adverse report on the whole incident.

When they were alone, Palfreyman said immediately that Hennessey should not have admitted to anything.

"I had nothing to hide. It was obvious—"

"Nothing's *ever* obvious to a good policeman," said Palfreyman. "All Powell had to go on was your confession and the fact that you had disturbed the crime scene. That was enough as far as he was concerned. He believed what he believed because he had no reason to believe otherwise."

"So, what happens now?"

"We get you out of here before they change their mind. What you need right now is a shower and a change of clothes. You look awful, John, and you smell worse."

"What happens if Giffard dies?"

"That would complicate things. We'd be forced to build a defence on other terms. We got you into this and we'll do everything in our power to get you out of it." Before Hennessey could reply, Palfreyman added, "Thanks to Harrenstein we can now directly link the gun found in the shack with Dean."

"Harrenstein?"

"He claims to have been threatened with what sounds like the same firearm as found in the shack." Hennessey's expression suggested cynicism. "He did you a favour, John, don't knock it. We wouldn't have known anything was wrong but for the call he put through to your hotel." A pained look. "You still think he's part of it?"

"Dean got to me."

"Yes, but that was just bad luck. You weren't there when Harrenstein's call came through. It was logged, then forgotten about."

"What time was logged in for?"

"Two-forty-five on the dot. We checked."

"When does Harrenstein say Dean left Aranda to go after me?"

"Just prior to that. Immediately prior."

"Then he's lying, David. Dean picked me off the street around two-thirty-five. I know that for a fact. I left the hotel at exactly two-thirty and hadn't gone a hundred yards when he struck." Hennessey's look was triumphant. "That suggests I was abducted by Dean *before* he left Harrenstein's office."

"You're sure about that?"

"As sure as I can be about anything," said Hennessey.

***

Norman Giffard remained unconscious, not because of the shoulder wound, which was serious enough, but because one of the two shots loosed by Dean while on the floor had deeply grazed the already fallen man's skull; he was stable, but only just.

There was a uniformed officer in the hospital corridor.

"Mary," said Hennessey, when they entered Giffard's room. It was three in the afternoon of the same day; Hennessey having arranged with Palfreyman to take him to see Giffard after a shave and change of clothes.

Mary looked up but didn't immediately say anything. Then, as if coming out of a coma herself, she said, "You killed Dean?"

A nod from Hennessey and a flashing smile from Mary. She turned back to her comatose husband and stared at him. "Do you think he's dreaming?" she asked.

Hennessey smiled his ignorance down at her.

"He's a *big* dreamer."

"He saved my life, Mary."

She did not reply to that; it was as if she hadn't heard.

There was a camp bed on the floor under the window; she had spent the night by her husband's side.

"He's in good hands, Mary," Hennessey said, more as a prayer than a statement. "He's tough."

As they made their way down to the carpark, Palfreyman informed Hennessey that a remaining sliver of bone was lodged in Giffard's brain. A second operation would be necessary.

"He's tough," Hennessey said again "Tough as they come."

***

Green and shady Lindfield. Tree-lined Lindfield. The squawk and flurry of green and yellow parakeets as they manoeuvred their way through the maze of manicured back streets. Verandas and wooden shutters and semi-tropical gardens on all sides. Palm trees towering high above everything, their spiky heads black against a cloudless blue sky.

"I got lost the first time," said Palfreyman.

"Next street," said. Hennessey.

Emma was on the front veranda when they drew up. A hug and she was saying that Laura had been beside herself with worry.

As they entered the lounge, Laura looked up. She was wearing a light summer frock with a small pattern and appeared even thinner than before. She came to Hennessey, and they embraced.

"What have they done to you? You look awful!"

"So, I'm told."

"Dean's behind bars?"

"Dean's dead."

Her shock was theatrical. "Really?" She let go of him and stood with her hands by her sides. "You're in one piece, that's all that matters."

"It's not quite over yet," said Palfreyman. "There are complications that have yet to be sorted out."

"And I have to get back to Tasmania," Laura said, apropos of nothing.

"How did he die?" asked Michael.

"We can't go into that at the moment," Palfreyman said. He turned to Laura. "We'll need John for a few more days. Debriefing, stuff like that."

Hennessey said he would like a word with Laura and Emma suggested the veranda; she would bring them coffee.

When they were alone, Laura continued to fuss over Hennessey's physical state and complain about his involvement with Palfreyman. He ought to have known better. He ought to have extricated himself when it became obvious that Dean was dangerous. He himself could have been killed, and for what, a book that was already back in his control. Hennessey waited for her to finish, but she seemed intent on avoiding the main issue, and he eventually had to say so.

"Suddenly the main issue is us?" she replied.

"It's always been us; you know that."

She turned away, leaned on the broad wooden balustrade and stared out into the garden where Dean had primed his home-made petrol bomb. He had been too busy with his Boy's Own Adventures to worry about what was happening to them, she said, glancing at him.

"I had no way of knowing how things would turn out."

"The last twenty-four hours have been an absolute nightmare for me!"

"And for me," he said softly.

"Grist to the mill?" She turned to face him. "You probably enjoyed every minute.

"I wouldn't wish what I've just experienced on my worst enemy." He measured his words carefully and continued. "I've never ever thought of life as being there solely for my artistic convenience, Laura. That's something you can't accuse me of."

Hammering at him with her eyes, she said that his autism was unbearable at times.

"My what?"

"People have commented on it."

"What people?"

"Friends."

"No one's ever said anything to me."

"Well, they wouldn't, would they."

He stared at her. "I don't believe you, Laura," he said, the code of her reasoning beyond his grasp. "You say whatever the hell comes into that head of yours."

"Now I'm a liar?"

"No, not a liar, just *lazy*. You accuse me of living in a little world all of my own, but it's you that's cut off from people, Laura, not me. Tuffnell isn't your enemy, you're *his* enemy. You've surrounded yourself with enemies of your own making. And now you've made me into an enemy. Well, I'm sorry, but I am *not* your enemy, and I refuse to be classified as one. You accuse me of living too internal a life, too self-involved a life, but I'll tell you something for nothing, I'd rather live the way I live than the way you do any time."

That was the moment Emma chose to appear with their coffees. Laura's reaction was to turn away and stand very straight. Taking the mug from Emma, Hennessey said that they were stuck, that the needle on the record would not leave its groove. Laura spun round at that.

"Speak for yourself!"

That was when Emma turned on Laura with a vehemence that few had ever witnessed. It was time she stopped holding everyone to ransom for her own selfish ends, she said blisteringly. She did not know how she had managed to hold her tongue for so long, but that was now over. The words kept coming, and they were not pretty words. And then just as suddenly Emma apologised, not in the sense of being sorry for what she had said, but as someone who had been left with no option but to say what was on her mind. Marvelling at the outburst, Hennessey watched Emma walk back across the veranda and into the house.

"Well," said Laura. Then with an expression Hennessey would never forget, she shouted, "Bitch!"

***

"I've met someone," Palfreyman said, after a long, heavy silence. They were back in the busyness of Sydney and heading, unbeknownst to Hennessey, for Edgecliff Road. A scene of emotional devastation lay behind them, Emma stony-faced and Laura upstairs packing her suitcase with tears.

"When? Where?" said Hennessey.

"At a conference. Knew her years ago and lost contact." A nervous laugh, and a glance. "I'm taking her out to dinner this evening. I haven't told Emmi yet."

"Will she be pleased?"

"Don't know. She seldom refers to Lynne."

It was the first time he had mentioned his dead wife's name. Another glance. "She's a redhead," he said, giving a little laugh.

"Life goes on," said Hennessey. "Where are we headed?"

"Emmi's; I'm under orders."

"I thought—"

"You'd prefer another cell?"

A silence: then, "It's over between Laura and me," Hennessey said, his world dissolving as he faced that fact. "Her parting words were that I was an arrogant sod."

"If that were the case Emmi would have laid you low at your first meeting," said Palfreyman.

And so, they arrived, Hennessey somewhat repaired by Palfreyman's words, but not absolved, and blindingly tired. He had killed a man. His partner had given up on him and he had all but given up on himself. They put him in the spare room, and he was asleep instantly. When he woke, it was nine-thirty in the evening and intolerably hot. Pulling back the drape he was confronted by an extraordinary sight: a magenta sky and clouds with black streaks twisted into gigantic whorls; it was about to rain like blazes.

23
Sinister Benefaction

There was no sign of Palfreyman when he emerged from the spare room. Emmi was in the lounge reading and it was so dark outside she had been forced to switch on the light.

"He's gone off to meet a woman he likes," she said. And then, "A little something to eat?" She got up. "There's wine here; the glasses are over there."

He watched as she went through to the kitchen and was reminded of Emma. Emma. Emmi. Almost thirty years between them, but the same calm certainty. A sheet of blue-white light exploded across the window followed by an ear-fracturing clap of thunder. He saw the panes flatten inward, buckle inward under the pressure, and was reminded of a café window in London. And then the rain started, the roar of it penetrating right into the building. Standing at the lounge window, his mind momentarily empty of Dean, he watched fascinated as bolts of lightning ricocheted across the horizon.

Emmi returned with a plate of lamb and potatoes topped with a rich, thick gravy. With the plate before him and a glass of wine at hand, he said that he would be eternally grateful to her for putting him up on that particular evening.

"A bad business," she said. "How are you feeling now?"

"Numb," he said, everything that had happened hanging in his mind like a black flag. And then, "What are you reading?"

Her words were lost in another roar. She waited for nature to settle; when it did not, she held up the book so that he could see the cover. "I have favourite chapters," she said, when things had quietened.

"Today's chapter?"

"Snow," she said, but in German.

He noted the change but continued in English. "I know it well," he said. "A death within a death. Well, almost."

And again, she spoke in German. "Have you met her?"

"No."

"Her name is Linda. She's got red hair… Is he in love, do you think?"

"Certainly enamoured," he said, sticking to English.

"It's in his voice." She doubled back. "He's mentioned Lynne to you. How she died?" He gave a little nod and she looked towards the window where the rain was beating out a wave-like rhythm. "It's taken him three years to recover from the shock of that. If one ever recovers, fully."

Three years was how long he and Laura had been together. He pushed that fact aside. Such happenings were always the more difficult to handle, he said.

"Better to have divorced," she said, accepting his reasoning and extending it in an unexpected direction. "A little more wine?"

"Please," he said.

She poured the wine carefully, and he noted the dark red crust at the bottle's nape.

Another flash; another blast.

"Life is so dramatic, isn't it," she said, Palfreyman's smile playing at the corners of her sculpted mouth.

"I've had more than my fair share of drama over the last twenty-four hours."

The revolver raised by Dean swivelling away as Giffard charged.

"Lynne was lovely. Getting used to someone else won't be easy."

"Life moves on," he said again.

His fist bashing down, down, down…

"Sounds bright enough; not just a pretty face."

"Mary has a room at the hospital," he said, her flashing smile dislodging Dean from his thoughts. "I don't think she realises how serious the situation is."

"She writes poetry; she confided in me."

The rain had dragged some of the heat out of the air and the sky was no longer quite as brooding.

"I didn't know that," he said.

A longish silence. Emmi returned to her book.

"I'm on my own again, Emmi," he said in German. "My partner and I have just split for good." Before she could reply, he added, "Is needing someone in your life for the sake of focus selfishness?"

"If you neglect them, then yes." She laid her book aside. "Have you neglected her?"

Hennessey did not reply.

"Then death is perhaps the kinder of the two," she said, reading his silence correctly.

Wrenching himself away from his thoughts, he said that his father had died of tuberculosis. The joke in the sanatorium had been… TB or not TB.

"They're all dying at the Berghof," she replied, picking up on his allusion to the book's central theme. "But I think you're right; I think perhaps Castorp wanted to taste the possibility of a natural death." She gave a little laugh. "He thinks he's testing life through his adventure in the snow, but he may have been testing death itself, hunting it down before it hunted him down." The childlike transparency of her look captured him for a moment, as did her next statement. "Your partner isn't interested in her death?"

It was a very German kind of thing to say. In response, he said that Laura had not yet acknowledged the need. Could he have her book for a moment? When he had it, he set about finding a particular passage, and on finding it read a few lines out loud: '*A wood loomed, misty, far off to the right.*' He looked up and caught

Emmi's smile. *'He turned that way, to the end of having some goal before his eyes, instead of sheer white transcendence.'*

"Wonderful," she whispered. She beckoned, and he returned the book to her, watched her scan the dense, German type. *'Here we have the typical reaction of a man who loses himself in the mountains in a snow-storm and never finds his way home... Whoever hears about it afterwards imagines it as horrible; but he forgets that disease — and the state I am in is, in a way of speaking, disease — so adjusts its man that it and he can come to terms; there are sensory appeasements, short circuits, a merciful narcosis — yes, oh yes, yes. But one must fight against them, after all, for they are two-faced, they are in the highest degree equivocal, everything depends upon the point of view. If you are not meant to get home, they are a benefaction; but if you are meant to get home, they become sinister.'*

It began to rain again, not as forcefully, but heavily enough to be heard. Emmi read on silently, then, looking up, her expression full of sadness, she said, "Sensory appeasement and conscious stupor, John. The two great deaths that have to be avoided." She was playing with the passage's literal meaning. "The merciful narcosis is only merciful if you're already half dead."

"Half alive in spite of being conscious?"

"Correct. Even when we consider our concerns as ultimate, they are meaningless. It's the fact that we have them that's important, not what they consist of." She laughed to herself. "Wittgenstein understood this. He tells us that it is not how the world is that constitutes the mystical, but that it is. When we understand that, we're halfway home."

"And if that doesn't occur to us?"

"Then our benefactions are sinister."

She put the book down and they talked on for half an hour or so, and as they talked the sky darkened again, the storm re-establishing itself over the city. And then the doorbell rang, and Emmi answered it, and he heard the sound of male voices coming down the corridor and was confronted by two men.

"John Hennessey?"

"That's me," he said.

"I'm Detective Inspector Curtis, this is Detective Sergeant Pirrie." A smile from Curtis as he displayed his credentials. Then the bombshell. "We would like you to accompany us to Redfern police station for further questioning concerning the death of Gavin Dean."

"I'm to be interviewed about that by Inspector Palfreyman first thing in the morning."

"Really?" said Curtis. Then, "So what are you doing here?"

"This is Inspector Palfreyman's mother, as I'm sure you're well aware. She has kindly allowed me to stay here this evening."

"Which is highly irregular."

"It was a welcome kindness."

"But well outside the guidelines for someone in your position." With a gestured puzzlement, Curtis said, "Inspector Palfreyman's… here, somewhere?"

"He's out for the evening."

"Oh, that's nice," said Curtis. Then, to clarify things, he said, "A complaint has been lodged by an officer against Inspector Palfreyman. It's a serious complaint. It requires your return to Redfern police station. We have a warrant to that effect."

"This is *ridiculous*!" said Emmi. "David will be furious."

"We would welcome Inspector Palfreyman's presence at any time," said Curtis.

"I'll ring him now," said Emmi.

"Tell him we've taken Mr Hennessey back to Redfern police station."

"Why don't you tell him yourself."

"We've tried; he's not contactable."

"How did you know where to find me?" asked Hennessey.

"We didn't. All we knew was that you were not where you ought to have been in custody somewhere. Inspector Palfreyman's chief could not explain that anomaly. It took Mary Giffard to sort things out for us."

"You've been harassing Mary?"

"Hardly harassing, Mr Hennessey. A simple question, a simple answer and here we are. She guessed, and she guessed correctly."

Directing their attention back to Hennessey, Emmi said, "Look at him? He's in no fit state for this."

"On your feet," said Curtis.

Hennessey got up, struggled up, the calm of his evening shattered. "This is going to get Powell absolutely nowhere," he said, squinting a look at Curtis. "I can tell you that right now."

"Oh, I wouldn't be too sure about that," Curtis replied.

***

Information transposed obliquely from one medium into another undergoes intrinsic change; this was Hennessey's discovery as his life and recent happenings underwent reassembly. As he listened to the case against him and attempted to argue his innocence in the face of questions put with skill, the strain of what he had been through began to show. But not in the fashion they were used to: Hennessey's way of cracking was to become faintly acerbic, his replies scrupulously sculpted. Had Palfreyman's approach in Hobart been used by him to pursue his own interests? When had he and Giffard decided to rip Dean off? On it went, getting sillier and sillier. He had no idea what they were talking about, and he suspected they didn't either. And still the questions kept coming, his replies evaluated in such a fashion as to form an alternative reality with a logic of its own.

"We think you and Dean had a nice little arrangement going at first, then things went wrong between you. Isn't that what happened?"

"There was no relationship; my meeting with Dean was purely accidental."

"Not according to the memo sent down to Hobart from the Bondi drug division. We have a copy of that memo. It links you directly to Dean."

"That was a misunderstanding; the Hobart squad sorted that out."

"You mean you spun them some yarn and they accepted it."

"Detective Sergeant Brownley of the Hobart drug squad will explain what happened; he was present when Inspector Palfreyman first interviewed me."

"We've already spoken to Brownley. He was not privy to the arrangement you claim to have had with Palfreyman. He was in fact kept away from what was going on."

"It was Palfreyman who got me out of here this morning! Does that count for nothing?"

"Yes, it was, wasn't it."

"So?"

"You tell me?"

"Tell you what?"

"What's going on between the two of you."

At a loss as to what the detective was getting at, Hennessey said that it was the OSI's chief who had arranged his release, not Palfreyman.

"At Palfreyman's instigation."

"Then speak to Murchinson; he has the whole story."

"All Murchinson knows is what Palfreyman told him."

"That isn't enough?"

"Bit one-sided, don't you think? All we know is that Dean was so annoyed with you he wanted to kill you, but that you ended up killing him."

"Yes, in self-defence."

"But why was he so annoyed with you?"

"It started with the manuscript he stole from me and ended up as a personal vendetta. I got under his skin, and he came after me. The book was only a factor in a situation that rapidly ran out of control."

"What were the other factors?"

"That's not for me to say."

"And that's exactly what Detective Sergeant Powell said you would say. Doesn't move us forward much, does it?"

"I wouldn't have been released if there had been any doubt in your chief's mind. Does he know you've dragged me in here at this time of night?"

"He sanctioned the warrant, Mr Hennessey."

"On what basis?"

"On our not having enough of your story to properly make up our minds about you."

"We're going round in circles," said Hennessey. "There's a situation working itself out here and I'm not at liberty to say what that situation is. Nor Palfreyman, for that matter. Which causes me to ask how a complaint made by Powell against Inspector Palfreyman necessitates my being arrested all over again?"

"Because nothing hangs together properly; it's all loose ends. Insinuation without substance."

"Insinuation *with* substance would be a non sequitur."

His composure ruffled, Curtis was silent for a moment, then with contrived patience, he said, "Palfreyman seems to have hung you out to dry this time. No one can find him. He's switched off his mobile."

"He's taken someone out to dinner, and no one knows which restaurant — it's *that* simple."

"Ignorance and privilege do not constitute a defence, Mr Hennessey. You played that game with Detective Sergeant Powell and that's why you're back here."

"I do not consider this a game by any measure."

"Yet you're quite good at it, aren't you? How come?"

"I think therefore I speak; not the other way round." A sigh of impatience from Hennessey. "Look, you're barking up the wrong tree with this kind of approach. "

"You've admitted to killing a man with your bare hands, Mr Hennessey. That is not an easy thing to do."

"I was fighting for my life and did what I had to do to survive. And let me tell you, *that* isn't an easy thing to live with."

"We know who you've been working with, what we don't know is who you're working for."

"I don't know what you mean by that."

"Palfreyman is OSI, but what are you?"

"I'm John Hennessey, I'm a novelist, and I'm completely out of my depth with all of this."

"You don't sound as if you're out of your depth, quite the opposite in fact. You're batting back replies like an old hand and that's unusual given the trouble you're in."

"I'm sorry, you'll to have to do better than that to earn your keep."

"*That* is a prime example of what I've just referred to."

"As I said, I'm a novelist; *dialogue* is the novelist's sweetheart."

Curtis and Perrie were not used to being spoken to like that; it raised their ire to be verbally outgunned by a suspect. On that basis Curtis decided to draw Hennessey out of his comfort zone. "You're an ex-intelligence officer, Mr Hennessey. Isn't that, right?"

Hennessey's reaction was to laugh and keep on laughing.

"What's so funny about that?"

"Seems everyone has access to my military file."

"Our investigations have been thorough."

"And your conclusion?"

"No conclusion as yet, just questions."

"Questions that will get you nowhere, so you might as well put me to bed."

"Oh, I don't think so," said Curtis. And as if nothing had been said to disturb his equanimity, he went on to ask Hennessey how he had come to be friendly with Norman Giffard.

After a pause, Hennessey said that he had been asked by Palfreyman to question Giffard, as he had Harrenstein, in the hope of eliciting information on Dean's whereabouts helpful to the OSI.

"Don't you mean helpful to Palfreyman in particular." Hennessey's frown conveyed bemusement. "Well, the two of you are very close, aren't you? At home with his mother drinking wine when you ought to have been in a cell?"

"Oh, for God's sake!"

"It may have slipped your notice, Mr Hennessey, but you've admitted to killing a man. We know *how* you killed him; we just don't know why."

"He was about to kill me, and I defended myself."

"The three of you had been drinking whisky together. What went wrong?"

"That's not how it was. Dean was playing games; I was playing for time."

"He was forcing an Irishman to drink whisky. Pull the other one."

"I wasn't being forced on that occasion. That was earlier. It was his way of saying a permanent farewell to me."

"Why? What had you done to him to make him so angry?"

"I stood up to him," said Hennessey, eyeing Curtis. "That's all it takes with some people."

Curtis absorbed Hennessey's swipe and came straight back at him. The man Palfreyman had asked him to question had ended up putting his life on the line for him? Why would he do such a thing?

"I'd hoped he would move earlier, but there wasn't a flicker until that moment. He must have realised he'd be implicated in my death if he didn't do something. What's missing from your story is that Dean also abducted Giffard and his wife earlier and only let her go on the provision that Giffard came back into his employ. His wife Mary overheard the whole thing. Ask her. Prior to that Giffard had been hunting all over Sydney looking for Dean. They came together in Rosie's Steak Bar at the Cross by accident and there was a fight. Giffard was drunk and Dean got the better of him; Giffard ended up in a cell. A female officer asked Dean if he wanted to press charges, but he declined."

"How the hell do you know all that?"

"Giffard. Palfreyman."

"You obviously had a thing going with Giffard."

"He wasn't a colleague, if that's what you mean."

"Then Dean hires him again?"

"It was Dean's way of taming Giffard; he was a control freak. He played with human beings, toyed with them; hence the whisky in my case." Hennessey's exasperation was now evident. "It was Dean who put Giffard in prison. He dobbed him in, because he'd tried to rip off some drugs during a delivery. He boasted to me that he had a thing going with the police."

"You said a minute ago that he wasn't forcing you to drink whisky. Which is it?"

"That was after being brought back to the shack; my first visit there was a completely different scenario."

"You were drinking together; that's known for certain."

"I was being *intimidated*."

"Make up your mind."

"Open your *fucking* ears!"

Curtis rocked back on his chair as if struck. "Cheek like that does not fit with the kind of person you want us to think you are, Mr Hennessey."

"Oh, I'm so sorry, it's just that you bring the best out in me. Did you know Dean had a thing going with the force? Did you know the Bondi station leaks like a sieve?"

"*Don't* go there," said Pirrie.

"Ah! It speaks," said Hennessey.

Curtis's expression was a warning.

"Dean told me he knew everything that was going on in the Bondi station, which means he also probably knew what was happening around here as well."

"That is a serious accusation," said Curtis.

"Yes, I thought it might interest you."

With a glance at Pirrie, Curtis returned to what he believed to be the heart of the investigation. "What we're trying to do is get to the bottom of a very murky business here and you are the only person who can tell us what really happened. And why. Problem is, you aren't doing that; you're doing the exact opposite and we want to know why."

"The 'why' of the situation is admittedly ambiguous," said Hennessey, "and it will remain that way until I'm informed to the contrary."

"That's an ex-intelligence officer speaking; you just can't help yourself, can you? You tampered with the crime scene and your ongoing affiliation with Dean and Giffard suggests a different scenario from the one you're at pains to paint. It's Dean this and Dean that without a glimmer of why he was about to kill you. There's no *context,* Mr Hennessey. Why is that?"

"I ended up knowing too much about him and his associates."

"A crime syndicate? You can't be serious?"

"There are things about that syndicate of which I cannot yet speak."

"All we know, Mr Hennessey, is that Dean is dead, Giffard is in a coma and you're wandering around scot-free! How can that be? Your being where we found you wasn't just irregular; it was subversion of the rules. Your Mr Palfreyman has broken just about every rule in the book. You were spirited out of here, not placed in custody as you ought to have been, then shuffled off to his mother's for wine and a little something to eat? I ask you; how do you think that looks?"

"Dicey?" admitted Hennessey.

"And all that fuss about being debriefed by Palfreyman and no one else? It didn't happen, did it?"

"I was to be officially debriefed tomorrow morning. *This* morning. I was exhausted; I still am. They had to put me to bed. I was not long up when you two arrived. Palfreyman was gone by then. I'd already given him a rough outline of what I'd been through."

"Which was?"

"That's *not* for me to say in this moment of time."

"So, you keep saying. But why? What's so bloody important that you can't speak about it? Or is all of this just you covering up for Palfreyman who will in turn cover up for you? Is that it? He can't still be in some restaurant, not at this time in the morning."

"I have no explanation for that."

"In bed with his girlfriend, perhaps?"

"What I've been privy to is not for this station's ears. Sorry, but that's just how it is."

"Now he's big-noting," said Pirrie.

"Who said we belonged to this station?" Curtis's look was innocently Machiavellian. "You were passed on to us because of the nature of Detective Powell's complaint. We're drug squad, Mr Hennessey, Bondi division. The one that leaks like a sieve. Let me put you in the picture. We thought it judicious to not waste any more time on your imaginative offerings, hence the warrant." A smile. Hennessey did not like its shape. "This isn't a novel, Mr Hennessey, it's real life, and right this minute it isn't going too well for you." Curtis then produced some photographs from a drawer and handed them to Hennessey. "Would you like to comment on how Dean got to look like that?"

His fist bashing down, down, down into Dean's face.

"As I said, I was fighting for my life."

"You pulped his face. That goes way beyond anger in my book."

"Believing that you're about to die energises you," said Hennessey, remembering. "I wouldn't have got out of that room alive if I'd held back." He took a breath, let it out slowly. "I didn't know whether he was conscious or not, that's why I kept on hitting him. He was a tricky bastard. I couldn't take the chance of his suddenly coming back at me. He had tried to shoot me through the table."

"But why? What had you and Giffard done to get him so worked up?"

"He was under the impression he had been ordered to shoot me."

"By whom?"

Hennessey had had enough. Looking straight at Curtis, he said that the two of them would look utterly ridiculous when everything sorted itself out. Eyeballing

Hennessey straight back, Curtis said they were just beginning to get at the truth of the situation.

"Enlighten me," said Hennessey.

"You and Palfreyman were about to take over Dean's patch, run it for yourself and make a bundle. Right?" Curtis was serious, Hennessey realised. "God knows what you and he were up to."

"That is a truly lunatic suggestion."

"Lunatic? It's called *policing*," Mr Hennessey. "It's putting two and two together and getting a good solid *four* out of the veiled nonsense you've been spouting."

"The mess of pottage is of your own making," said Hennessey. "You're so far off beam it would be funny if it weren't so pathetic." The room swam suddenly, and he lurched forward. "I don't feel well," he said.

"No problem," said Curtis. "Just tell us what we want to know, and we'll have you seen to."

"You're plainly idiots. I have no more to say."

"Now you listen to me," said Curtis, his patience finally gone. "I'd never heard of Inspector Palfreyman or of the OSI until I read Powell's report. Do you know what Palfreyman's an inspector of? A bunch of nutters chasing eighty-year-old men who can't remember their own fucking name. That's what. Whatever the hell it is you two are up to, it's over, so you might as well start talking."

Hennessey managed a laugh in spite of how he felt. A simple procedural mistake at Bondi over his stolen book had escalated into a bureaucratic farce of Biblical proportions.

"What's so bloody funny, mate?"

"Nothing's *remotely* funny; *that's* what's so funny."

"You're weird," said Pirrie.

"Just a couple of questions more, Mr Hennessey. Bear with me." A smile not altogether lacking in sympathy formed on Curtis's face. "It's thought your book was used as a cover to bring hard drugs into Australia from Hong Kong. Right?"

"The books were brought in from UK, not from Hong Kong, and no drugs were ever found. Gunther Harrenstein of Aranda had them in storage. They were picked up by a friend of mine and stored at his place."

"Where exactly?"

"Lindfield. I'll give you the address." Then, "C'mon! Ask yourselves why Dean would do that. Why put his name on my book? What could he possibly gain from that, given that I reported its having been stolen to the police the moment I found out? You really think he would have chanced a drug shipment with his name on it?"

"You tell me," said Curtis.

"I don't know the answer to that. I wish I did."

"The way I see it is this: you double-crossed Dean in some way, he sussed what was going on while you were having a drink together and decided to sort you out there and then."

"And my stolen book? How do you explain that?"

"Publishing that book with his name on it resulted in the unexpected: you and he getting together. You must have come to some kind of arrangement over the book, an arrangement that backfired."

"I'd be careful with plots if you ever do decide to write a novel," said Hennessey."

"*Then* he gets the reviews you ought to have had and you get mad all over again," said Pirrie, rallying. A glance at Curtis before he delivered his *coup de grâce*. "It could be said he *became* you, in a sense, and you didn't like that one little bit?"

Hennessey's silence surprised Pirrie

"What?" said Pirrie.

"You're a brilliant dolt," said Hennessey. "Dean was setting himself up with a new identity. Opportunism turned into something much more useful, the chance to transform himself into the opposite of what he was. The reviews and articles for my book describe him as a sensitive writer; he must have loved that. Particularly the review in *The Australian* where he was said to have made *not a bad fist at empathy*. He wasn't importing drugs; he was importing a new psychological profile for himself as a backup position."

In response, Curtis said sourly that what Dean had been up to in his head was of no interest to him.

"Well, it damn well ought to be," said an enlightened Hennessey. "Do you know why? Because it explains the *context* of his so-called relationship to me

— the context none of us could identify. He published my book under his own name as a future escape route, a visible credential that he could flash around in some other clime: probably the US. He was a chameleon, an actor and a killer. He fooled me on our first meeting — even had me convinced for a few minutes that he was a tax office official on one occasion."

"It's you who's the chameleon," said Pirrie.

"Oh, *shut up!*" said Hennessey.

"What a *fucking* cheek!"

"I don't know how you've got to thinking the way you do," said Hennessey, his attention on Curtis, "but the case you're building is so daft it has to have been hatched for you. You couldn't have arrived at this nonsense on your own."

Something about Hennessey's reasoning made Curtis hesitate, and Hennessey picked up on that hesitation. Not so Pirrie, who was suddenly animated and cocksure. "Harrenstein's in this with you, isn't he?" he said, as if about to unfold another revelation for Hennessey's benefit. "The drugs that came in with the books must have been syphoned off by him."

"There were no drugs!"

"So, you want us to believe, but only because you and Harrenstein intended to split the profits."

"It's me and Harrenstein now, is it?" Hennessey laughed to himself. "He's certainly a suspect, I'll give you that, but not because of drugs."

"Why else would he warn you?"

"Warn me?" said Hennessey. "Where the hell did you pick up on that?"

"Around."

"Around *where*, may I ask?"

"Well, he did, didn't he?" said Pirrie, but he could sense a black hole looming. "If that doesn't tell us something then I don't know what does." He was suddenly floundering; his tongue had outgunned his brain and Curtis was staring at him fixedly.

"I'll tell you what it tells *me*," said Hennessey. "It tells me that you are in someone's loop and that your colleague here isn't."

Pirrie's face sort of collapsed in on itself in that moment; it was as if he had had a mini stroke. Supplying the missing piece for Curtis's sake, Hennessey said that knowing about that warning meant Pirrie knew more than he was letting on.

"Rubbish!" said Pirrie.

"Okay, then let's work it out," said Hennessey, more to Curtis than to Pirrie. "Did Powell approach your division with his complaint, or did you approach Powell's?

"We were approached," said Curtis.

"Are you sure about that?"

"It was brought to our attention *by* Detective Sergeant Powell," said Curtis. "Powell was really annoyed with the way Palfreyman had treated him and asked Detective Sergeant Pirrie for advice."

"That might *just* be true," said Hennessey, "but knowing about Harrenstein's warning puts him way ahead of the pack. Let me spell it out for you. Only three people had access to that bit of information: Harrenstein, Palfreyman and myself. As Harrenstein has admitted telling Dean that he'd warn me, that makes four, and your colleague's knowledge of that warning makes it an unbalanced five. Now you either got that snippet from Harrenstein direct, which I think unlikely given that you've just dobbed him in, or from Dean, which is a possibility, or, from those lurking in the shadows of this whole affair."

"Poppycock," said Pirrie.

"Okay, I'll be fair," said Hennessey. "I'll give you the benefit of the doubt on who spoke to whom first, but please tell us where you picked up on Harrenstein having warned me that Dean was heading in my direction?"

"Oh, I don't know," said Pirrie, agitated. "A colleague? There's a lot going on in our division. You pick up on all kinds of stuff."

"The OSI has been dealing with Special Branch from the very start," said Hennessey, opening the door a little for Curtis's sake. "Your lot haven't been in the loop since you sent that memo to the Hobart squad implicating me in Dean's affairs." Before Pirrie could reply, Hennessey closed in on him. "So why dump his grievances on the drug squad? Why not go further up the chain of command?" Pirrie did not reply, so

Hennessey answered his own question. "Because it was *you* who approached him, not *he* who approached you, and that tells me you were under orders to do just that."

"Don't be ridiculous!" said Pirrie, trying to bluff it out, but there was no conviction in his tone. "Dean was well known to the squad; he's on file for all kinds of shit. Rumours spread fast in our business."

"You're treading water, and you know it," said Hennessey. "You were instructed to approach Powell, the intention being to stitch me up so as to destroy my credibility as a witness. Which suggests a series of moves made post Dean's death on the basis of information supplied to you by Dean's puppet-masters."

Pirrie opened his mouth to speak but was again overridden by Hennessey.

"So how deep in are you? Are you a soldier, or just a stooge selling information on the side?"

"You've flipped your bloody lid, mate!"

"Was it him who came up with my having been an intelligence officer? If he did, I know where he got it from, and it wasn't from my military file."

Curtis was staring hard at Hennessey. After a glance at Pirrie, he said, "If you're lying about this, I'll have your guts for garters."

"I am *not* lying," Hennessey said.

"Interview terminated at... one-forty-eight a.m.," said Curtis, pressing the stop button on the interview clock. Then to Pirrie, he said, "A word in your ear, mate."

***

Inspector David Palfreyman turned up at three-thirty a.m. Hennessey was fast asleep in the holding cells. Roused from his slumbers, he had a cup of coffee shoved at him and was instructed to dress. When he walked into the interview room, he found Palfreyman and Curtis deep in conversation. There was no sign of Pirrie.

"John," said Palfreyman. "Christ! You look awful!"

"I've felt better," said Hennessey.

"Inspector Palfreyman has been filling in a few details," said Curtis, his tone carrying the hint of an apology. Then with a shake of his head, he said, "What a bloody mess."

"Where's Pirrie?"

"Undergoing questioning and considering his future," said Palfreyman. Then, with a touch of alarm, "Sit down, John, you're wobbling."

After two sips of coffee, Hennessey directed a question at Curtis: why had Redfern's station chief allowed the drug squad to intervene?

"We were led to believe the issue of Dean's death revolved around drugs, and that you were deeply implicated. But as the complaint against Inspector Palfreyman had originated at Redfern, there was also a need to keep tabs on it this end of the chain. It was our intention to move you out the moment we had established a link between you, Dean and his network."

"The good news is that Giffard's regained consciousness, John," said Palfreyman. "He's talking. Boy, is he talking!"

"Is he going to be, okay?"

"As okay as one would expect. He regained consciousness immediately after the second operation."

"So, what happens now?"

"In your case, a re-evaluation on all levels. Everything you claimed, and have yet to claim, has been confirmed by Giffard."

"He wasn't present during my interrogation, and he wasn't conscious when I killed Dean."

"No, but he's given us a pretty detailed description of what you went through prior to that moment, and what happened seconds before he himself got shot. He couldn't believe you had survived, and that Dean was dead. He wanted to know how you'd pulled it off. I told him you had defended yourself with the only weapon you had at your disposal, your fists. He said it was lucky for you that you knew how to use them. What did he mean by that?"

"I boxed at university; not that that helped me. I flailed at him like any amateur. Having him jammed under that table gave me the advantage. My first two, three punches were straight down into his face and seemed to do the trick, but he was a cunning bugger, so

I kept hitting him until I was sure he wouldn't come back at me."

"That explains the mess he was in," said Curtis.

"Which, if you care to remember, is what I told you earlier," said Hennessey.

A smiling Palfreyman waved this moment of contention aside. His chief was again upstairs. They'd been at it for some time, so the missing pieces must be falling into place by now.

"Plain bizarre, all of it," said Curtis.

"Nice juxtaposition," said Hennessey.

Curtis looked at Palfreyman and Palfreyman said, "Forget it."

"Harrenstein?" asked Hennessey.

"More than a bit player, it seems. Up there with the big boys."

"He's been arrested?" A nod from Palfreyman. "Pirrie?"

"He was Dean's ears and eyes at Bondi. Been at for years."

"He's admitted as much?"

"You've been asleep for a couple of hours, John. Raids are about to take place in Melbourne and Perth as we speak; they may in fact be underway. The bunch you had to deal with were still in situ and have been nabbed." A weary sigh from Palfreyman. "If it had just been madcap politics behind closed doors, I doubt anyone would have taken much attention, but it's turned out to be much more than that. This bunch had quite extraordinary plans. We already knew about their American links, what we didn't know was that they were also in contact with like-minded citizens in Britain *and* in Europe. Frank put together a rough outline of what they might be up to, but what's surfaced goes way beyond even his projections. Their ambitions were monumental, probably still are elsewhere."

"Realisable?"

"Not to the extent of this mob's projected imaginings having an immediate impact, but certainly dangerous in terms of driving the right into the arms of the far-right. With the tenor of the election coming up, they could have created a backgrounding climate of opinion and pushed small 'c' conservatives into the ultra-conservative camp against their will. The nutcases would have followed."

"Dean believed he'd been given an order to kill me. I think that doubtful. He was told to take me back to my hotel."

"There are things yet to be determined, John. The people you were dealing with are known right-wing advocates, but they're also upright citizens and pillars of Australian society. Butter wouldn't melt with the top echelon; they're squeaky clean on the surface."

"They're nuts," said Hennessey, the memory of Arthur's face as he struck him down never to be forgotten. "They're selling pragmatism run amok. It's Ayn Rand utilitarianism pushed off the bloody planet. I couldn't believe what I was hearing."

"You might be called on to testify to that effect."

"I'd be happy to if anyone's willing to listen." Hennessey cracked a smile. "Your evening out? How did that go?"

"I got a call *en route* and that was that. Hence my leaving you to this lot's tender mercies. Things were moving too fast, and as you have ably demonstrated, there was the possibility of an intercept."

"Pirrie was too busy trying to entangle me in his nonsense."

"As I was," said Curtis, by way of a *mea culpa*. Getting to his feet, he added, "I'm out of here. I'm bushed."

Hennessey extended a hand and Curtis, surprised, grasped it, saying that interviewing him had been an interesting experience. The experience had been mutual, Hennessey said. As the door closed behind the detective, Palfreyman said that the coroner had asked for an autopsy on Dean. A pathologist's report would determine the cause of Dean's rather sudden demise.

"We already know the answer to that."

"It's just procedure, John."

"I was *there*, David."

"It could have been a heart attack."

"Yes, caused by *me* beating his brains out if it was."

"Straws, John. Straws."

"I can't get that moment out of my mind; it keeps recurring. It's horrible."

"Murchinson will argue for an acquittal, as will I. The circumstances are on your side, John. Any idiot can see that." Hennessey was about to reply but didn't get the chance. "C'mon, let's get out of here," said Palfreyman.

When they left the building's dour corridors twenty or so minutes later, Hennessey glanced back at Redfern police station, half-expecting a uniformed officer to run out arms flailing, but that did not happen.

"Emmi has insisted that I take you back to Edgecliff. I think you deserve that after what you've been through."

"Did she manage to contact you?"

"Yes, eventually, but I was embroiled with Special Branch over the raids. We only had a small window of opportunity and had to move fast."

"She and I demolished a bottle of shiraz together. I think it helped me see the funny side of things."

***

It was four-thirty in the morning when they reached Edgecliff. Hennessey undressed in Emmi's spare room, conscious of how light it had become outside. In response, he pulled the drapes shut and stood for a moment in the inky darkness. Emmi coughed in that moment, just a little cough, but he heard it through the wall. What had she said about Wittgenstein? He could not remember. But he could remember what she had said about ultimate concerns. They were meaningless, she had said. It was the fact that we had them that was important. He closed his eyes, so enclosing darkness within darkness. Then, quite involuntarily, he let his breath flow out into the room's silence until his lungs were empty.

Postscript

The pathologist's report revealed Gavin Dean to have died as the result of a subdural haematoma in the left hemisphere of his brain. A subdural haematoma, Hennessey learned, was an accumulation of blood clots beneath the fibrous membrane of the brain due to injury, but in this case not the injuries inflicted by himself. The report was quite specific. The reason for death was the reception of a blow or blows — termed 'insults' in the pathologist's quaint terminology — approximately one week or so before death occurred. The reason for this delay was that bleeding in the subdural haematoma was venous in nature, not arterial, and as such took longer to clot. As was nature's way, small capillary-sized blood vessels had extended into the clot from the brain's fibrous surround, and from the appearance and structure of the membrane that formed, an approximate timing of the initial injury had been possible. One further observation had fixed this interpretation in place, for although it was possible for chronic alcoholics and predisposed people to experience spontaneous subdural bleeding, close examination of Dean's skull had revealed bruising of deep soft tissue unrelated to the surface lesions, but closely related to the subdural haemorrhage. This finding confirmed the previous blow theory.

Giffard smiled one of his rare smiles when Hennessey turned up at the hospital. Mary, too. For a brief moment he felt like the hero they thought him to be. But only for a moment, for having bashed even an already dead man so severely had left its mark on him. It was Giffard, not he, who had set the clock ticking for Dean, he, John Hennessey, the one favoured by the fickle laws of chance to witness that clock falter and fall silent. The arc of brutality had come full circle, Heather Barton's merciless bashing at the hands of Dean paid for in full. Then had come the news that Gunther Harrenstein's automatic had killed Dave Hollows, and that Detective Sergeant Perrie's involvement in the whole affair had been much more than that of a petty informer: he had worked undercover for some months, got used to breaking the rules and telling lies and allowed himself to be corrupted.

Hennessey remained at Emmi's for a few days, then returned to his hotel. And during it all not a peep out of Laura, who was apparently back at work. But not for long, as he was soon to discover she of the new hairdo had modified her ambitions and secured a plum job in publishing.

Charged with attempting to pervert the political landscape, and with sundry other crimes, James Atherton and Gerald Korn faced the cameras with almost comical bravado, their chests stuck out in defiance, their political and cultural manifesto a curious mixture of sense and nonsense. Korn's talent was for generalisation, his weakness a tendency to see nothing other than what he wanted to see. "What you do not seem to understand," he said, staring into the camera with almost scary intensity, "is that there are already people in high places with enough sense to see what has to be done to save this country from itself. The saving of Australia from wishy-washy political ideas may have been delayed, but postponement is not victory. Our time will come." Only much later, when trying to talk his way out of sedition and murder charges, would Atherton reveal Korn's directive to have Dean *look after* Hennessey, and Harrenstein *look after* Dean.

Hennessey, as Laura had surmised, but mistakenly timed, began to sketch out the bones of the story he intended to write. All he had on paper was the layout of Rosie's Steak Bar, but it was a story backgrounded distantly by the escalating violence in his homeland. The Americans were telling the Irish to stop haggling and get on with the peace process, but on the streets of Londonderry and parts of Belfast serious rioting was still taking place. The headings were, as usual, eye-catching: ULSTER LOOKS INTO THE MOUTH OF HELL; TWO YEARS OF PEACE HOPES TRAMPLED IN PORTADOWN; ULSTER'S FALSE DAWN OF PEACE, and so on. Given how deep the fracture went, would it ever end?

Only a short period of time since his return from London, a period during which his relationship with Laura had collapsed and he had almost lost his life. It was too much to take in, too difficult to accept that he had become something of a catalyst in such an outrageous affair. And in the midst of it all that deliciously dangerous moment with Emma, that moment when their eyes had met, and a kind of electricity had passed between them. What to make of that? Shaking his head as if to dislodge the thought, Hennessey stared blindly at his scribbled notes.

A visit from David Palfreyman brought a cake from Emmi and news of a bizarre document that had surfaced in the German federal archive. In his infinite wisdom, Adolf Hitler had apparently planned to remove the entire Anglo-Saxon population of Tasmania and repopulate the island with Australians of German descent, true believers who would have stamped — in every sense of that word — the Third Reich's mores into the soul of the Apple Isle. According to this document, Tasmania's thousands would have been shipped out to Victoria and left to the tender mercies of the by then triumphant Japanese.

Hennessey left for Hobart on a Saturday morning at the civilised hour of ten, and as the plane fought its way up into the sky, closed his eyes and tried to ignore the sounds that he, and probably only he, could hear. Then came the empty, stifling flat where he and Laura had spent their passion to the point of bankruptcy. Laura had already moved her stuff out, leaving what Hennessey described to someone as 'possession holes' everywhere. Her computer gear and desk were gone, and some bric-a-brac, and not a few books. He stood for an age looking at what was left of their life together, his thoughts drifting, by degree, in one direction, then another. Anger. Hopelessness. Self-recrimination. Anger. The note in her scrawly handwriting informed him that she had no need of furniture, crockery or bedding: she would start fresh. All that remained of her now was a dark score on the corridor wall indicating the passage of her desk — *her* desk — from lounge to front door.

He made himself a coffee and stood at the window contemplating what had happened to him, then again broached the unthinkable: Emma's look and the tenderness of her parting hug. Had he imagined it? Had she really communicated something deeply personal? The touch of her hand on his sleeve. The look she had given him. The fact that she had not looked back as Michael waved goodbye. Projection? Misunderstanding? Fantasy? Whatever meaning it all had was quite immaterial, for in his heart of hearts he knew Emma would remain Michael's faithful wife, and that he, John Hennessey, would remain Michael's trusted friend.

The End